MARLENE CAMPBELL

NAME YOUR GAME

FAMILY, COMMUNITY, AND THE TIES THAT BIND THEM

Name Your Game

ISBN: 9781773661667

Printed in Canada

Cover: Tracy Belsher
Design: Rudi Tusek
Editor: Robin Sutherland

Library and Archives Canada Cataloguing in Publication

Title: Name your game : family, community, and the ties that bind them / Marlene Campbell.
Names: Campbell, Marlene, author
Identifiers: Canadiana (print) 20240459210 | Canadiana (ebook) 20240459245 | ISBN 9781773661667 (softcover) | ISBN 9781773661674 (EPUB)
Subjects: LCGFT: Novels.
Classification: LCC PS8605.A54743 N36 2024 | DDC C813/.6—dc23

The publisher acknowledges the support of the Government of Canada, the Canada Council for the Arts and the Province of Prince Edward Island for our publishing program.

ACORNPRESS

P.O. Box 22024
Charlottetown, Prince Edward Island
C1A 9J2
acornpresscanada.com

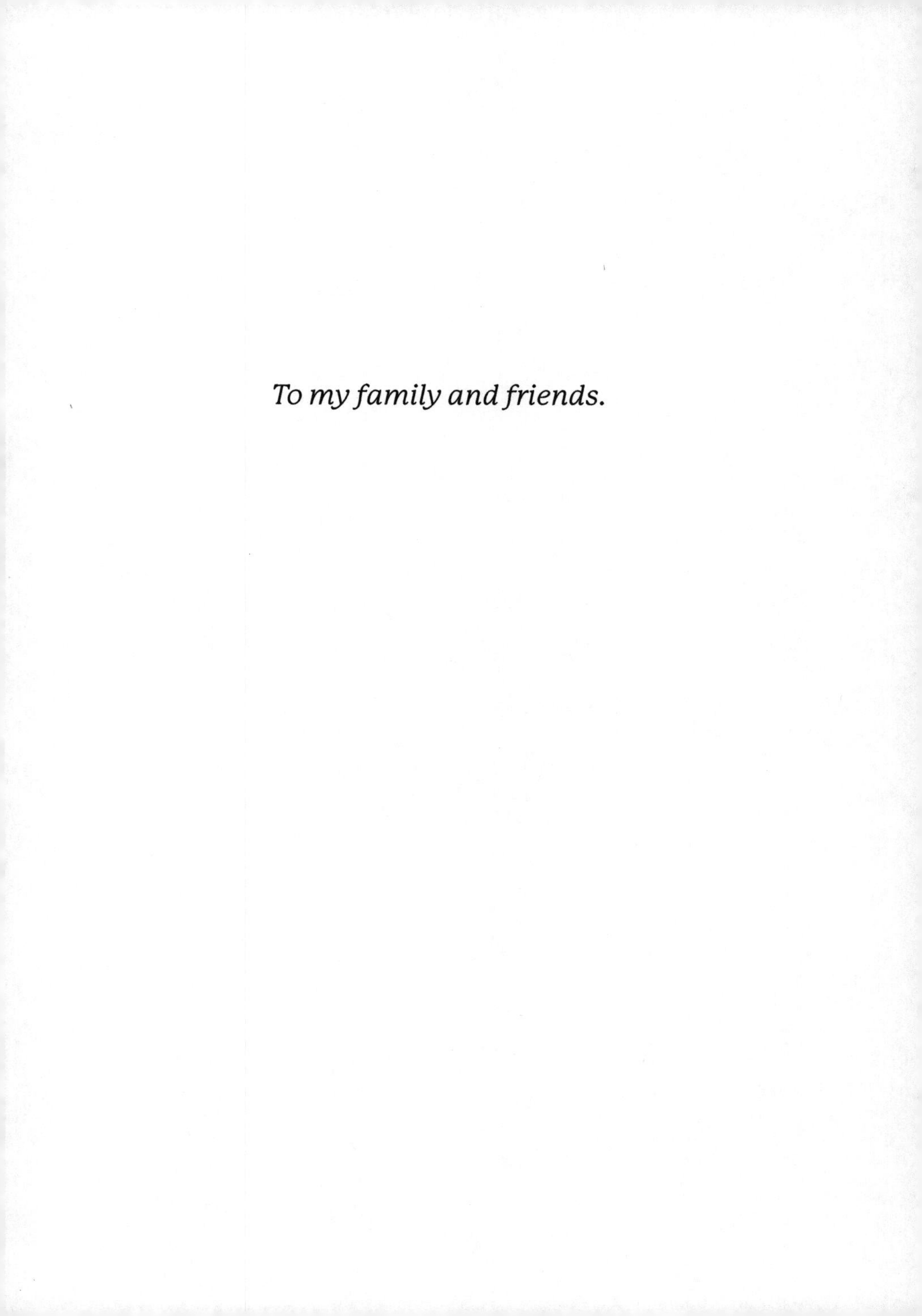

To my family and friends.

CHAPTER 1

Daniel woke from sleep two minutes ahead of the six am alarm set on the Baby Ben clock. He quickly turned it off. Isabel did not need to be up this early. Glancing at his wife's sleeping form, Daniel wished he could curl against her warmth and drift back to sleep rather than face crawling out from under the blankets to be assaulted by the frigid cold of the unheated bedroom. But his day had begun. He slid from the bed, pulled on thick woolen socks, and covered his long johns with work pants and shirt.

Daniel quietly left the second-floor bedroom of the Prince Edward Island ell-shaped farmhouse, descended the stairs, and entered the large kitchen. The green and white tile floor felt like ice beneath his sock feet. "I'll bet it's warmer outside than in here," he muttered as he flicked the light switch, and crossed to the wood range.

Opening the cover of the stove's firebox, Daniel noted no flame among the embers. Deftly, he cleaned out the ashes, and placed them in the metal bucket for spreading later in the pile behind the farm buildings. He gathered some paper and kindling that had been left to dry behind the stove overnight and layered them in the firebox. He took a match from the tin container and struck it against the side. When it lit, Daniel held it against the edge of the paper and watched the flame increase in size as the paper and then the thin slivers of wood caught.

He waited until the kindling was well-ignited before taking several pieces of larger wood from the wood box at the side of the stove and adding them to the fire. Leaving the cover off for several minutes, Daniel held his hands over the gaping hole to try and warm them.

Once certain the fire was gaining momentum, Daniel replaced the cover of the stove and crossed to the small pantry off the kitchen. There, he removed a loaf of homemade bread from the breadbox and cut a slice as thick as two slices cut by his mother-in-law's hand and smeared it with her homemade strawberry jam. While eating, Daniel went back into the kitchen and removed a lunch box from the small refrigerator, along with the milk bottle he had filled the previous evening when he milked the one cow kept in production for the winter months. Swallowing the last bite of bread and jam, Daniel shook the bottle to mix the cream that had separated and risen to the top, then poured half a glass of the frothy cold liquid and downed it in several large swigs.

Daniel reached for his winter coat hanging on the row of hooks next to the exterior kitchen door and placed it on the oven door to warm. He added more wood to the fire and stopped for a moment to listen to the crackling sound before going back up the stairs to the bedroom. He crossed to Isabel's side of the bed and bent over to place a kiss softly on her cheek and gently shook her arm to wake her.

When Isabel's eyes opened, Daniel smiled at her and said in a low voice, "The fire's going. The kitchen will be warm soon."

Isabel's appreciation showed in the smile that spread from her lips to her eyes.

"Thanks. It's so hard to get up in the cold. Did you eat something?"

Standing straight, he nodded. "I was hard on your mother's bread. Don't leave the fire long, okay? I've gotta go."

"Okay, take care. I love you." Isabel reached up to stroke his arm.

Though they were both twenty-eight, Daniel always felt Isabel's face looked younger than his, and the thought went through his head again as he looked down at her. "I love you, too," he said. "Thanks for doing my barn chores."

"No problem—we're a team," she was quick to reply.

"We are indeed." Daniel nodded his head.

He slipped from the room and crossed the hallway and quietly opened a second bedroom door and went over to the double bed to look down at his two daughters, deep in sleep. Five-year-old Jeannie was flat on her back, while Mary, three, was curled on her side. Daniel bent to retrieve the blankets that had been kicked to the bottom of the bed, and tucked them under each girl's chin. Neither stirred as he kissed them. Daniel stood watching the girls for a moment before leaving the room, and then softly crept past the bedroom door of his in-laws and down the stairs.

Dressed in his winter gear, Daniel walked out into the crisp morning air. He paused to pull the coat collar closer about his neck and then began to walk the long farm lane towards the road where his old car was parked. He gave a sigh of relief when the engine rolled over and caught on the first turn of the ignition key. It was going to be a good day.

CHAPTER 2

Daniel met no one on the short drive and didn't expect to. Farms lined the road, and the commute to work for a farmer was a walk across the yard from the house to the barn. Daniel couldn't wait for the day when that would also be his path. Two miles down the road, he pulled the car into the narrow lane of a field and killed the engine. Daniel's eyes hungrily absorbed the sight as he sat back in his car. Not far off the road, perched on a footing, sat a one-and-a-half-storey house, dwarfed by the size of the field. The tracks of the teams of horses that had hauled the structure to the location were still visible in the hardened snow. A pile of fresh lumber sat off to one side, ready to be used to replace the missing back wall of the house, which was the kitchen wing of a much larger farmhouse the owner was downsizing. The downstairs had a porch, pantry, large kitchen, and a bedroom that Daniel would convert to a living room. The upstairs was one open room that he would frame up for individual bedrooms and bath.

Daniel exited the car, and with his eyes fixed on the house, walked slowly towards it. Before starting to work, he needed a moment to savour the fact that the house was his and sat on land that was also his. Well, at least almost his land. Soon he would make it a working farm. Daniel stood quietly in the stillness with a look of pride on his face. He jumped when a voice rang out from behind him.

"Sorry, I didn't mean to scare you. I thought you would have heard the car and my footsteps on the snow." Peter, his younger brother, stood there with a toolbox in hand. "She stood the move in good shape."

Daniel thumped the side of the building with his fist. "They didn't always build these old houses straight, but they sure built them strong."

Peter nodded in agreement as he set down the toolbox, opened it, and took out the hammer. Daniel retrieved his tools from where he had hidden them inside the house. The girt, which tied the house together, was intact between the first and second floors. The 6 × 6 rough timber beam, at least a hundred years old, showed no sign of rot. Daniel and Peter would nail the replacement wall studs from the sill to the girt for the first floor and from the girt to the beginning of the roof line for the second floor. As though in sync, the two brothers each grabbed a freshly sawn stud and proceeded to the missing wall. They positioned the first stud and Peter nailed it into place, while Daniel measured the distance for the second one.

Peter continued the conversation over the hammering. "Seems kind of funny Clarence tore the kitchen wing from their house. I bet his father was none too impressed."

Placing a stud, Daniel replied, "Harry wasn't, but then it is just one more thing for him to add to the list of his life work that he feels Clarence has destroyed since taking over."

For a moment Peter was silent. "It must be hard to work your whole life for something, and when you give it to a child, they change it all."

Daniel looked up from his measuring. "Yeah, but times change, and one has to keep up or get left behind."

Peter grunted. "Well, it worked in your favour. Trust you to get a house minus a wall for seventy-five dollars."

Daniel grinned. "She's not much yet, but by the time we finish, my family will have a home to call its very own."

Peter straightened the next stud. "Living with the in-laws can't be that bad."

"Spoken like a man who has never had the pleasure," retorted Daniel.

Peter gave his brother a sideways glance before picking up a nail that held the winter cold. "Considering you had to get married without a cent to your name, you're lucky they put a roof over your heads these past five and a half years."

Daniel stopped hammering and looked directly at his brother. "I didn't say I wasn't grateful. Isabel's parents have done a lot for me under the circumstances, but a guy doesn't need a daily reminder that he put the cart before the horse and caused disappointment."

Peter appreciated Daniel's plight. "Well, brother, tough as it is, you usually land on your feet."

Daniel snorted, "It's called hard work and a little charm, Peter. Let's see a little more work right now. We only have a short time before we have to leave for work, and we need to get her boarded in before a storm hits. I really appreciate the help you're giving me. It's a big sacrifice for you."

Peter flashed a grin. "You're right, but it's what brothers do."

For a time, the two men worked in comfortable silence. Then Peter remembered something he wanted to tell Daniel. "Guess what?" he said. "I had a letter from Edgar yesterday."

Daniel removed a spike from his mouth. "Is that so? How are things in Montreal?"

Peter stopped hammering as he wanted Daniel to hear the news, for it was good. "Fine. He says there are jobs for both of us on the crew the first of May. The company is building a new subdivision in Dorval."

Daniel took his time answering. "I've decided I'm not going back this spring."

Shocked, Peter demanded. "What do you mean you're not going back? You can't make money like that round here. Need I remind you that Montreal is the reason you have paid off the majority of the mortgage on this land that you want to farm? It would have taken you years of work here on PEI."

Daniel didn't disagree. What Peter said was true. He could never have earned that kind of money, as quickly (at least not legally), other than working a job in construction in Montreal. Building was booming there, and the two brothers made good money working from early spring to late fall. But Daniel's mind was made up. The homesickness the past season had been almost unbearable. Even working as many hours as possible could not block Jeannie, Mary, and Isabel from his mind. He knew that every day, the girls were growing and changing and he was missing it all. At night in bed, surrounded by the sounds of the snoring of the other men in the room, Daniel would often let the tears run down his face. It was different for Peter, who was single and loved the work and the crew, many of whom were from the Island.

"I'm not leaving Isabel and the girls again." Daniel drove a nail into the stud with more force than necessary. "Besides, I'm far enough ahead on the mortgage to get the farm started this season."

Peter sensed Daniel's sudden tension, but was unwilling to stay quiet. "Who're you kidding? The sooner you have that five thousand dollars and interest paid in full to Charles Elliott, the better. I don't trust him not to pull the rug out from under you."

Daniel tried not to feel uneasy at Peter's words. He had approached many people to secure the mortgage money, and only Charles Elliott, who owned the general store in the community, had been willing to lend it to him. The interest rate was higher than the going rate, but Elliott had explained the increase was necessary because Daniel was a financial risk, being without permanent employment and owning nothing other than an old car.

Not that Daniel had proved any risk. Every payment was on time, with additional money on the principle. "Relax, Peter, that's the thing about your time in Montreal, you're starting to think big city. No trust for anybody," he said, envisioning the home he was so close to calling his own.

But Peter pointed his hammer at his brother. "It's not about trust. It's about the reality of lenders like Charles Elliott, who let people pay for years on a mortgage, then with the end in sight, call for the remaining money knowing full well the borrowers don't have it and can't get it. These crooks repossess the properties and start the whole deal all over again with some other sod wanting to build a life. You saw it with our grandparents. The only difference was their lender was a woman shrewdly investing her dead husband's money." Peter stopped himself from voicing his real fear, which was that Daniel was the perfect target for a man like Elliott.

Daniel wasn't sure if it was for himself or Peter that he defended the storekeeper. "Elliott's not like that."

Peter gave a harsh laugh. "Elliott would sell his own mother for the right price."

Daniel had heard enough on the subject. "Listen, Peter, Elliott came through for me at a time when no one else would lend me a cent. I wouldn't have this land without him, and he has no reason to doubt I won't pay every cent back. But I won't leave the girls again."

Peter was not easily dissuaded. "Then take them to Montreal with you. With your skills, your life could be so much easier than all this."

Daniel stood another stud in place. "What you're saying makes practical sense, Peter, but the Island's home. My heart's here in the red soil, and the salt air. For you too, or else you wouldn't keep coming back in the winters. And don't try and tell me it's just for the hockey."

Peter fell silent. It was true what his brother said. There was something about the Island that got into a person's blood and became a part of their very essence. It was like a child who cried and clung to your coat tails when you tried to say goodbye, and smiled with forgiveness and warmth and embraced you when you returned. Yet, for generations, youth had been forced to leave the Island because its resources were limited in providing a livelihood. Peter admired his brother's determination to stay, despite all the challenges. He himself was not yet sure of his own course. He knew the Island was where he felt complete, but his vision on how to stay was not clear. For the moment, he was satisfied to share his brother's dream.

Peter glanced at his watch. "Damn! Come on, before we're late."

They quickly packed the tools, and Daniel, as though reading his brother's mind, said, "Instead of worrying about me, you should start thinking about firming up your own life direction. What about Jake Williams's offer to take over his farm and marry Alice? She's a great worker and a fine cook. Ever taste her apple pie?" Peter bolted to his car, desperate to avoid the conversation about Alice. "You can be such an ass, brother. See you at work," he hollered over his shoulder as he threw his toolbox in the trunk of his car.

A few steps behind, Daniel's laughter filled the air. There was nothing he liked better than to torment Peter, yet he had been serious. Old Jake's farm was to be envied. It was just too bad he was determined to tie the daughter to the deal. Everyone but Jake knew that Alice was waiting for the day she could hit the road and move to a mainland city to pursue what she called "a bigger kettle of fish in the career and male department."

Daniel got in his car and followed Peter onto the road. Not that it mattered about Alice, because Peter had no interest in her, anyway. Daniel wondered why love couldn't be practical. Their own parents had nothing material to give their sons to help them start out in life, and Peter could have had it made had he and Alice cared for each other. Daniel sighed. The same went for Alice. She would never find anyone more loyal than Peter. Or hardworking. Peter was always working. Daniel's thoughts turned to his paid work. He was annoyed that they had stayed at the new house too long. Now they only had minutes to spare getting to their worksite, and he hated the anxious feeling in the pit of his gut. Today, work had to go right.

Wrapped up in his thoughts, Daniel never noticed the car parked on the side of the road just up from the house, nor did he see it return to the road and travel the short distance before stopping right in front of the house. In it sat Charles Elliott, who took a drag on his cigarette and slowly exhaled the smoke as he contemplated the obvious work that was being done on the house. Elliott had to give the young bugger credit. Daniel MacDougall was undoubtedly a go-getter. Elliott narrowed his eyes and took another drag on the cigarette. Just maybe too much so. Such gumption could prove to be a problem and one thing Charles Elliott didn't like was a problem that involved someone else's ambition.

CHAPTER 3

One behind the other, Peter and Daniel pulled into the parking area of the Miscouche train station. This thriving Acadian village was located five miles west of the Prince County capital of Summerside. The small train station and miles of rail bed linked it to the major centres of North America. The distant sound of a whistle announced the imminent arrival of the train coming from the western end of the Island, which would make a brief passenger stop on its way east, but that was not Daniel and Peter's concern. The two brothers proceeded to the storage sheds by the switch line where two rail cars were waiting to be loaded with one-hundred-pound jute bags of potatoes destined for the Montreal market. The Irish had brought the potato to the Island, where it thrived and quickly became the main cash and export crop for farmers. The flavour of Island spuds couldn't be beaten.

The rest of the work crew, Keith MacKinnon, George Thompson, and Ernest Birch were already there waiting for the clock to strike the top of the hour. The young men were also from Daniel and Peter's home community of Lot 16, situated to the northwest of Miscouche. Several trucks and a horse with a sleigh, all heavily loaded with potatoes, had already formed a line.

Ralph MacLaren, the foreman, spotted the brothers and waved. "It's about time you two showed up! The day is already half over, and these cars need to be on their way before quitting time. Three of you get in the car and two on the load."

Peter jumped into the box car with Keith and George, and Daniel and Ernest took the sleigh. Daniel lifted a bag from the pile and heaved it up to the entrance of the rail car, where one of the men caught it and hefted it to the back of the car for packing. Ernest followed suit. Once the rhythm of the crew was established, the men fell into easy conversation.

"So how come you and Peter were almost late?" asked Ernest. "At the house, I imagine."

"Well, if you know, why are you asking?" quipped Daniel.

"I should know better than to expect a straight answer from you. I'll take that as a yes. It's a nice-looking house, Daniel. You did alright there." Ernest hoisted another bag on the ledge.

"She'll look even better with a fourth wall, and yes, I think I did do alright." Daniel lifted the final bag from the sleigh to the railcar, and the two men jumped to the ground. The farmer, who had been chewing the fat with another farmer, jumped into the sleigh and used the reins to move the horse along. The truck in the lineup pulled up and Daniel and Ernest jumped onboard. And so the day went. As one vehicle was unloaded, another pulled into place. The only breaks were the morning and afternoon snack times and lunch. Much as Ralph hated giving the two snack breaks, he realized the time lost was offset by the increased energy levels of the men.

The station clock showed four when Daniel placed the last bag of the last load on the lip of the rail car door. The boys pushed it into place, jumped to the frozen ground, and slid the heavy door into place. Ernest and Daniel got down from the truck bed and as the vehicle moved off, Daniel hollered, "We need to make tracks!"

As the men made for their cars, Ralph, clipboard in hand, stuck his head out the office door. "Hey! Where do you fellows think you're heading?"

Daniel shouted back, "Like you don't remember, Ralph. We're playing hockey in Mount Pleasant tonight. We'll be looking for you in the stands."

Ralph waved the clipboard. "You better make it worth my while. I got a dollar riding on a win. Oh, and make it a half hour earlier in the morning. A car has to be ready for Toronto by noon."

"We'll be here," said Peter, as he jumped in his car, mumbling "...of all the damn days to have to be early."

Ralph watched the men pull out of the yard. What he would give to be young again and have the energy to work all day and then play hockey at night. But at least he could watch and cheer them on. There was a lot of talent in the Intermediate C League, made up of teams from the central part of the county, and you never knew how a game would go. There was no better entertainment to be found when the cold winter temperatures allowed natural ice to be made in the old wooden country rinks. Ralph was telling the boys the truth that he was betting on them tonight. The Lot 16 Rangers was his first pick out of loyalty, but he had omitted the fact that he had also just made a bet on the opposing team in tonight's game with one of the farmers. Ralph reasoned he was only being practical, having watched half the Lot 16 team put in a hard day's work loading the railcars. Surely they had to be tired, and the Mount Pleasant team was made up of hefty young men who liked to play dirty. So, no matter what happened, Ralph was covered. He smiled and turned to watch the train engine hook onto the loaded cars.

The potato crew boys weren't the only ones anxious to be through with their day's work. Victor Yeo and Charlie Cann had laboured all day building lobster traps alongside the older fisherman, Johnny Williams. They were chomping at the bit to be on their way. If one of them wasn't looking at the clock, it was the other.

Finally, at four, Johnny took pity on them. "Away with you, boys. I'm just wasting my money having you here when all you can think about is the game."

Victor jumped to his feet and grabbed for his coat. He didn't need to be told twice. "Thanks, Johnny. We promise we will be here bright and early in the morning."

Johnny gave a grin that showed his white teeth against the redness of his beard, "If you don't win, you needn't bother coming."

Charlie, who was known for his optimism, tipped his hat at the old fisherman. "Well, Johnny, you'll be sure to see us then, and we'll expect a good fire for our efforts." As the young men closed the door of the shed behind them, Johnny shook his head and spoke to the empty room: "The cockiness of youth! You've got to admire it."

Several of the young farmers on the team were doing their best to get an early start on the evening barn chores. Ivan Campbell, who had gone to the feedmill with his father to have barley crushed, rushed the older man through his visiting ritual. John Cameron cut short his afternoon nap, while Wendell Smith told his mother she would have to wait another day for him to help her finish papering the hallway. Once the three made it to their respective barns, they hurried to feed the livestock and clean and bed them for the night. It was a fine balancing act of working quickly, satisfying their fathers' standards, and keeping track of the time on their wrist watches.

Team members weren't the only ones mindful of the time. Charles Elliott stood behind the counter of his general store, which he had proudly built from scratch and though customers still had a full hour left to increase his profits, he wished it was time to flip the sign to Closed and shut off the lights. His mind was on the night's hockey game to which he planned to take his wife and children. Elliott was a great fan of hockey, but going to the games was about more than the play—it was about meeting people and looking for business opportunities. The love of money, combined with a fear of putting all his eggs in one basket, prompted the storekeeper to have a number of irons in the fire.

While he waited for his sole customer, Mrs. Ethel Thompson, to finish gathering the items on her list, he glanced about the main floor of the store with its ornate plastered ceiling and brightly painted walls. It was an impressive establishment for a country store in the 1950s. There were two full floors, each averaging over a thousand square feet, filled with merchandise, plus a basement for storage. Charles kept the clothing and footwear area stocked with items as fashionable as anything that could be bought in the town of Summerside, some ten miles away, and he had a wide inventory of wallpaper, paint, nails, tools, furniture, pitch forks, shovels, rope, a little china, and a whole floor of groceries. The storekeeper looked approvingly over at the candy and cheese counters, which he knew were the envy of many other store owners. Yes, Charles concluded: if he didn't stock it, then no one needed it.

Finally, Mrs. Thompson made her way to the counter to pay for her goods. Charles was making small talk with her when the bell chimed on the door, and in rushed young Robert Phillips who headed for the rack with the boot and skate lace display. He quickly found the laces he wanted and brought them to the counter.

As Charles finished ringing in and bagging Mrs. Thompson's items, he glanced at Robert and said, "Big game tonight."

"Yeah, we're playing Mount Pleasant, so wish us luck." Robert dug money from his pocket, which he passed over to Elliot.

"Luck has nothing to do with it. It's all about heart, and skill, and the Lot 16 Rangers have plenty of that." Ethel Thompson knew the game as well as anyone else. She gathered her parcels as she spoke. Ringing in the laces, Charles offered his opinion. "That may well be, but a bit of luck goes a long way."

"When it comes to Mount Pleasant, it sure can." Robert pocketed his change.

"Well, I'm counting on the Rangers taking some of the stuffing out of Mount Pleasant tonight. It makes me mad when they play underhanded, so I'll be in the front row to see the smirk wiped off their faces. And will I see you there, Charles?" Ethel turned to ask the storekeeper.

"Wouldn't miss it. The team brings spirit to this community in a way that nothing else ever has. If my support in the stands can help the boys, I'm glad to give it," he replied.

Although Robert badly wanted to be on his way, he remembered his manners and carried Mrs. Thompson's parcels for her. At the door, they nearly crashed into Reverend Mark Johnson, the young minister who had arrived to serve the community three years ago after graduating from the theology school in Halifax, Nova Scotia.

The minister tipped his hat to Mrs. Thompson and turned to Robert. "Good luck on the ice tonight, Robert. And be sure to tell the boys to keep it clean."

"I'll be sure to do that, Reverend Johnson." Robert hurried Mrs. Thompson to her car.

"There's different degrees of clean you know, Robert." Mrs. Thompson took the bags from the sturdy farm boy she had known his entire life and settled them matter-of-factly into the trunk of her car.

"Yeees, Mrs. Thompson, there surely are." Robert looked at his former Sunday schoolteacher, puzzled for a few moments until he realized what she was saying. "Clean can most certainly come in many different degrees." The two laughed before parting ways.

Reverend Johnson stepped up to the counter. "Good evening, Mr. Elliott. It sure was a fine winter day." Without waiting for Elliot to respond, the Reverend continued: "Might you have some more of those throat soothing drops I bought last week?"

Charles looked at the young preacher who he felt was always secretly laughing at him. "I suppose you want them for the game tonight?"

"Yes. The cold air bothers my throat." Reverend Johnson reached into his pocket for some coins.

"Are you sure it's the cold air or the cheering you are doing in the stands that is bothering your throat, Reverend?" Charles handed over the drops in exchange for the money.

"I think it might be a bit of both, sir. I'm as determined as you to support the Rangers." Reverend Johnson dropped the tin can of drops into his coat pocket. "See you at the game, Mr. Elliott." He'd be dammed if Elliott's comments would tone down his cheering in the stands.

"A bit of both, indeed," Elliot muttered as he watched the Reverend leave the store.

One of the people who would not be going to the game, however, was Carol Ramsay. Instead, she stood at the kitchen sink washing the last of the supper dishes. She could hear her husband, Roland, upstairs getting ready for the game. The children were seated at the kitchen table finishing their homework so they could skate on the outdoor rink while she finished the barn work. Like most game nights, Carol completed the farm chores for her husband so he could be behind the bench of his beloved Lot 16 Rangers. Most times, she didn't mind staying home to do the work. She and Roland were a partnership and that was all there was to it. If coaching was important to him, she would support him. While there was no glamour in her side of the agreement, the payoff came in the form of a much happier husband. Plus, Carol was proud of both him and the players for what they achieved as a team. Still, sometimes she resented her sacrifice, especially when it meant she missed out on the excitement of being in the crowded rink and watching the game. Tonight was one of those times, but she wouldn't let it show.

Carol drained the water from the sink and turned to the children. "Get your skates on so Dad can tie your laces when he comes downstairs."

The two boys, Alex and Dale, slammed shut their books and rushed for their skates, which were warming behind the kitchen range. They seated themselves on the wooden bench by the door and pushed their feet into the skates. Carol filled the stove with wood and turned down the draft. She heard Roland thumping down the backstairs and waited for him to join her in the kitchen. He appeared just as she knew he would: freshly shaved, hair slicked back, dressed in his rink pants, shirt, and vest, and looking handsome. He went directly to the boys to lace up their skates.

"Is it a Rangers' win tonight, Dad?" Dale beat Alex to the same question they asked every game.

"That's the plan, boys." Their father answered just as he did, every time. As the boys stood to put on their outdoor gear, Roland turned to Carol, "It might be a late night. Don't worry about waiting up for me."

Wrapping her arms around her husband, Carol breathed in the faint smell of her husband's cologne. "Of course I'll wait up, Coach Ramsay. I'll be wanting a first-hand commentary of the game."

CHAPTER 4

Jeannie and Mary heard their father in the enclosed porch stamping the snow from his feet and then the creaking groan of the hand pump as he washed his hands. They jumped up from their play on the kitchen floor and rushed for the door.

"Daddy, Daddy! You're home! Pick us up, pick us up!" they shouted in unison and danced about him when he came through the door. He quickly removed his coat, hung it behind the stove, and scooped both girls into his arms.

"You're cold, Daddy." Mary clasped his face in her small hands.

"Too cold for a whisker rub?" Daniel leaned in and before his daughter could protest, he rubbed his bristled cheek against her soft one until she squirmed and laughed with glee.

"Now me, Daddy, now me," Jeannie demanded, and her father complied. He nodded a greeting to his father in-law, James, seated by the stove, reading the paper, and saw that the table was already set for supper.

Isabel entered the kitchen from the pantry and placed a pie on the table before turning to her family.

"Let your father be, girls. He needs to eat his supper and get ready for the game." She motioned at the chairs around the table. "Everybody sit in."

James took his place at the head of the table. "Is it a must-win game tonight, Daniel?"

Daniel took his own seat, and placed the two children on his knees. "If we want to stay on top, every win counts, but we especially want to beat Mount Pleasant."

Jessie, his mother-in-law, emerged from the pantry and removed a crock of beans from the oven of the kitchen range. "You would think after a man worked hard all day like you do, Daniel, he might be more interested in getting some rest, rather than..."

"Don't start, Mom. He deserves the break hockey gives him." Isabel cut off her mother as efficiently as she removed a bowl of fried potatoes from the warming closet.

She placed the bowl on the table and proceeded to serve her husband.

"I can speak for myself, Isabel," Daniel said, as he turned towards Jessie, a woman he greatly respected, but often butted heads with. She hadn't forgiven him for making Isabel's life harder than it needed to be, and yet his welfare seemed important to her.

"I'm just having a bit of fun when I play hockey, Mrs. MacArthur." He tore the slice of bread he had buttered in half and gave a piece to each girl, along with spoons to eat off his plate.

"The Rangers would not be the force they are without you. In fact, I might be inclined to say they would be nothing," offered James, spooning potatoes onto his plate.

Jessie took her place at the table and accepted the bowl of potatoes from James. "So would his family." She passed the green tomato chow to her son-in-law. "You need to remember, Daniel, that you have a wife and two children depending on you. What would happen if you got hurt having fun?"

It was not a discussion Daniel wanted to have, not then, and not with his mother-in-law, but her question was valid and one he had asked himself many times. "I'm the least likely player to get hurt, since I'm the only one who wears a helmet."

"Well, forgive me if I don't believe that a piece of leather strapped on your head is going to protect you. Especially when we all know that as the best player on the team, you're a likely target." Jessie stopped spooning mustard pickles onto her plate and looked Daniel right in the eye.

"Sometimes you have to have faith, Jessie, that all will be well," James interjected.

"And sometimes you have to have common sense." Jessie pointed a fork at her husband. Daniel and Isabel shared an uneasy glance at the brewing argument.

"Thank-you, Mrs. MacArthur, for calling me the best player on the team. That is quite a compliment." Daniel attempted to bring the conversation to safer ground.

Jessie looked up from her task of pouring tea into her cup. "You can save the malarkey, Daniel—I'm just repeating what the fans say, not to mention the fact that the players name you captain year after year."

"I'm not the only one to know a good thing when I see it." Isabel laughed.

Although no one would have guessed, Jessie's words played over and over in Daniel's mind throughout the meal. He concentrated on eating the food Jeannie and Mary were feeding him, and kept the conversation light, but he wondered, as he often did, if he was just being selfish by playing hockey. There was nothing in it for him other than the sheer love of the game. When he took to the ice, the responsibilities in his life melted away. Those rare moments of play that gave joy made it possible to carry his load. But the risk was real—he couldn't afford an injury if he wanted to achieve his dream and provide for his family. Maybe his father-in-law was right about having faith. It sounded better than living in fear. And Daniel surely knew plenty about fear.

CHAPTER 5

At six on the dot, Percy MacLean pulled his father's one-ton truck with its closed-in wooden box into the schoolyard. The truck, which hauled potatoes and grain by day, served as transportation for the team and fans on game nights. Percy had spread a couple of bales of straw on the floor of the box to keep feet warm and had put bales around the exterior walls for the passengers to sit on. He had hung an old blanket over the opening at the back of the box to keep the wind out. Both players and fans were already waiting for him, stamping their feet impatiently to keep warm. As soon as the truck braked, they surged forward. The rule was that players climbed on first, followed by fans, until the truck was full. The reality was that a spot was always found for anyone who needed a ride. Daniel and Peter made a dash for the cab and opened the door, but Percy was having none of it. "Get in the back, boys. I'm saving these seats for better-looking passengers than you two."

The men laughed, but Percy's plan of driving to the rink with a pretty and available girl in the front seat next to him was serious. It was also doomed when his sister, Beth, and their cousin Norma, skirted around Daniel and Peter and hopped into the cab seats that Percy was saving.

"What a considerate thing for you to do for your family, Percy." Beth patted her brother's disappointed face before settling in for the ride.

"Serves you right, you schemer," said Peter as he followed Daniel into the back of the cab. "But I'll be sure to keep things cozy in the back for you." Resigned, Percy watched as Wendell and John helped a few fair passengers climb in the box before hopping in themselves. Then he checked his watch.

"We have to go. Is everyone accounted for?"

When a sing-song of laughing voices yelled "Yes!" Percy put the truck in gear and began the trip to the Mount Pleasant rink. Though the distance wasn't great, the drive would take over an hour on rough narrow roads that were flanked by snowbanks often as high as the truck itself in some places. He sure hoped the wind wouldn't block the road with drifting snow before they had to head home. Maybe it was just as well his sister and cousin were in front. Percy needed to concentrate on driving.

The Lot 16 Rangers had eleven players: enough for two defence lines, and two forward lines. Daniel, Keith, Ernest, and John played defense, while Peter, George, Charlie, Wendell, Robert, and Victor made up the forward lines. The team's only goalie was Ivan, because no one else wanted to play nets, and Ivan, though less than stellar in the position, had come with the pads. The players ranged in age from twenty through to twenty-eight and had pretty well grown up together. A number of them had been raised on farms at the lower end of Southwest Lot 16, while the rest were children of fishers, small farmers, and labourers from the upper end of the settlement that bordered the Grand River. Only a couple had married and had families, which somewhat set them apart from the others, but they all got along well.

"Coach Ramsay must have left early on his own for the rink. His car was gone when I came by the farm, but there were still lights on in the barn." John, who liked to know the ins and outs of everything, reported this tidbit of information to those in the truck box.

"Yeah, that would be Carol doing the chores. Lucky for us, she sees herself as part of the team and pitches in with the work to free up Coach Ramsay."

Chewing on an apple, Wendell nodded though no one could see him. "Yeah, if it wasn't for Coach Ramsay, there wouldn't be the Lot 16 Rangers."

Don Baglole, a Rangers' fan who had grown up with the coach, and knew him better than most, interjected, "It's not like he isn't getting something out of it. Nobody likes to win more than Coach Roland Ramsay."

Don then stretched his long legs out in front of him to relax the muscles. He knew by the time the game was over his legs would be cramped from the tight fit in the cold stands. There was a lot more he could say about Coach Ramsay, but left it there.

At that moment, Percy took a bend in the road too fast and everyone seated on the right hand side was thrown against the person seated next to them. Wendell took the opportunity to scramble across the floor to squeeze himself between the two girls, Colleen and Evelyn. Still single at twenty-four, Wendell was always on the lookout for a possible girlfriend. He knew how to get one, just not how to keep one. The handsome young lad was all about catch and release.

Lawrence Smith, a middle-aged labourer who never missed a Rangers' game, spoke up. "You have that right, Don, but Roland has a lot of pride in the players, which is justified. I mean, he started with a few boys on the ice in a pasture field, and on the pond, and now they are one of the top teams in the South Shore division."

"Let's make sure we keep it that way tonight. We need to keep our heads up and be prepared for every dirty play in the book," said Peter.

"Do you really think Mount Pleasant plays any dirtier than Bedeque, Freetown, or us?" Daniel flashed a smile in the dark.

"Yes!" everyone answered in unison.

Peter continued, "They play dirty just for the sport of it, and to make up for their lack of skill. The rest of the teams only resort to it when nothing else is working."

This time, Percy swerved left, banging heads against the truck box wall and generating a lot of complaints. The passengers couldn't see that he had successfully avoided a fox on the road. Colleen and Evelyn took the opportunity to scurry to the right side of the truck box. Wendell had applied too much cologne for their liking.

With the hockey conversation disrupted, Victor turned in the dark towards the sound of Daniel's voice and said, "Peter tells me you're not going back to Montreal in the spring."

Trust Peter to go talking about his private business. "Not if I can help it." Daniel didn't try to keep the sound of annoyance out of his voice.

"Really? You're crazy not to go," piped up Robert. "If the old man would let me off the farm, I'd be gone in seconds." He leaned forward to try and see Daniel's face.

"You're sure it's him holding you back? It's easy enough to say you'll do something when you don't have to. And we all know, as the only son, you're set for life." The words came from Peter who, having caught the tone of his brother's voice, felt a need to get in on the conversation. He kicked Victor in the leg for his stupidity in revealing what he had been told in confidence.

Daniel spoke to Robert. “That’s all the more reason you should go— so you can get over thinking you’re missing out on something.”

“Are you saying I’m not? Look at what Montreal has that this place doesn’t.” Robert may have been the youngest player on the team, but he didn’t back down.

“I think you need to look at what this place has that Montreal doesn’t,” Daniel answered.

Ernest, not a fan of conflict, broke the heaviness of the mood. “I’m tempted to someday climb into one of the potato bags we’re loading on a rail car bound for Montreal and see what lovely French girl might take me home.”

“Once she peeled you, she’d be looking for a refund, because you ain’t no netted gem,” Daniel retorted.

Everyone’s laughter carried through to the cab. Percy glanced into the rearview window wondering what fun he was missing and stepped on the gas while thinking about all the responsibility he had transporting the team. Five minutes later, Percy pulled the truck into the rink parking lot and looked about for a good spot. There was going to be a crowd tonight. The lot was already over half full with still plenty of time before the puck dropped.

CHAPTER 6

The Mount Pleasant Rink was in an old hangar of the former Bombing and Gunnery School built as part of the British Commonwealth Air Training Plan during World War II. The servicemen and the planes were long gone, but the rink and hockey breathed an entirely different life into the space.

As soon as Percy parked the truck, everyone in the back unloaded and headed inside. While the fans joined the queue to pay their entrance fee, the team headed for the visitors' dressing room, where they could see Coach Ramsay waiting outside the door. Daniel brought up the rear of the team, and as they walked along, he carefully checked out the surroundings. Whenever Daniel went somewhere, he paid attention to what was around him, be it landscape, streetscape, interiors of buildings, or people. He especially loved watching people, although sometimes the habit evoked an unfathomable sadness. Still, Daniel couldn't understand people who didn't look about them, but just kept their heads down and went about their business. In his opinion, they were missing out seeing so many of life's offerings that helped make a person feel alive. Daniel quickly scanned the stands. Mount Pleasant fans clearly outnumbered the Rangers' fans, but that was only to be expected at an away game. There were all ages in the stands, including many children and women. That fact gave Daniel a sense of peace.

Once inside the dressing room, the players dropped their bags on the benches and began to dress for the game. The process was quick, for they had little gear. Most of them simply pulled their jerseys over their undershirts and shirts. The men were proud of the jerseys, especially how they were acquired. A Summerside merchant had stocked up on NHL jerseys one Christmas, only to find those emblazoned with the Rangers name didn't sell. He had given the Lot 16 hockey team a great price to take them off the clearance rack. Mothers and wives had stitched Lot 16 over the top of "Rangers", and a new team was born. Each player had hockey pants, socks, gloves, and, of course, skates—the pride and joy of their equipment. Only Daniel had a helmet. It was the last item he self-consciously pulled from his bag and strapped on his head. He had initially debated whether the expense was worth it, but the sense of protection he felt wearing the thin piece of leather was empowering. All the players knew better than to say anything about the helmet. Several of them secretly would have liked to have had one if it meant Daniel's confidence on the ice.

As soon as the men were dressed, they sat down on the dressing room benches. Conversation was sparse, since they had talked all the way to the rink. Now was the time to get their heads in the game, gain control over nerves, and listen to their coach. "Okay, boys, we are going to win this game tonight by working as a team." Coach Ramsay was all business. "Let's stay away from the fancy individual stuff."

"Does that mean you aren't going to let Ivan play?" Keith looked up from where he was adjusting his laces.

"Bite me, Keith. Be careful where I put this when you're covering the net." Ivan brandished his thick goalie stick at Keith.

"Listen." Coach Ramsay held up his hand to stop the chatter. "Make sure we headman the puck and provide strong forechecking in Mount Pleasant's end."

Coach Ramsay started pacing as he talked. "Remember, we are a faster skating team and should be able to tire them out. Also, and perhaps most importantly, let's stay out of the penalty box. We've worked hard to get to this point—don't let yourselves down. Finally, let's make our fans proud." He nodded at Daniel, the team's captain, to give any final instructions to the group.

"Okay players, let's show the Mount Pleasant Flyers how hockey is really played!" Daniel stamped his feet and whooped.

Inspired, the players got to their feet, and began to chant: "Lot 16 is lean and clean. They're ready to make a scene. Let's goooooo, Lot 16!" Their voices grew so loud, no one heard the knock at the door until it turned into a bang. It was time to play hockey.

As the Lot 16 Rangers filed out of the dressing room and walked to the visitors' box, the air pulsed with a roar of thunder as the fans stamped their feet and clapped their hands.

Peter, playing centre, took the first faceoff for the Rangers. From the moment the puck dropped, the play was fast and the fans were right there in the game, slapping the boards and yelling, "Go, Rangers, go!" or "Go, Flyers, go!"

Daniel was clearly in his element. His grace and skill were immediately apparent. Within minutes, he broke through centre ice, gracefully picked up a long pass, split the defencemen, and deposited the puck between the legs of the Mount Pleasant goaltender. "Let's go, everyone, make a scene!" The Rangers' fans screamed at the top of their lungs, and those standing by the boards thumped them with their hands. The cheers were met by a round of booing from the Mount Pleasant Flyers' fans.

One of the Mount Pleasant team members, Chester Craig, had hockey skills of a lesser calibre than many of the other players, but he was large in stature, and his intimidation skills had been well honed. Mount Pleasant's Coach Dyment placed Craig on the ice to shadow Daniel and hamper his play. Several times, Craig succeeded in slamming Daniel into the boards, much to the delight of the Flyers' fans, but was unable to slow him down or prevent him from setting up plays. George, playing left wing for the Rangers, scored the next goal, followed by Charlie on right wing. Then Mount Pleasant quickly scored two goals on the Rangers' net just as the first period ended.

With a 3-2 score in favour of the Rangers, the second period got underway with another warning from Coach Ramsay to stay out of the penalty box. Mount Pleasant was doing their best to provoke the Rangers, but cool heads prevailed, and no one took the bait. Coach Ramsay held his breath every time his second lines raced out onto the ice. If anyone was going to slip up, it would be one of them, but they played clean and did him proud.

"Lot 16, it's time to shine!" The anxiety of the fans grew with each shot on the respective nets. People jumped to their feet in anticipation of a goal, only to slump down again with the goalie's save. No doubt the rafters vibrated from the impact of the cheering. Daniel set up two good opportunities for the forward line to score, but the Mount Pleasant goalie was giving nothing up. The fact didn't upset Daniel. There was still plenty of time on the clock and he was having fun. Mount Pleasant got more shots on goal, but the Rangers held onto the lead. The period ended with no change on the scoreboard.

At the start of the third period, the tension in the rink thickened like smoke rising from a chimney on a mild day. Fans were banging on the boards and hollering insults in an attempt to distract the players: "Call the undertaker, cause the number 10 Ranger is a stiff!" ... "Who let the skunks in? Never mind, the stink is coming from the home team!" ... "You're an embarrassment to your mother!" ... "Throw away your stick, and use your long nose. You might get a goal!" ... "Jesus, you call that puck handling?" No one was safe from the roaring fans. Coach Ramsay paced behind the Rangers' bench chewing gum a mile a minute. He wanted the win so badly he could taste it. The man had dedicated hours of time away from the farm and family for this team that he had built from nothing. He might be middle-aged, but part of him was out on that ice taking every check and scoring every goal. Often, Coach Ramsay was amazed at the talent in those country boys, and wondered how far some of them could have gone with the big teams had opportunity presented itself. But the scouts weren't among the crowd in the Mount Pleasant rink. And maybe that was a good thing, because what Ramsay and his players had going in the Island league likely felt as good and as challenging as the big times. And the fans were giving all of them their moment of glory. Coach Ramsay tried to let his muscles relax, but it was of no use.

The game continued to move quickly as both teams made skilled shift changes. The fans' necks rotated side to side following the puck as it shot from one end of the ice to the other at lightning speed. The goaltenders deflected shot after shot as the minutes on the clock ticked away. Finally, Daniel, carrying the puck with Craig in pursuit, broke away and skated into the Mount Pleasant end. With no forward player in place to pass to, he realized if a goal was going to happen, it was up to him. The goalie came out to meet him, and Daniel gave the impression he would shoot to the left. The goalie took the bait and moved forward to the left. In that moment, Daniel moved the puck a little to the right, and with a powerful wrist shot, put it into the net. As the fans erupted with cheers, the siren blared. The game was over.

The Mount Pleasant Flyers' players ignored their coach's signal to return to their box and dropped their gloves on the ice. But Coach Ramsay quickly called his players in and ushered them back to the dressing room. The boys relished the win as they undressed, and Coach Ramsay was full of praise. "Way to go, boys! Ivan, you were solid in nets, great game."

"Thanks, Coach," said Ivan as he stripped off his goalie pads. Bending over he turned his backside to Keith. "Bite me."

Coach Ramsay rolled his eyes. "And Daniel was hot. What did you have for supper? Beans?"

"Yeah, as a matter of fact I did." Daniel lifted a butt cheek and let one rip.

When the laughter subsided, Coach Ramsay spoke. "The Mount Pleasant crowd was upset about the loss, so take your time changing and let them clear the building before we leave. Percy, it might be a good idea for you to go start the truck and get it warmed up."

Five minutes later, Coach Ramsay opened the dressing room door, and seeing that the coast was clear, signalled to everyone that it was safe to leave. The Rangers filed out into the corridor, with Daniel and Peter bringing up the rear. As the door slammed shut behind them, the rink lights were cut, and in the darkness, the team was jumped.

"Christ Almighty!" someone cursed, and soon the pitch black was full of grunts and yelps and the sound of fists making contact with various body parts. Daniel, his arms wrapped around someone's middle from behind, shouted, "There's a side door about ten feet up on the left! Make for it and get out in the open!"

An intoxicated voice shouted out, "Is that the best you cowardly bastards can fight or cuss?" The man grunted as Peter gave him a solid punch in the gut before scrambling for the door, but it was Keith who managed to wrench it open, and the brawling players and a number of Mount Pleasant fans spilled into the parking lot. As he threw a punch and felt his fist crunch into the side of someone's head, Daniel suddenly knew security and survival were two reasons he checked his surroundings.

The moment he saw the commotion, Percy put the truck in gear and edged forward as close to the mob as he dared. He laid on the horn to let his team know where he was, and those who could, broke free of the fight and made a run for the truck. After the first few people scrambled into the box, they helped haul others in and pushed them aside to make way for the next person. Coach Ramsay ran for his car, got it started, and pulled up next to the truck.

Several Mount Pleasant players and fans were down on the ground unable to get up, while a couple of others limped their way back into the rink. Some simply backed off when they saw most of the Rangers had made it to the truck or Ramsay's car, but the two men entangled with Daniel and George were determined to fight to the bitter end. Finally, Daniel and George broke free and ran for the truck. The other players hauled them in, and after a quick headcount, Peter shouted "Go!" Percy already had the truck in gear and was letting out the clutch when those in the back spotted Mark Manderson, one of their fans, pinned to the side of his car by two big men. Inside the car, their faces pressed to the window crying, were

Mark's two preteen girls. They loved the Rangers and constantly begged their father to take them to the games. Mark was holding his hands out in front of him trying to ward the men off. One of the men hit him square in the mouth and Mark dropped to his knees.

"Wait! Percy, stop!" Daniel hammered on the box wall. "Quick! We need out! Peter—Keith—let's go!" The three men leapt from the truck and ran to Mark's car. Daniel and Keith took on the attackers, while Peter helped Mark to his feet and into the car. Mark's girls screamed for Peter to close the door before the men could hit their father again, but that was unlikely. Daniel's man was on the ground with blood flowing from his nose. Keith had aimed a blow to the groin that had buckled his fighter's knees and sucked the breath from his body. Even Keith felt the pain of the blow, but he hadn't started the fight. He was just finishing it. Mark had the keys in the ignition, but made no move to put the car in gear.

"Gun it, Mark! Get the hell out of here!" Peter pounded on the window.

Finally Mark sprang into action and peeled out of the parking lot. Keith, Peter, and Daniel ran to the truck, where they were hauled into the box by the other players. "Everyone is in!" yelled Robert. Seeing several men spill out of the rink and head toward the truck, Percy stepped on the gas and tore out of the parking lot, the engine, in first gear, roaring in protest. Coach Ramsay was right behind.

For a moment, shocked silence filled the back of the truck. Charlie broke the tension. "Holy Hell! That was a sure instant cure for constipation!" He wiped his brow. "Let's give ourselves a round of applause for winning the game and living to tell the tale." Everyone clapped and hooted.

Daniel seated himself on a bale and leaned against the wall for support. He fought to steady his breathing, and then removed a mitten to watch the blood oozing from the knuckles of his left hand. He grimaced at the thought of hefting potato bags the next day. He quickly put the mitten back on and placed his hand under his jacket for warmth. Suddenly, he began to laugh. All in all, it had been a good night.

CHAPTER 7

Isabel had waited up for Daniel. The moment she saw his hand, she sighed deeply, uncurled herself from the blanket she was wrapped in, and rose from her chair by the stove. She retrieved the basin from the nail where it hung on the kitchen wall, and poured salt into it, followed by hot water from the kettle and just enough cold water to make the mixture lukewarm. She placed the basin on the kitchen table and motioned Daniel to be seated.

"You promised at this very table to be careful. I can hear my mother now." Isabel examined his swollen hand before placing it in the water.

"I was careful on the ice. I never promised anything about off the ice. A couple of guys tried to put a beating on Mark while the two girls were watching in the car. Would you have wanted me to leave them in that situation?" The saltwater solution stung and Daniel tried to remove his hand, but Isabel carefully pushed it back into the water, and held it under for a good minute or so.

"Don't ask stupid questions. You know one of the reasons I love you is because you're there for others." Isabel removed her husband's hand from the water and gently dried it. She then reached for the Watkins salve, the go-to-medicine in the house for nearly every ailment.

"You defend my playing to your mother, but you'd be happy if I'd quit, wouldn't you?" Daniel watched Isabel's face as she worked.

"Honestly— yes. I'm afraid you'll get hurt. But— no. You shine on the ice, and I know that playing hockey lets you escape your responsibilities and burdens. At least for a little while." Isabel began wrapping Daniel's injured hand in one of the strips of flannel bandages that her mother always kept at the ready.

"You and the girls are no burden, Isabel. I can't imagine my life without the three of you." With his free hand, Daniel reached up and stroked Isabel's cheek.

For a moment, he thought about telling her about the job waiting in Montreal, but only for a moment. Rarely did he keep anything from Isabel, but this was something he couldn't voice just yet. She might encourage him to go, and those were words he couldn't hear right then.

"Did you make the punch count?" Isabel covered Daniel's hand with hers to hold it to her face a moment longer.

"I sure did." Daniel grinned the endearing smile of a young boy.

"I can just imagine. Go up to bed, Daniel. I'll see to the fire."

Isabel put away her nursing supplies and put another stick on the fire and turned down the draft. She wished she could have seen the fight.

Though his hand was swelled and stiff the next morning, Daniel was at the new house before first light. The throbbing throughout the night had not made for a peaceful sleep, so he had arisen earlier than usual with plans to start putting up staging. Daniel had hoped swinging a hammer would take out the stiffness, but it was already clear it was going to be a long workday and he'd have to just suck up the pain. From the second storey staging, he watched his brother pull into the driveway. Peter had been pretty certain Daniel would be there early as it would be far too sensible to take the day off and let his hand heal.

As Peter hopped out of the car, toolbox in hand, he didn't bother to broach the subject of the injury, but just started in on the game. "I think last night's game was the best one of the season," he said.

"You say that every time we beat Mount Pleasant." Daniel paused his hammering and flexed his stiff fingers.

"Yeah! It sure feels good to take them out." Peter slid a stud onto the staging.

"Especially in the parking lot," responded Daniel.

"You're right. It was especially good in the parking lot," Peter chuckled as he put a little more force behind the hammer than needed.

The men fell silent, each absorbed in his own thoughts. For Peter, it was the game and how unimpressed his mother would be to learn of yet another fight. Not that he had any intentions of telling her, but she'd hear about it somewhere today, and would be reminding him at the supper table that she had raised her boys better than that. Peter could hear her now. "What did you fellows do to that other team to get a fight going?" It had been that way his whole life, but he was no longer the child bullied in the schoolyard whose lack of support from his mother left him questioning if he did indeed deserve the beatings. These days, Peter listened to his gut, which never lied to him about when to stand up for himself. There was no one he needed to apologize to for last night's fight.

Daniel's mind was also running a mile a minute as he remembered everything that had happened in the past twenty-four hours: hockey, the fight, the likely condition of Mark's face today, the house, Montreal and the job, and Isabel and the girls. It was a wonder Daniel could drive a nail straight.

"Morning, boys. You're hard at it early." Both men jumped when a voice spoke to them from beneath the staging.

The brothers looked down to see Charles Elliott.

"We need to make every minute count if we are going to be in by spring. It's good of you to stop by and see the progress. I'll come down and show you around." Daniel climbed from the staging onto the ladder and made his way down to the ground. Peter stayed where he was, but didn't resume his work. Instead, he watched the storekeeper.

Elliott took a deep drag on his cigarette, then dropped the butt and ground it beneath his foot. He pulled his coat collar up around his ears before ramming his hands in the pockets and stared at the ground.

"I'm afraid it's rather an unpleasant call this morning, Daniel. I wish I had known just how serious things were before you hauled the house over here, but it's like this— I'm experiencing a cash flow problem at the store, and the only way I see out of it is to call in the money I loaned you for this place." Elliott removed the cigarette package from his coat pocket and made a show of withdrawing another cigarette, which he lit with an expensive gold lighter. He took a deep drag and made eye contact with Daniel.

"You're calling in my mortgage?" Disbelief and shock sounded in Daniel's voice.

"Please understand. It's not that I want to— rather, I need to. If you remember the terms, I need only to give you a month's notice, but knowing how much you have put into the place, I'm willing to give you an extra week to raise the money." Elliott took one last drag of the cigarette before grinding it beneath his foot.

"Big of you, Charles!" Peter cleared his throat, and from his place above on the staging, spit. The gob just missed Elliott's leather boots.

Daniel stood as though frozen to the spot on which he stood, with the hammer still clenched in his hand. He swung it back and forth unaware that he did so. He didn't speak.

"Well, I'll leave you to it. Hopefully, you can work something out in the next five weeks. I would really hate to take the land from you." Elliott kept his eyes on the two brothers as he tipped his hat farewell and stepped back a few paces. Returning to his car parked at the side of the road Elliott kept glancing over his shoulder as he walked. But Daniel continued to stand motionless, and Peter made no move from the staging. Only when Elliott disappeared from sight did Daniel throw his hammer onto the frozen ground and began to pound the wall with his bare fists.

CHAPTER 8

It was when the blood broke through the bandage that Daniel stopped beating the wall. Then he slumped against the wooden structure and allowed his body to slide until his bottom rested on the cold, snow-covered ground. His shoulder and head supported by the wall, Daniel fought to keep from crying in front of his brother. But he could not stop the tears from coming. Peter stayed silent. Only when Daniel's sobs grew softer and his breathing less ragged, did Peter finally climb down the ladder to stand helplessly at the bottom.

"Charles Elliott has as much of a cash flow problem as the Bank of Montreal. What better time to come looking for his money than mid-winter when the land can't give you anything." Peter badly wanted to put an arm around his brother's shoulder to comfort him, but this wasn't hockey, where such a move was acceptable.

"Don't," Daniel said.

"I'm willing to bet he already has a buyer lined up for spring and your money will be a handsome profit." Peter continued as though he hadn't heard Daniel. Perhaps in his anger, he hadn't.

"I knew he couldn't be trusted." He kicked at the snow with his boot, and knew it was foolish and hurtful to voice his thoughts, but he just couldn't hold back.

"So why didn't I?" Daniel lifted his head to look at his younger brother.

"Because you wanted him to be trustworthy." Peter looked into his brother's eyes. "You needed to believe he would behave like you. It makes you the better person, although that doesn't count for much at the moment."

The two men fell quiet. All that could be heard in the silence of the early morning was their breathing, which spoke volumes. Then Daniel raised himself slowly from the cold, hard ground.

"I've worked hard and sacrificed plenty for this land, and if Elliott thinks he can take it without a fight, then he has another thought coming." Daniel stood a little straighter and brushed the snow from his backside, as though his resolve had risen with him.

"Come on, we can't be late for work." He reached for his hammer lying where he had thrown it on the ground.

Peter retrieved his toolbox and fell into step as they walked towards their cars. Suddenly, Daniel stopped, turned, and looked back at the house. "We'll be back in the morning."

"Why put anything more into it now? It will just increase the value for Elliott," questioned Peter.

Daniel turned away and continued to walk to his car. His words carried back to Peter. "Because I can't lose hope."

Peter took one last look at the house, shook his head, and silently followed. He reflected on how fast life could turn on a guy. One moment, Daniel had been elated about a hockey win and building a home, and a moment later, had the rug pulled out from under him. Their father would no doubt justify the unfairness by saying God only allowed a man to get so high before He knocked him down. Daniel should have known his place. Peter shook his head. What a crock of bullshit that was. God had played no role in this mess. If He had, He would have struck Elliott dead with a bolt of lightning. As usual, though,

He was nowhere to be seen or heard. Not that Peter was really watching or listening.

Daniel and Peter were the last of the crew to arrive at the railyard. Ernest, and George, each sporting a shiner, were sitting on the edge of the platform. Keith was leaning against a post rubbing his hip. Two trucks were already waiting to be unloaded.

Ralph exited the office ready for a little fun. "I was thinking I might take the day off to spend the money you boys won for me last night, but I can see by your sorry asses I might need to take over loading the cars myself." The foreman laughed at his own joke, but still he was concerned that the Toronto order might not be loaded on time. The shiners that Ernest and George were sporting weren't an issue, but Daniel's banged up hand could be.

Daniel wasn't in the mood for casual banter. "About the only thing you can lift Ralph is your clipboard, so move aside and let some real men show you what work really is."

"Well, I guess not all the spunk got left in Mount Pleasant. You're still able to flap your gums," snorted Ralph.

"The only reason we all showed up today Ralph, is because of the respect we have for you, so have a little mercy on us," Keith begged.

"Maybe you could spend some of your winnings on a steak to take the swelling down on Ernest and George's eyes," suggested Peter.

"If I buy a steak, it'll be to eat, because nothing will make those boys look pretty. Now quit talking and get those trucks unloaded." Ralph strummed his fingers on the clipboard, and turned towards the office, the sign for the men to get to work.

Daniel took his place on the back of the truck. Ernest joined him, and the other three climbed into the boxcar. Daniel hoped the others would take Ralph's words seriously about not talking, but questioned himself on why that would even be a possibility. As soon as the work rhythm was established, the chatter started up again as the players dissected the game and moved onto the fight.

"I'm not afraid to admit I was plenty scared when we were trapped in the rink passage," Ernest said, as he placed a bag on the lip of the railcar. "And you boys know that it takes a lot to scare me."

"Really? From what I remember of our school days, you were scared of your own shadow," Daniel bantered as he lifted his bag up to the ledge. The men nearby chuckled causing the hefty Ernest to bristle.

"Well, it's one thing to fight in the open, but another thing altogether to be caught in a confined space. Last night could have turned out really bad."

"Fair enough, Ernest. It was a dangerous trick to play. But at least we know they are also suffering today."

"Oh yeah, ain't justice great?" Keith hollered from inside the railcar. "Oh, damn! it hurts to laugh."

For the rest of the morning, Daniel distanced himself from the conversation. For every truck to be unloaded there was a driver wanting to hear about the game and the fight. The rest of the crew were only too willing to tell the story. They put their captain's quietness down to his injured hand, not a war with a private demon.

The aspirin Daniel swallowed did nothing more than dull his physical and mental pain. Still, he carried his workload like any day, and breathed a sigh of relief when Ralph rang the quitting bell. Only after he got in the car and was driving home did Daniel allow Elliott's voice to play in his head:

"I'm afraid it's rather an unpleasant call this morning, Daniel. I wish I had known just how serious things were before you hauled the house over here, but it's like this - I'm experiencing a cash flow problem at the store, and the only way I see out of it is to call in the money I loaned you for this place."

Daniel gripped the steering wheel as Elliot's voice continued talking in his head. "Please understand. It's not that I want to—rather, I need to. If you remember the terms, I need only to give you a month's notice, but knowing how much you have put into the place, I'm willing to give you an extra week to raise the money."

At home, Daniel behaved no differently. He ate supper with the girls on his lap, and answered every question James and Jessie threw at him about the game and the parking lot brawl. Jessie had heard all about it at the afternoon meeting of the church ladies. Daniel figured she would rip him a new one, but to his surprise, she was all for the action he had taken.

"Just imagine," said Jessie. "Poor Mark could have been seriously injured or even killed by those hooligans, and in front of the children at that."

"I thought you didn't approve of fighting, Mom?" Isabel couldn't help stoking the fire.

"Sometimes, you just have to fight, Isabel, and then ask the Lord for forgiveness."

"You must spend a lot of time asking forgiveness, missus." James chuckled as he reached for a sugar cookie, then closed his eyes after he took a bite. "My! What good cookies, dear."

The only time Daniel came close to giving in to his emotions was when Isabel changed the dressing on his hand. The girls were in bed, but the adults were all still up and within earshot of one another: Jessie sewing at her machine in the corner of the dining room, James reading by the dining room stove, and Isabel and Daniel seated at the kitchen table.

After removing the bandage from his hand, Isabel turned it first one way and then the other. "I think your hand actually looks much worse today."

Daniel clenched his teeth when she lowered his hand into the dreaded saltwater bath. "It's from scraping against the jute bags all day."

Isabel nodded. As she put salve on his hand and re-bandaged it, Daniel counted the minutes until he could escape to the privacy of their bedroom. It was really the only place in the house where they were ever truly alone.

Finally, Isabel followed her parents upstairs while Daniel saw to the fire. He added a hardwood stick, turned down the draft, and took the kindling, now dry, from the oven and put it behind the stove for the morning. Isabel was already in her flannel nightdress and sitting up in bed reading when he entered the room. It was her ritual to be ready for bed ahead of Daniel. Unknown to him, she enjoyed watching him strip down for sleep. Daniel always turned his back to her, and she would watch the muscles in his arms and shoulders ripple as he removed his shirt. She secretly thought that the way Daniel removed his pants was an art form. Of course, in winter, he left his long underwear on for warmth, but their close fit only contributed to defining the shape of his lean, powerful body.

Tonight, though, Isabel had news she was excited to share. She put down the book. "Aunt Edith is getting a new sofa and chair for her front room. She offered us their old ones. Of course, I said yes. How lucky is that?"

Busy unbuckling his belt, Daniel inwardly groaned. The timing of the gift couldn't be worse. Isabel grew inpatient for him to share her excitement.

"Daniel? Are you listening to me?" Isabel sat up straighter in the bed.

He savagely kicked his pants aside.

"Daniel?"

"I heard you, Isabel. It is very generous of Edith, but...."

"But what? There are no buts, Daniel. I accepted the furniture."

"Please stop talking and listen to me." Daniel spun around to face his wife. Elliott, he... called in the mortgage this morning."

Isabel stared at him, stunned, as Daniel walked to his side of the bed.

"We have five weeks to come up with the money or he takes the place."

"No, that is not possible. He can't just do that!" Isabel shook her head in defiance.

"Unfortunately, he can." Daniel wearily lowered himself to a sitting position, his back to her, so he didn't have to see her face.

"That miserable skunk! What are we going to do?" Isabel scrambled across the bed and grabbed his shoulders to force him to look her in the eye.

"I don't know yet." Daniel kept his head lowered so he didn't have to see her hurt and outrage.

"Well, I know. We have to talk to our families. Between them, we should be able to raise the money." Isabel released her grip and cupped his chin to force him to make eye contact.

But Daniel pulled her hand away and got back to his feet to pace the length of the room several times before coming around to her side of the bed. Seating himself to look directly at her, Daniel spoke. "No. I'm not taking anything more from our families. They have already sacrificed enough for us. This is between us, Isabel. I'll find a way. We'll find a way."

"And if you don't? Because I know you expect it to be you that will solve the problem, not us." Isabel gave him a look filled with fury and determination.

Daniel sat back down on the bed and took her small hand in his. He gently stroked her soft palm with his thumb. "I need you to believe in me now— more than you ever have, Isabel."

Isabel was tempted to argue. Instead, she closed her eyes, nodded in agreement, and pulled him down on the bed. She wrapped her arms around her husband and held him close. They were far from beaten. Still, it was a long and restless night for both of them. When Daniel did sleep, he dreamed of Elliott's laughing face dancing before him, calling out, "Here, you stupid man. I have something for you." Then it was Peter circling him with a warning: "Don't believe him, don't believe him." Daniel had walked towards Elliott, anyway.

The next day, Daniel stayed true to his word. He returned to the house first thing in the morning, and Peter joined him not long after.

"Each morning brings more daylight," Peter noted.

"We can use the lengthening days," said Daniel, thinking of all that needed doing.

"What's the plan this morning?" Peter decided today was not the time for deep conversation. He would follow Daniel's lead.

"Get started on closing in the bottom wall," was Daniel's short answer.

As they fitted the boards and nailed them in place, Daniel thought of how satisfying this moment should have been, and felt the anger stir in his gut. The one thing Daniel did understand in the light of day was that Charles Elliott, whatever his circumstances, did not actually regret calling in the mortgage. The more Daniel had thought about Elliott's words, the more he realized the tone was not that of a man who was sorry. If Elliott had been indeed nervous and upset, Daniel decided it was only out of fear for his own safety about being alone with him and Peter.

Daniel fumed that he had stood there and let Elliott have his say with no real comeback. Why hadn't he challenged the man and asked for more details about the cashflow problems? Why hadn't he asked for more time instead of standing there like a lump of coal? As he drove another nail in the board, Daniel answered his own questions. It wasn't just shock on his part. He would have been wasting his breath. Elliott had made the mortgage rules, and Daniel had eagerly agreed to them.

With each stroke of the hammer Daniel berated himself for being such a fool for getting involved with Elliott. Peter was right. Daniel had wanted to believe the storekeeper could be trusted so he ignored the subtle comments he had heard about the man— things like how he usually came out on top. Daniel had thought people were only jealous of Elliott's thriving business.

Daniel recalled the day he had approached the storekeeper for the money. Elliott had been all ears. He listened intently to Daniel's plans and had even offered a few suggestions on cash cropping and animal husbandry. Daniel clearly remembered what Elliott had said that day: "Your working in Montreal for good money makes you a sound investment. Still, the interest rate will have to be higher."

Daniel replayed those words over and over as he and Peter nailed boards into place. He could now see how Elliott's words could be taken several ways. Daniel didn't want to be like his father, Duncan, so scarred from his own parents' loss that he never took a financial chance. When the old lady lender had called in his grandparents' mortgage during the recession, they were two years from having it paid after a lifetime of work. The heartbreak killed his grandfather, Cecil MacDougall. Daniel's father was spending his working career working for others, giving them his labour, being at their beck and call, and making good money for them, instead of working for himself. That wasn't the life Daniel wanted, but at the moment, it felt like it might be his destiny. How Elliott must have laughed every time Daniel paid extra money on the mortgage. Why hadn't he just made the regular payments and banked the extra until he could pay the remaining balance in one sum?

Daniel thought of all those lonely nights in Montreal, and he could hardly breathe. His family's sacrifice could not be for nothing. Isabel and the girls shouldn't have to suffer for his stupidity. Suddenly, as Daniel fit the last board of the morning in place, he recognized his anger as a good thing. Anger brought clarity. He wasn't stupid to want something better, but he was naïve to believe others behaved like he did. So he needed to make the anger work for him and remove the blinders from his eyes. Peter was right. Elliott was out to cheat him, and the anger generated from that knowledge would be the fuel to take him to the finish line. Daniel wasn't going to hand the place over to Elliott without a fight. As he drove the last nail in the board, he imagined it was Elliott's head he was pounding the hammer against, and it felt damn good.

"It's probably time for us to make tracks." Daniel tossed his hammer in his toolbox and turned to his brother. He then paused. "Thanks for coming this morning, Peter. You were right about Elliott, but the game isn't over."

Knowing his brother, Peter hadn't thought otherwise. Bending to pick up his tools, he wondered what was coming next.

CHAPTER 9

When Ralph came out of the office and rang the lunch bell, Daniel jumped down from the railcar and walked over to speak to the foreman.

"Ralph? I have an appointment in town. I might be a bit late getting back, but I'll make up the time." Daniel pushed his gloves into a coat pocket.

"No problem." Ralph waved him clear, and Daniel hurried to his car. Peter stood by the railcar and watched his brother drive out of the parking lot. He had no idea what Daniel was up to. He sighed. Maybe his brother was right, and Peter needed to start sorting out his own life. But first, he wanted an answer for his older brother.

Daniel pushed the old car as hard as the road would allow and made good time getting to Summerside. He parked on Main Street, and quickly walked through the door of the Bank of Nova Scotia. Anyone observing him would have realized he was a man on a mission. He gave the receptionist his biggest smile, which she returned before glancing down to his ring finger. She looked up with less enthusiasm, and indicated Daniel should follow her down the hall and into the office of the loans officer, David Foley.

Daniel quickly scanned the room and the loans officer himself, noting the man's fine suit and manicured hands. Foley stood, but ignored Daniel's outstretched hand. Instead, he indicated the chair in which Daniel should sit.

"Is that potatoes and jute I'm smelling?" As Foley took his own chair, he sniffed about him and grimaced.

Daniel felt his stomach churn. Foley, the pompous ass, was making it clear he felt superior to Daniel. The paunch that fell over the top of David Foley's fine suit pants suggested that he enjoyed a bountiful table, so he obviously wasn't disdainful of food production. Just the people producing it.

"Yes. I'm loading potatoes onto the railcars." Daniel had little choice but to humour Foley, but he had no intention of apologizing for bringing the smell of honest work with him.

"Toronto or Montreal market?" Foley perked up, always one to follow the scent of money.

"Toronto today. We loaded for Montreal earlier in the week. Both markets are hungry for Island potatoes," Daniel replied. Foley considered the information and nodded.

"So, what can I do for you today, Mr...." he paused, returning to the business at hand. He looked at the paper on his desk to check the name "MacDougall?"

Good sportsmanship obviously wasn't going to be a part of the encounter. Daniel could see that Foley saw him as a weak opponent that he could toy with. Daniel leaned forward. "I'm looking to borrow $1,200 to pay out my mortgage."

A look of boredom flickered across the banker's face as he leaned back in the comfortable leather chair and raised his arms to interlock his hands behind his head. The action pushed his gut outward, straining the buttons on his dress shirt.

"I see. Now, why would that be?" Foley finally said, looking up at the ceiling.

Daniel forced himself to relax in his chair. He couldn't afford to appear desperate. Since Foley wouldn't make eye contact, Daniel looked at the straining buttons. The crude thought leaped into his head of when Foley might have last seen his stick without the aid of a mirror.

"My private lender is having some cash flow problems and has called in my loan, which has more paid on it than required. The land and house are worth far more than what's left owing," Daniel explained.

This time, Foley leaned forward.

"Oh? Why didn't you acquire a mortgage from the Bank of Nova Scotia in the beginning?" His words were acid.

"You obviously don't remember turning me down for the lack of a down payment. When the banks wouldn't deal with me, I went private. The majority of the mortgage is paid, so I figure I'm no risk to you now." Daniel struggled to stay composed and keep his tone pleasant.

Foley picked up his ball point pen, a silver one with his name engraved on the side and rolled it between the fingers of his right hand. "Have you ever had any type of loan with us or any other bank?"

"No. I believe, when possible, in paying cash." Daniel felt like tearing the pen out of Foley's hand, forcing him to take the conversation seriously. The man knew damn well Daniel never had a loan with the Bank of Nova Scotia.

"Then we have no credit record to show your ability and dependability to make repayment now, do we?" Foley dropped the pen to the desk with a force that sent it rolling towards Daniel.

Only when the pen reached the edge of the desk directly in front of him did Daniel flick it back at Foley.

"Charles Elliott holds my mortgage. He can vouch that I always make my payments on time—and pay extra." Daniel fought to keep his tone of voice calm and neutral.

Foley lunged for the pen before it shot past him and onto the floor.

"Private lenders don't work on the same credit scale as the banks. Do you have fulltime work with one employer?"

"No, but I'm always working somewhere." Daniel knew that Foley was enjoying the mind game and getting off on the power play, but he tamped down the anger in his gut. Now was not the time to lose sight of the goal.

The loans officer lined up another shot. "Do you have the money to plant a crop come spring?" He smirked.

"I have an agreement with an older farmer to plant his crop for payment in seed and fertilizer." Daniel shot back.

The answer caught Foley off-guard. He stopped the play and went silent, letting the seconds tick by.

"I would like to help you, Mr. MacDougall. But your lack of a credit rating doesn't meet the bank's criteria for loaning money. I wish you luck elsewhere." He flipped the file folder shut.

"The value of the property makes me no risk to you, and how am I supposed to get a credit rating if you won't loan me any money?" Daniel slammed his fist down on the desk, now desperate.

But Foley stood, to indicate the meeting was at an end.

"I don't make the rules. I just follow them." He walked to his office door and opened it.

"I'm sure you have some leeway, especially when there is no risk to the bank." Daniel remained seated and made one last attempt.

"Good day, Mr. MacDougall." Foley pulled the door a little wider and gestured outward with his arm.

Resigned, Daniel stood up and walked from the office, then stopped and turned to speak again. But Foley shut the door in his face. As Daniel pulled on his hat and gloves and left the bank, he angrily hoped the smell of earth and potatoes lingered in the office for the afternoon. He felt sure the stench of Foley's aftershave clung to him.

Daniel returned to Summerside the following noon hour to try his luck at the Bank of Montreal. Before leaving the railway station, he had gone into the washroom and changed his clothing, and washed his hands, in an attempt to remove any of the earthy smell of potatoes. He also brought his good coat to wear. His teammates and co-workers, now eating their lunches, whistled at him as he walked by, although no one asked where he was going two days running. They knew Daniel and knew they wouldn't get a straight answer, no matter how curious they were. Peter was the better option for information.

"Where's your big brother going these days, Peter?" Ernest picked up his second baloney sandwich and casually threw out the question before taking a bite.

"Not a clue. I thought you might know." Peter put down his lobster sandwich and wiped his mouth with his sleeve before answering.

"Yeah right! Like you don't know your brother's every move." George gulped milk from a quart mason jar, and upon lowering it, didn't bother wiping off the milk mustache.

"If Daniel wanted me to know, he would tell me, although that doesn't necessarily mean I'd tell you guys", Peter griped.

"I'm sure we'll all find out soon enough." Keith held out one of his mother's sugar doughnuts to Peter.

Upon arriving at the bank, Daniel stopped for a moment outside the front door, and discreetly raised his arm to his face to check again for smell but could detect nothing. Robert Sanderson, the loans officer, greeted Daniel with respect and listened attentively to his request.

"I just wish, young fellow, you had banked the money you made those extra payments with and borrowed against it to build a credit rating." Sanderson seemed genuinely saddened by Daniel's situation.

"Why can't the land be my collateral?" Daniel appealed to the banker.

Sanderson shook his head. "The banks aren't interested in land, although I imagine the day will come when they will be hungering for it, but not in time to help you. The best I can do for you, Mr. MacDougall, is to advise you to apply for a small loan with us to establish a credit rating once you have secured full-time employment." He stood to indicate the meeting was over.

A disappointed Daniel stood outside the bank door. So much for the effort with the clothing, and he had certainly wasted his time washing away the smell of potatoes. A look could only take a man so far.

When Daniel returned home that evening, the family was just settling down to eat. As he took his seat, Isabel caught his eye, tilted her head to the side and raised her brows inquisitively as if to say, "Well?" Aloud she spoke, "How was your day?"

"Just the usual. We filled an order for Boston." Daniel gave a slight sideway movement of his head and frowned.

"Do you think we could go to Boston someday?" Isabel passed him his supper plate, trying to keep the conversation light.

"That would be nice, but not in a railcar." Daniel smiled at her.

“Passenger car, Daniel. We could go in a passenger car, not freight.” Isabel smiled back.

“I spend so much time in freight, I never thought of the passenger car,” Daniel laughed.

Jessie looked from one to the other but made no comment about their obviously staged conversation. She just hoped that whatever was up was not serious. Nobody in the family needed anything serious to deal with. Jeannie climbed down from her chair and tapped on her father’s knee to be picked up. Mary tried to follow suit, but her older sister pushed her back.

“Share.” Daniel’s one-word put an instant end to the sibling struggle, and both girls were soon on his knees.

“So, the Rangers take on Tyne Valley tonight?” James had seen Jessie’s face and knew it was up to him to get the conversation back on track.

“Yes, it should be a good game.” Daniel answered between mouthfuls. “We are pretty evenly matched.”

“Hopefully, the action stays on the ice.” James had no time for unsportsmanlike ambushes.

“There will be no trouble with Tyne Valley. At least not in the parking lot.” Jessie held a high opinion of the people of the small village, many of whom were relatives.

Daniel hoped Jessie was right. He didn’t think he had a brawl in him tonight. All he wanted was the freedom that a great game of hockey brought him.

Though it was a precious waste of fuel, Daniel decided to travel to the game on his own. He didn’t feel he could handle making small talk travelling to the game in the truck with the rest of the team. He also wanted to avoid Peter, who would certainly want an update on the noon trips to Summerside. But Daniel wasn’t ready to talk about the rejections and listen to Peter’s inevitable opinions. He hadn’t expected to feel ashamed for being turned down by the banks, and he didn't know what he was supposed to do about that feeling. The rules were bigger than Daniel, but that was no comfort. The rejection felt personal, because it likely was. Rules could always be broken for the right people.

CHAPTER 10

The Tyne Valley Rink was quickly filling up with fans, and the Rangers were already in the dressing room when Daniel arrived. He paused for a moment outside the door before going in. For the sake of the team Daniel needed to put his personal life on the backburner for a couple of hours.

Once in the dressing room, Daniel changed without a word and then sat quietly on the bench. John was seated across from him dressed and ready but sporting a wool hat. It struck Daniel as strange since John rarely wore a hat. He had curly dark hair of which he was very proud. Wishing to distract himself from his own troubles, Daniel asked, "Why the hat, John? It holding all that wisdom in?" Everyone else laughed and started badgering John with the same question.

Knowing his teammates, John knew the gig was up. He reached up and slowly pulled off the hat. He was completely bald.

"Damn! What the hell happened to you?" Ivan practically shouted.

"Yeah. Your head looks like a calf that had all the hair burnt off its arse from the shits," said Wendell.

"Esther was home on the weekend and asked if she could trim my hair for practice for her hairdressing course." John ran his hand over his bald head as if he were searching for his lost hair.

"Is that what they call a trim at beauty school these days?" asked Robert, grinning.

"Double damn. Remind me to never get your sister to trim my hair," Victor said, as he grabbed John's head and roughly rubbed his knuckles over the top. "Smooth as a loaf of bread and just as dense."

"It was an accident, okay." John was getting stressed. "Esther was talking to Mom while trimming my neckline with new electric clippers she bought. She gestured upward to explain something and cut out a whole patch of my hair on the way up. She had to shave my whole head to make it look right."

Not wanting to miss the fun, Charlie piled on. "Daniel, can John borrow your helmet tonight, so Tyne Valley won't mistaken him for the puck?"

Everyone immediately focused on Daniel, anticipating how he might answer. Nobody could come up with a deadly quip faster than Daniel. But he didn't look up from relacing his skates, as if he hadn't even been listening to the banter. His teammates shifted uneasily in their seats, but no one dared ask outright what was biting him.

"Screw off guys or I tell Esther you are all looking for a haircut." John put his hat back on. "I guess I'll play with my hat on. It'll give the girls something to think about."

"Like the girls spend anytime thinking about you John Boy," chuckled Peter. "But you just keep on dreaming."

"Dreams are good, especially when it comes to hockey," said Coach Ramsay. "That haircut will make you more streamlined on the ice, John, so button it, boys, or I'll order a crewcut for all of you."

Daniel only half listened to Coach Ramsay's usual pep talk. He was thinking how it would be nice if a shaved head was a guy's biggest problem.

As the players filed out of the dressing room, Coach Ramsay motioned with his hand that he wanted Daniel to hang back for a word. The two men silently looked at each other. Then Coach Ramsay asked, "Are you okay, Daniel? You seem a little off."

"Just tired, Coach. I have a lot going on." Even if he had wanted to talk about it, Daniel knew the dressing room, a couple of minutes from the puck dropping at centre ice, was not the time or place. For a moment, it appeared the older man had something more to say. Then he simply nodded his head and held open the door for the captain to pass through.

Daniel's line was on the first shift, and from the moment the clock started, he chased the puck hard, an equal to anyone on the ice. He had decided walking out of the dressing room that a shift in attitude was needed, and the game was the place to find it. He set up the first goal for Charlie at the five-minute mark, and on his second shift, delivered the second goal into the Tyne Valley net himself. The Rangers had a 2-0 lead and their fans couldn't have hollered any louder or pounded the boards any harder if they tried. An instant later, everything changed.

A Tyne Valley player followed Daniel into the corner of the Rangers' end and knocked him hard against the boards. Daniel wasn't hurt, but when the opponent skated away, all he could see was Foley's smirking face. "Is that potatoes and jute I'm smelling?" Daniel grit his teeth as rage exploded in the pit of his gut and burned through his entire body. Rage scared Daniel. He could usually keep it down, keep control over it, and toss it away with a sarcastic word. But this time, it boiled over.

"I don't make the rules. I just follow them."

He slammed the blade of his stick against the boards, seeing only Foley's face. Hearing Foley's dismissive little voice.

"Good day, Mr. MacDougall."

Daniel dug in. His smooth skating style, which effortlessly carried him over the frozen surface, was replaced with measured force that pushed his blades into the ice and propelled him aggressively forward. He kept his body low as though ready to body check in an instant and skated up the ice to meet the incoming forwards rather than letting them come to him, as was his usual practice. Daniel got so close to them that he saw both puzzlement and fear in their eyes. The captain of the Rangers, who prided himself on his power skating and puck control and clean checking, seemed like he was looking for a fight. Daniel checked clean, but hard, and took one player into the corner, but no one would give him that fight. Perhaps the Tyne Valley team, too, sensed that something was amiss with the Rangers' captain. This was not their usual opponent who delighted in the skill and beauty of the game rather than brute force.

When the whistle blew for the shift change, Daniel skated to the Rangers' box and wiped the sweat from his brow. Coach Ramsay was on him before he was seated.

"What the hell, Daniel? Stop playing like a goon."

"I'm playing to win." Daniel took a drink from the water bucket.

"Bullshit. You're playing to get hurt, and you're no good to yourself or us that way. I need you to play smart. Whatever's bugging you, deal with it off the ice. Don't make me bench you for the rest of the game."

Sitting on the bench, Daniel felt the anger dissipate as fast as it had risen. He leaned forward and rested his head on his stick. He had taken his anger out on the wrong people. He could have unnecessarily hurt someone or himself. And for what? It wasn't going to change the situation. Strength seeped from his muscles and tears gathered in his eyes, which he abruptly wiped away.

Daniel was ready to ask Coach Ramsay to bench him for the rest of the game when he felt a hand on his shoulder. He looked up to see his brother.

"Come on. We've got a game to win," Peter said.

Daniel slowly nodded, accepting that he had more than one game to win. Back on the ice, and with three minutes on the clock of the third period, Daniel passed the puck to George, who shot it to Peter, who neatly placed it in the Tyne Valley net. The clock ran out with a 3-0 score for the Rangers. The fans began to chant, "Now Lot 16 can rest. They've proven they are the best."

Tyne Valley was gracious in the loss. As Jessie had predicted, there was no trouble in the parking lot.

With a win under his belt, and a good night's sleep, Daniel felt confident and energized to continue the search for money. What he received, though, was a now-familiar answer at the Bank of Commerce and the Royal Bank. Daniel should have put the extra money in the bank and used it as collateral to take out a couple of small loans along the way. He would have developed a credit rating when he repaid them. Because he didn't, he had no credit history with the banks, and they weren't interested in talking with Charles Elliott. It was all fine and dandy in theory, Daniel thought bitterly, but no one had ever taught him such money skills.

Daniel was thoroughly kicking himself for taking pride in saving up and paying cash for consumer items. He had learned well his father's lesson that if you didn't have the money, you didn't buy something until you did. But there were limitations on how far one could get ahead living that way. The mortgage was good debt, even if the banks were underestimating the worth of the land. But now it was all meaningless. One thing he knew was that if he found a way through this mess, he wouldn't make the same mistake twice. Yet the days were slipping by, and he was losing precious time.

Daniel's mind never stopped churning and thinking about how he could get the money. He worked on the house in the morning, loaded potatoes all day, and played hockey at night. He was struggling to stay connected to Isabel. Each time Daniel came home from a bank appointment and saw the questioning look in her eyes, followed by disappointment, a part of him felt smothered by failure. It was his job to take care of his family, and he was letting Isabel and the girls down no matter how much she tried to pretend otherwise. James and Jessie also needed to be told soon. It was getting difficult to keep up the pretense that all was well. In Daniel's mind, facing a banker was nothing compared to facing Jessie.

And then there was Peter, who had finally confronted him about his progress on finding the money for Elliott. Daniel saw how his brother's body deflated when he told him where things stood. It was one more person he had let down, because Daniel knew his own success would give Peter the confidence to believe he too deserved and could achieve good things.

Along with the rest of the crew, Daniel had agreed to work late to finish loading a shipment bound for Boston. He was actually relieved, because it meant there was no time to go home before heading to hockey. Anticipating the long workday, Daniel had put his hockey gear in the car, and Isabel had packed him a supper as well as a lunch. It was six o'clock before Daniel and his crew mates finished loading the last railcar, and they barely had time to inhale their supper before Percy pulled up in front of the station.

"My arse is going to be dragging on the ice tonight," said Keith as they walked to the truck.

"It should be your normal game, then." It was the first time in days that a light-hearted taunt came off Daniel's tongue. Everyone chuckled, pleased to see their captain behaving more like his old self. Keith hauled himself into the truck without trying to think of a cutting reply.

The Lot 16 Rangers were playing the Freetown Royals, a fast-paced team that preferred scoring to fighting. They were Daniel's favourite team to play against in the league. A game with the Royals was always a recipe for high-calibre hockey and a close game.

When the Rangers entered the rink, they could see that seats were quickly filling. The cold air was full of the smell of french fries and vinegar. Daniel took an appreciative sniff and wondered how many fans came to the games more for the fries than the hockey itself. At least the fries, freshly cut from Island potatoes, never disappointed.

Within minutes of the puck dropping, the fans could clearly see that neither the Rangers nor the Royals were playing their usual game. Energy seemed to have been sucked out of both. The Rangers were giving the Royals too many opportunities to carry the puck into the Rangers' end, but when they got there, the Royals were slow to capitalize on their advantage.

Keith was indeed dragging his arse. He barely prevented the Royals' left winger from scoring when Ivan was caught off to the side. Daniel felt as though his legs were cement and no matter his will, he couldn't gain speed. He couldn't recall feeling this way on the ice and maybe he had an excuse, but what the hell was wrong with the rest of them?

"Do you have lead in your pants?" Coach Ramsay bellowed at each shift that came off the ice. "Get out there and play like you have liniment in your underwear. Give the fans what they paid for. Give 'em some game. Show us what you're made of!" But he might as well have been talking to a sack of potatoes for all the good it did.

The Rangers held the Royals to two goals in the first period, but they couldn't seem to move the puck to the Royals' end. The second period was painfully slow with neither team scoring.

It took until the third period for Peter, assisted by John, then Wendell, assisted by Victor, to tie the game. Both teams seemed satisfied with that result and coasted through the rest of the period much to the displeasure of the fans.

"I didn't get my money's worth tonight, boys! Shame on you!" an older man yelled, as the two teams left the ice.

"I spent my allowance on this game. Where was the fight?" hollered a young boy from the top of the stands.

"So now I have a rink full of disappointed people to add to my list," Daniel said to Peter. "Sure. Why not?

"You know the saying: go big or stay home, brother boy," Peter replied.

The return trip home in the back of the truck was unusually quiet. No one knew what to say, and Coach Ramsay didn't even have the energy for a lecture. It was as though a spell of heaviness hung over everyone, but no one knew why.

Daniel wondered if it was his fault that things had gone so badly. He was supposed to be the inspiring captain and yet tonight, caught up as he was in himself, he had done nothing to lead his team. Daniel leaned his head back against the wall of the truck box and listened to the hum of the tires. Suddenly, he missed his girls, all three of them. He closed his eyes and allowed images of them to flash into his mind. Was the extra work worth losing out on supper with them? Yet every cent counted right now. Maybe he needed to work, but did he need to play hockey and deny them that time? Daniel opened his eyes and sat straight. He needed to turn off his damn mind and give it a rest.

CHAPTER 11

The next morning, Daniel skipped going to the house before work. Tough as it was to do so, he finally realized he needed a break in order to juggle all of the demands on him. Peter went alone and enjoyed making progress boarding in the wall. Especially enjoyable was watching the sun put on an orange and red light show as it rose for the day.

Daniel also took the day off from trying to search out money. Instead, he simply showed up at the Miscouche Railway Station and concentrated on loading the railcars. It had been an amazing stretch of work with no signs of letting up, and for that Daniel was grateful. He even joked with the other crewmembers, which made them happy. Secretly, they loved when Daniel tormented them, because the captain only joked with people he liked. The crew and Ralph figured he must love them. If Daniel told the truth, he did.

The workday even ended with a decent quitting time and he headed straight home to face an unpleasant task. There was nothing for it: tonight, he and Isabel had to tell his in-laws what was happening. To say the words aloud would be a great relief for both of them.

Daniel waited until everyone was served supper and had begun to eat. The girls were quietly seated on his lap, their presence giving him a sense of security and calm. He exchanged an "it's now or never" look with Isabel and began.

"Isabel and I need to share something with you." Daniel looked directly at James and Jessie. "A few days ago, Charles Elliott called in our mortgage. He gave us five weeks to come up with the remaining money, but so far, I've had no luck."

Silence filled the room. Even the girls made no sound other than that of their small jaws chewing. Daniel couldn't recall having heard that sound before. He watched as James reached for his water glass and Jessie put down her fork and knife.

"We knew there was something, the way both of you were going around here with long faces. Since dealing with the devil would get one a fairer shake than dealing with Charles Elliott, I guessed it was likely the mortgage." Jessie said.

Jesus, thought Daniel, even my mother-in-law had Elliott pegged.

James put down his glass, and respectfully asked for more details. Daniel and Isabel complied, telling how extra payments had been made, and the remaining amount. For a time, James didn't speak. Jessie didn't push him. James knew the character of his son-in-law, as well as his pride and the belief he had to shoulder things on his own. Help from his in-laws would have to be carefully offered.

James hoped his wife would stay quiet for the next few minutes while he asked a few questions. "What have you done to try and get the money, Daniel?"

But Isabel jumped in to answer, listing every bank Daniel had been to, and why none of them would make the loan.

"I wish Jessie and I had the money to give you outright, but we don't." James looked from Isabel to Daniel as he spoke. "But I'm thinking perhaps I can sign a note at the bank for you." He looked at his silent wife.

Jessie's face didn't give away what she was thinking, but James knew that while she would not be comfortable with such a move, she would never refuse to help the young couple, who were so close to reaching the mortgage finish line. Isabel's face immediately brightened, but Daniel's expression remained sombre.

"I appreciate your offer, but I can't accept." He looked squarely at his father-in-law and shook his head no.

"Why not? It's the answer to our prayers." Isabel looked in disbelief across the table at her husband.

"Because your parents have already done more than enough for us. They've put a roof over our heads these past five and a half years. Your father has given me space in the barn for stock and use of some land to grow feed. I'm not asking for more, especially if it means putting your parents at risk." Daniel slapped the palm of a hand to the table, startling Mary, who stopped eating. Her lower lip trembled as she stared at her father.

"Is that the real reason? Or is it because it hurts your pride to ask for help?" Isabel's voice went up a dangerous octave. Jeannie looked over at her mother, alarmed.

"And when does asking for help stop, Isabel? When I'm nothing but a shell of the man I want to be? When I have it all, but can't look at myself? Is that when it stops?"

"You're being ridiculous. There's nothing weak about asking for help—not this close to the goal. They're not just handing you the money, you know." Isabel was now on her feet.

Daniel abruptly pushed back from the table, stood, and resettled the girls on his chair. He, too, was now shouting.

"No, but the worry would be there for them every moment until the debt was paid in full. It would change everything. Just the offer already has. The answer is thanks, but no thanks." He turned and left the room and as his family heard his heavy footsteps on the stairs, the girls started to cry.

“Shhh. It’s okay, girls. Daddy is not mad at you.” Isabel came round the table to gather them in her arms. The girls had never seen her and Daniel fight like this. Isabel wished they hadn’t seen it tonight.

“Is he mad with you?” Jeannie looked up at her mother.

“Not really. Daddy is mad and sad about something that happened, but it will be okay. I promise.” Isabel hugged her close and wiped away the tears. She then sat both of her daughters down to finish their suppers

“I’m truly sorry, Isabel. Daniel needs to do this his way.” James reached for a biscuit and resumed his meal.

“A man’s way.” Jessie spoke to no one in particular as she considered a forkful of her now-cold meal.

“Just give him some space to figure it out, Isabel. Work with him, not against him,” James advised his daughter.

Upstairs, Daniel threw himself onto the bed and looked up at the ceiling, lit only by moonlight. He took deep breaths and released each one slowly to calm down. Daniel felt angry and embarrassed for having lost his cool in front of his in-laws and especially his children. But Isabel shouldn’t have pushed him. He groaned and covered his face with his hands. His reaction wasn’t her fault. The worst of it was he had shared her excitement for a brief moment. Yet there was just no way Daniel was taking another thing from his in-laws. They had given more than enough by sharing their rambling farmhouse. It was a kindness they likely had not expected to go on for years. Daniel knew how they felt about him for getting Isabel pregnant before marriage and before the young couple had a place of their own. Jessie had freely voiced her disappointment and displeasure, while James reflected the deepest sadness Daniel never wanted to see again. And then there was the disappointment on his own parents’ faces when Daniel told them that he and

Isabel were getting married and expecting. The MacDougalls had counted on their oldest son breaking that particular cycle of family history and choosing an easier path in life. Perhaps their biggest disappointment was they were in no position to help the young couple financially.

If Daniel couldn't get the mortgage money, they would be back to square one unless he took the job in Montreal and moved Isabel and the girls. Yet that was the last thing he wanted. He'd take living with the MacArthurs over that, but he wasn't imposing any further by putting them at financial risk.

Daniel finally drifted off to sleep only to wake sometime later to the sound of creaking floorboards. Memories of the supper table fight came rushing back as he lay, still fully clothed, cold and shivering on top of the bedcovers. Daniel sensed rather than saw that he was not alone. He quickly turned to look at Isabel's side of the bed and saw her sitting there dressed in her night clothing quietly watching him. Daniel went to speak, to say he was sorry, but Isabel placed her hand on his lips. "I understand. Now, let's get under the covers and warm each other up."

Daniel got up from the bed to allow Isabel to pull back the covers and get under them. He quickly undressed and slipped into bed pulling her close. "I saw you sneak that hot water bottle in at your feet Mrs. MacDougall, so share or I'll put my cold feet on you."

Isabel laughed and pushed over the bottle so that both of their feet rested on its warm surface. She stroked his jawline as Daniel stroked her hair. It was a familiar position when they wanted to talk before sleeping, but all either wanted to say was, "I love you." As Daniel drifted off to sleep, he was grateful that the next day was Saturday and he could sleep in an extra hour.

Come morning, Daniel woke to a beautiful winter day. He could tell by the lack of frost on the windowpane that the temperature was good for outside activity. Mending the divide with his wife gave Daniel the confidence that he could handle the world again.

After breakfast, he attended to some neglected chores around the barn before heading to the house for a day's work with Peter before the night hockey game.

Much to his annoyance, Peter was unable to sleep in on Saturday morning. Grumbling about the unfairness of it, he had gotten up at the usual weekday time and completed the outdoor chores of chopping wood and clearing the walkway, along with feeding and cleaning the few animals in his father's small barn. Peter spent time grooming his filly and filling her in on the week's happenings.

After breakfast, Peter headed to Daniel's house to start work well ahead of the appointed hour to meet, all the while berating himself for being as contrary as his brother in investing labour and material into the place until they knew the final outcome. It was not a day of hope for Peter. He talked to himself about how what he was doing was totally stupid. Was he really helping Daniel or just enabling the man? Peter debated the difference between the two, and decided he was helping. He threw another board on the staging. He was doing what he was doing because Charles Elliott had to be shown the game wasn't over yet. He needed to know Daniel might be able to be knocked down, but not easily. Elliott deserved to sweat a little.

When Daniel arrived, the brothers determined their objective for the day: to finish the boarding in of the wall, and, with a little luck, get a start on the windows. One thing Peter did know for certain was that Daniel always overestimated the amount of work that could be done in a given time slot. It was like their mother always said: "That boy does three days work in one and then needs two to recover."

"By the end of next week, we should have the outside shingled and then we can move inside and start the flue. Once we can get a fire going, it will be a lot more comfortable working inside." Daniel fired boards up to Peter on the staging as rapidly as he was speaking. Peter wondered where the optimism was coming from.

"Yeah, but maybe you need to take a break from the house, Daniel, so you can get some rest and concentrate on finding the money. I think that should be your only focus right now." Peter felt Daniel needed a dose of reality.

"No, I can't stop now. I promised myself the house would be ready to move into right after we win the league championship."

"Maybe you're taking this optimism thing too far," Peter said.

Daniel gave him a sideways glance. "And maybe you don't take it far enough."

Peter didn't disagree. He often envied his brother, who seemed to have more of the optimistic outlook of their mother. Peter had a little too much of his father's cautiousness. "What if the money doesn't happen, though?" he asked.

"I still have a couple of cards up my sleeve. Somebody is going to bite." Daniel, who even looked like his mother, was sounding all confidence.

"But if they don't, it's more work for nothing."

"No one's forcing you to be here." Daniel stopped working and turned to look directly at Peter.

"You want me to leave?" Peter looked crushed.

"No. I just want you to believe in me." Daniel drove a spike with such force that it split the board.

"You want me to believe in you! What the hell have I been doing? It's not you that I don't believe in." Peter threw down his hammer and raised his arms in frustration.

"I know, I know. I'm sorry." Daniel had the sense to look sheepish. "I just need to know you and Isabel won't give up on me."

"Believing in you is one thing. Going to hell with you is another," Peter snapped, before he could help himself.

"I won't take you there, Peter. I promise. Please just stick with me a little longer," Daniel pleaded.

Peter's response was to pick up his hammer and go back to work.

When they called its quits for the day, the two men felt pleased with their work. The wall was boarded in against the elements and the four windows were in place. The tarpapering and shingling would come next. Peter already knew Daniel would have to have the rows perfectly straight or else he would be bothered every day of his life.

However, all that mattered right now was for both men to get home. They had a lot of work to do before they had to leave for the hockey game.

When Daniel arrived at the MacArthur farm, he discovered that Isabel, with the girls in tow, had done his barn work. Grateful, Daniel now had time to enjoy his supper, help give the girls their Saturday night bath, and read them a couple of stories before he got ready for the game. The day couldn't have gone better.

When he was ready to leave, Daniel swung Mary and Jeannie up into his arms. He gave them a real good whisker rub and covered their faces in kisses while they begged for more.

"Don't you get them all riled up and then leave, mister." Isabel crossed the kitchen to shepherd the girls to bed.

"Do you want your whisker rub before I go?" he asked.

"Of course, but go easy on my tender skin."

Daniel pulled her close, loving the feel of her curvy body against the strength of his, and made the rub count.

"Ouch, not so hard, I tell you!" Isabel squealed. The girls laughed and circled their parents' legs, jumping up and down and calling in unison, "Do it again, Daddy, do it again!"

Daniel looked into Isabel's eyes. "Maybe you would like this better," and he gently kissed her lips.

"I believe I would," she smiled, as the girls danced around, hollering, "Yuck, yuck, yuck!"

James, seated by the fire reading the paper, laughed. It lifted his spirits to see the young family having a bit of fun. However, more than fun was on his mind.

"I would say by the feel of the air there is weather brewing. You boys keep an eye out and get on the road home if the snow starts."

CHAPTER 12

As Daniel set out to meet up with his teammates, he felt a softness in the air that had been missing just a couple of hours earlier. Turning back for one last look at the house and the welcoming light shining from the windows, he wondered if he should stay home with the family. For a moment, he lingered, torn. As much as he wanted to go back inside, the team was counting on him. It was unfortunate that the game was in Borden, the small community situated on the Northumberland Strait. If a storm came in off the water, the drive would be bad. He pulled up his collar and started the walk to the school, the last one to arrive. Everyone else was loaded in the truck box waiting to go. The few fans in the box were another indication weather was brewing. Percy had lucked out tonight, as neither of the two girls seated in the cab were related to him. Daniel wondered what it would be like to have one's biggest worry be what girl would be seated beside you on the drive to a hockey game.

When the team reached Borden, there was still no sign of snow, but the temperature was rising. With the puck drop to start the game, the Rangers discovered the temperature change was just enough to soften the natural ice in the rink and slow down the play. Fast skaters, the Rangers were used to controlling the puck, but not tonight. They couldn't seem to get their feet under them on the slow ice and the game was starting to look like it would be a repeat of the Freetown game.

Borden scored two quick goals in the first period, thanks to Daniel. He had already been distracted by the worry of being caught in a storm, and then had spotted Charles Elliott in the stands. The storekeeper had slightly tipped his hat at him, which unnerved the captain causing him to allow a couple of easy plays by him.

"Get a grip, MacDougall!" Daniel grit his teeth as he dug his blades into the ice, reminding himself that the rink was his domain.

The Borden fans were elated with the goals and shouted their approval, but they got an even bigger charge shouting at the Rangers. "The Rangers suck when handling the puck. Oh, what bad luck!" The Rangers' fans were mystified about what was happening.

The Rangers prided themselves on making sure to take the lead in a game, but for the second straight game, they failed to do so. Now that they had blown it, they were finding it a struggle to come back, but Peter—with help from Keith, and George, assisted by Wendell, tied the game in the second period.

"Go, Rangers, Go! Make the score grow!" Finally, the Rangers' fans had something to cheer about, and cheer they did. A fight broke out in the stands.

Within minutes, Ivan let another goal into the Rangers' net. Coach Ramsay was pacing behind the bench and periodically taking off his wide-brimmed hat to run his hand through his hair. The pain on his face was clear.

Daniel was sure the roaring of the Borden fans could be heard on the other side of the Northumberland Strait: "The Rangers suck when handling the puck. Oh, what bad luck!"

With the scoreboard reading 4-2 in favour of Borden, Daniel managed a goal just before the clock ran out on the game. Unbelievable! The first-place Rangers had just gone down to a 4-3 defeat to Borden, the last-place team in the league. The Borden players raced to centre ice to huddle and pound each other on the backs, then skate away and come back to do it all over again. The Borden fans got equally excited in the stands, stamping their feet, clapping, and hurling more abuse at the Rangers. Both the players and the fans knew the win changed nothing for them in the standings, but the win sure felt empowering after a dismal season. The Rangers retreated to their dressing room.

In the dressing room, Coach Ramsay paced back and forth like a man ready to explode. It was obvious to the players he was fighting to get himself under control. They quietly undressed and put away their gear. They were not used to seeing him like this.

"Borden! Last place in the league, and we lose? Can you explain that to me, boys?" Coach Ramsay planted himself in front of Daniel and spit out the words. No one answered him.

"Of course you can't. How would any of you know since you didn't show up for the game," the Coach raged on. "And Daniel? Your grandmother could've played a better game than you did tonight."

"I'm tired. I've been working hard." Daniel didn't appreciate the Coach's words, even if they were true.

"Is that so? You need to remember, Daniel, that until this championship is ours, your number one focus has to be this team."

"I've got a life outside of hockey." Daniel did not back down.

Neither did Ramsay. "Yes, you do. Make sure you bloody keep it off the ice!"

Thankfully, Percy chose that moment to appear in the doorway. "Make it fast, guys. We got ourselves a snowstorm."

When the team walked out into the parking lot, they were hit by a horizontal wall of snow blowing in off the Northumberland Strait. Though the storm was only minutes old, it was apparent the snow was coming down fast and the flakes were small, perfect to be blown about by the howling wind. Daniel thought of his grandmother's saying, "Big snow, little snow—little snow, big snow." This was going to be a big storm, and they were miles from home.

Percy had the truck running to warm the cab and was brushing snow from the windshield as fast as it fell. Team members cleaned off Coach Ramsay's car while he got in and started the engine.

"This looks really bad, boys. I can't see driving in this." Percy was panicking.

"What choice do we have?" Daniel hollered, squinting through the pellets of ice and snow. "There's no place to stay around here, except the rink, and it looks as though the Borden crew has left, so it's locked.

"If we don't get home tonight, we could be storm-stayed for days," Peter shouted over the wind.

"Let's get going." Coach Ramsay stepped from his car and took charge. "Percy, put Daniel and Peter up front with you for extra eyes. George, Victor, Keith, and John, get in with me for weight. We'll follow right behind the truck. For God's sake, be careful."

Percy pulled the truck out onto the road, with Coach Ramsay following close behind. The truck box blocked some of the wind, giving Coach Ramsay more visibility than Percy. When the whiteouts hit, Percy, Daniel, and Peter saw nothing up ahead. Percy gripped the steering wheel for dear life and held the truck steady and plowed through one drift after another.

"You're doing great, Percy. Just keep your speed steady." Daniel spoke as calmly as he could to help keep Percy's nerves grounded.

"I have no idea if Coach Ramsay is still following behind." Percy tried looking in the rearview mirror.

"He's still there but let me worry about him. I'll look behind, and you and Daniel keep your eyes on the road ahead," Peter advised.

"We need to pray no one is stuck on the road ahead of us," said Daniel, staring into the kaleidoscope of snow in front of them.

"Oh, so now you're a praying man?" Percy kept his eyes glued ahead of him.

"Driving to hockey games with you behind the wheel has taught me to be one, Percy old boy!"

"I'll think of a response when things are calmer," Percy said as he stepped on the gas to plow through a deep drift. And then another. He made it about ten miles up the road before the truck hit a drift she wasn't able to plow through. She bogged down.

"God damn it all to hell." Percy swore as he tried rocking the truck back and forth to free it, but it was going nowhere. They were stuck solid.

"Well look who's praying now," said Daniel.

"At least Coach Ramsay's car is behind us, and not part of us." Peter pulled his head back into the truck and rolled up the window.

The three men piled out of the truck, as did those in the car, and waded through the deep blowing snow to assess the situation. Those in the truck box pulled aside the blanket to crawl out, but Coach Ramsay commanded them to stay put and stay dry.

"We'll have to shovel her out," Daniel hollered, his voice barely audible over the howling wind.

"What's the point? It's filling in so fast we'll just be stuck a little farther up the road. We gotta find a place to shelter. It's too cold to stay with the vehicles." Coach Ramsay advised.

"I think the vehicles are the best place for us. We could easily get lost in the storm. We can all huddle in the straw in the truck box. I vote we stay put." George yelled over the howling wind as he fought to stay on his feet.

"We're on the main highway. What if another vehicle runs into us? There has to be a house close by that will give us warm shelter." Coach Ramsay was used to calling the play for his team.

Daniel struggled to see through the blinding snow and the dark of the night. He could see a faint outline of trees and what appeared to be a barn off to his right. Straining to be heard over the wind, he yelled: "If we're where I think we are, there's a farmhouse off to the right. An old bachelor lives there. I delivered fertilizer to him last spring."

"I wonder how he feels about company." Coach Ramsay was determined to find shelter regardless of the snow having grown deeper in mere minutes. "Get back in the truck box, boys, so we can get organized."

Once inside the box, which felt like a haven from the storm, Coach Ramsay told its occupants the plan. "We're going to form a human chain and make our way to a house in the distance. I need everybody to stay calm and focused. Our safety depends on us working together. Thankfully, we only have two fans to worry about, besides the team." He didn't voice his concern that they were girls. "I'm putting Daniel at the front.

Everyone is to hold on to the next person's hand to form the chain. I'll take up the rear. Don't anybody let go."

Daniel felt panic rise in his chest. If he was wrong, this whole thing could turn out to be a disaster. Maybe they should do what George wanted, but Coach Ramsay was signalling for him to get out. Daniel pulled aside the blanket and was instantly hit by the driving snow. It hurt his bare face as badly as the slap of an open hand. He jumped down from the box and fought to walk through the snow to move ahead enough for the next person to exit the truck. Robert climbed out and Daniel grabbed his hand and moved ahead again. They repeated the movement over and over until the team of eleven, the two female teenage fans, and Coach Ramsay were lined up.

"Okay, we have the chain formed. Lead the way," Ernest shouted as he waved to Daniel.

For every step they went ahead, the wind drove them two steps back or three to the side. One moment, the snow was knee-deep, then waist deep, and back to knee or ankle deep, throwing people off balance and plunging them into a drift. Every tumble brought the line to a halt. Precious moments were lost to the elements as the downed person regained their footing, and once again, gripped the hands of those ahead and behind them. As hands numbed in the cold it became harder to hold on. Snow crept over the top of boots to freeze calves and ankles, and the wind tried its best to rip through the layers of clothing. Minutes felt like hours, as each person feared that Daniel had lost his way or never knew it to begin with.

Suddenly, one after another, they miraculously slammed into the old farmhouse. They just stood there for a time, weak with relief and fighting for breath. A few cleared tears from their eyes.

"I'd kiss these shingles if I wasn't scared my lips would freeze to them." Victor spread his arms on the house as though trying to embrace the entire structure.

As a unit, they felt their way along the side of the house until they found the door. Everyone huddled around, shivering with cold, while Coach Ramsay pounded on the door with his fist, and shouted to make his voice heard over the wind, "Is anyone home? Is anyone home?"

When there was no answer to Coach Ramsay's knock or call, the others joined in pounding their fists on the wall and shouting, "Is anyone home?"

After what seemed like an eternity, an old man dressed in red long johns, woolen socks, a heavy sweater, and a wool hat opened the door a crack and peered out. If all the snow-covered faces on his front porch terrified him, he gave no sign. "Of course, I'm home. It's where anyone with a lick of sense would be in this weather," he said.

"We're the hockey team from Lot 16. We've just finished playing Borden, and we can't get any further on the road. We need shelter." Coach Ramsay managed a faint smile though his chin was encrusted with ice, and his cheeks beet-red from the cold.

The old man, fighting against the wind that threatened to rip the door from his hands, peered out at the huddled group. He looked hard at Coach Ramsay. "Who won?"

"Borden, 4-3." Daniel answered.

"Well, lucky for you guys, they did. I'll let you sleep on the kitchen floor." The old man smiled a toothless grin. He opened the door a little wider and motioned them in. He had at least several days' growth of whiskers on him, and tobacco juice staining one side of his chin. "But be quick before the wind blows the snow in."

The stranded travellers found themselves in a massive kitchen that held nothing more than a wooden table, several chairs, a day bed, and an old kitchen range in which the coals had burned down. They could hear the wind howl through the frost covered windows. Everyone looked about them in dismay. The old man's house wasn't much of an improvement over the truck.

"Good grief," Wendell muttered. Coach Ramsay cast him a withering look. "Is there a phone we could use?" Daniel asked as he scanned the threadbare room.

"Don't believe in having one," the old fellow spit tobacco juice into the tin can by the stove. "Anyhow, I'm back to my bed. Just so you know, I ain't got nothing worth stealing."

"You have nothing to fear from us. We are mighty grateful for the shelter," Coach Ramsay reassured their crusty host. "But I wonder if you have another room the women can sleep in?"

"Nay, what you see is what you get. And don't touch that stove. I let the fire die down cause of the wind." A blast of cold air hit the kitchen when he opened the door that led to the hallway. He passed through, shutting the door behind him.

As Coach Ramsay stared at the closed door, the others stared at him. He could feel the eyes on his back and slowly turned to face the group. Knowing the need to be reassuring, he took a deep breath before speaking,

"The main thing to remember is that we are all safe. Everyone at home knows we are sensible people who would get ourselves to safety. Let's try to make the best of a bad situation. It's good we only have Grace and Sylvia with us tonight. See if the two of you can squeeze onto the day bed and the rest of us will sleep on the floor."

"We're not sleeping on that! It could be full of fleas. We'll sleep on the floor like the rest of you." Grace looked at him with horror on her face.

"We should have gone home early, like the other girls did, with Mr. Elliott." Sylvia sounded like she was about to cry.

"You mean he knew the weather had turned, and left without telling the rest of us?" Daniel asked, incredulous.

"He went out for a smoke and when he came back, he said a flurry had started and perhaps it was time to head home, but we didn't want to miss the game, so we stayed," Grace confirmed.

"How considerate of him to have informed me." Coach Ramsay's voice was ice cold.

"He thought of it but decided that you wouldn't want to forfeit the game by leaving early, and the snow might not amount to anything anyways." Sylvia pulled her coat tighter to her body and wished she had gone home in Mr. Elliott's warm car.

"I guess it wouldn't have mattered if we had forfeited tonight, eh, boys?" Coach Ramsay said quietly.

It was a question for which no answer was expected, and thus none was given.

The girls huddled over by the now cool stove, fully dressed. The men took off their boots and coats, and to conserve heat, got as close to each other on the floor as felt comfortable. They left their mitts and hats on and covered themselves with their half-wet coats.

"Some of that fresh straw on the truck box would feel mighty good right now." George tried to get comfortable on the cold hard floor, resentful that his suggestion to stay with the truck had been overridden.

"Look everyone, I'm not happy about this either, but let's just try and get through the night." Coach Ramsay also wished to be in the truck box but knew that at least in the old kitchen the team was safe off the road.

Daniel stood alone by the window looking out into the stormy night praying Coach Ramsay was right and Isabel would assume they were safe somewhere. Finally, knowing that worrying would change nothing, he turned away from the window and positioned himself at the end of the line to put his back against Peter's. He could feel his brother shiver. It was going to be a long, cold night. Daniel had to agree with George. If they had stayed in the truck, at least they could have curled up in the straw.

Miles away at the MacArthur farmhouse, Isabel had gone up to bed with the girls, intending to stay with them until they fell asleep, but curled against the warmth of their small bodies, she had drifted off. She woke to the shuddering of the window as the wind beat against it. Isabel climbed from the bed and covered the girls, and then tiptoed to her and Daniel's own room. She opened the door hoping that it was much later than she thought, and that he had come home and gone to bed without waking her. But Daniel wasn't there. She tiptoed down to the kitchen. The clock said eleven thirty. She frowned. He should have been home about eleven. Isabel went to the window and peered out into the darkness and raging storm. Daniel would not be home tonight. She leaned her forehead against the window casing and felt the strength of the cold. Prayer was all that was within her power at that moment. So that is what she did. As the whole house shook in the howling wind, Isabel prayed. "God, please keep Daniel and the team safe and warm through this storm. Please bring them safely home."

It was not a restful night for Isabel. She missed Daniel curled up against her. It was a reminder of the long, lonely nights she endured when he was in Montreal.

While the Lord may have answered her pray to keep Daniel and the team safe, he didn't keep them warm. Huddled against Peter, Daniel thought of Isabel's warmth in comparison to his brother's. He acknowledged it wasn't a fair comparison. The thick mattress, flannel sheets, and quilts were missing. Still, it was Isabel he missed the most.

The sound of a plow penetrated Daniel's light sleep. He listened intently, fearful it was wishful thinking, but in the distance, the faint sound was there. Day had come and sunlight was trying to force its way through the frost-covered glass. The exterior wall of the kitchen was also covered with thick frost. Daniel was curled in a tight ball, and it hurt to stretch out his legs. Even though he had known plenty of cold in his life, he couldn't remember ever being this cold.

"Come on, you guys. It's the plow. We need to get the vehicles shovelled out." Daniel forced himself to his feet and looked at the rest of the group still sleeping, their exhaled breaths frozen by the frigid air.

"I swear I'm frozen to the floor. Someone help me up." George tried to straighten out his curled-up legs. He groaned from the pain of muscle spasms.

Daniel gave him a hand and then reached for John and Wendell. When he got them up, Daniel went down the line and then over to Grace and Sylvia, who sometime through the night had moved from the floor to the daybed. The driving cold had obviously defeated the fear of fleas.

"Grace? Sylvia?" Daniel called until the girls stirred.

"Oh!" Grace cried as she tried to straighten her legs. "I wish I had listened to my grandmother when she said her joints knew a storm was brewing."

"We went through all of this and the team didn't even win." Sylvia stretched and winced as she swung her feet to the floor.

Daniel bit his tongue and turned away. They were just kids, after all. Victor went to stand by the stove, which was stone cold. Embarrassed, he looked around to see if anyone had noticed, then reached out to look in the kettle. The water in it was frozen solid.

"There's no sign of the old fellow. Should we wake him up before leaving to say thanks?" Peter pounded his mittened hands against his thighs to try and warm his fingers.

"I ain't going up there. He's probably frozen stiffer than a board." John did a little dance to try and get circulation in his feet.

"I guess that would make him, what? A real stiff?" Charlie cupped his hands to his mouth and blew on them.

"Well, if he is, he'll stay fresh till they find him." Despite himself, Daniel had to laugh.

"He took us in for the night so everyone can leave a quarter on the table for the hospitality." Coach Ramsay rotated his neck to try and ease some of the stiffness in it.

"A quarter!" Ivan grunted. "That's highway robbery for what we got. He didn't even stoke the fire." But, like the others, he dug into his pocket and pulled out a shiny coin and dropped it on the table.

As Peter added a coin to the growing pile, he thought about the old fellow upstairs. He sure as hell didn't want to end up like that. The very thought was enough to give him the willies.

The group quietly left the house and made their way out into the beauty of the crisp winter morning, where the sun's rays were dancing off the now-still snowflakes. When the wind had dropped through the night, so had the temperature.

Daniel pulled his coat collar up around his neck and said to no one in particular, "It's cold enough to freeze the nuts off a bridge."

"Yeah, but it's still warmer than it was inside that old house." Peter responded as everyone began the trudge through the deep snow to the road and their abandoned vehicles.

The plow had manoeuvred around the truck and car, piling the snow high about them. Coach Ramsay's car was buried to the bottom of the windows.

Ernest let a curse word out under his breath. "Good grief! It'll take half the day to dig out."

"Then let's get a move on," Daniel commanded.

"Who wants to call me an old woman now for keeping five shovels on board?" Percy scrambled into the back of the truck to retrieve them.

"Not I," said Coach Ramsay. "I've a couple more in the trunk, but the back end of my car will have to be dug out first to get to them. This will be better than a practice for you boys. We'll take five-minute shifts."

The shovelling warmed the men up, and Grace and Sylvia took turns, so they too could drive the cold from their bodies.

"Ernest, I can hear your stomach rumbling from here." Daniel threw a shovelful of snow over his shoulder.

"Damn right you can. I'm two hours past a serving of six man-sized pancakes, and four sausages drowning in maple syrup. That is my Sunday morning breakfast treat."

"I should be eating Mom's baked beans and fresh bread dripping in molasses, with a big cup of tea." Keith leaned on his shovel and sighed.

"Sunday morning breakfast is hot cocoa and fresh biscuits. It's the best," said George.

"No," said John, "The best is three poached eggs sandwiched between two thick slices of toast washed down with coffee."

"Okay, enough," thundered Coach Ramsay. "No more talk of food. It's cruel." He thought about the big piece of chocolate cake and ice cream he liked to have for Sunday breakfast.

It took them over an hour with seven shovels to clear the last of the snow from around and under the vehicles. They opened the hoods and cleaned the snow from the fan belts and wires. Then Percy and Coach Ramsay crawled into their vehicles. Everyone waited with bated breath as the two men turned the keys in the ignitions. Both engines fired to life and a group cheer went up as people scrambled aboard. Seated on a bale of straw, Daniel felt the truck tires vibrating on the snow-packed road. He was on his way home to his family. Never mind breakfast, he hoped dinner was going to be a good one.

"Daniel! You're home!" Isabel and the girls met him at the door for a group hug, and a smothering of kisses. To Daniel's surprise, even Jessie and James were pleased and relieved to see him.

"You must be cold. Take your coat off and stand by the fire," Jessie ordered.

Daniel stood close to the range with his hands stretched out over the top and welcomed the heat into his body. He inhaled deeply to breath in the smell of roasting chicken. Jessie had killed and dressed one from her flock early that morning. Warming his hands over the top of the kitchen range Daniel watched the vegetables simmering in pots at the back of the stove. He saw a lemon pie cooling on the table. Daniel's stomach growled. He was indeed all set for an excellent dinner.

Daniel washed and shaved in the small bathroom off the kitchen and changed into fresh clothing before joining the family at the table. Jeannie and Mary crawled onto his knee, and Isabel handed him a heaping plate of food. Throughout the meal, the adults peppered him with questions about the game, the storm, and the night. The cold bare kitchen of the old man's home appeared in his mind, so different from the colourful life-filled MacArthur kitchen. Daniel wondered when a meal such as he was enjoying had last graced the old man's table.

He spent the afternoon with Jeannie and Mary, sledding out on the hills and then sharing hot cocoa by the stove. When the barn work was done, he made it an early night. Never had lying on an actual bed with a feather-tick mattress buried beneath thick quilts felt so good. He curled up against Isabel and held her tight. Daniel realized there was much to be thankful for.

CHAPTER 13

Monday morning dawned clear and crisp. The temperature had risen a few degrees and there was no wind, which made for comfortable working conditions at the house. Daniel and Peter prepared to shingle the wall. First, they nailed a strip of tarpaper to the bottom boards and attached the kickboard. Then they were ready to shingle.

Daniel held a shingle to his nose and inhaled. "I don't think there is a much better smell than a cedar shingle. It pleases the nose, but also makes you think about newness and going forward."

"Well, aren't you a profound thinker on a Monday morning. I don't disagree, but my vote for the best smell is that of a roast beef dinner." The smell was not one Peter had experienced often enough in life. He had promised himself that would occur far more often in his future. But right now, there was a railway car waiting to be loaded with Island spuds.

The crew finished loading the railcar at three in the afternoon. Ralph told them they were done for the day, but new cars would be waiting in the morning.

"All of you are to be fresh and eager when you arrive tomorrow," were his final words before he disappeared into the office.

Daniel couldn't believe his luck. He had an appointment in town at 4 pm and now he didn't have to lose time off work. He was sure it was a sign—today was his day. The rest of the crew was equally pleased with the early end of their workday.

"I know! Let's head to the Nebraska Creek for a game of hockey. It'll be good to get an extra practice in and figure out some of the mistakes from the Saturday night game," Ernest proposed, as they walked to their cars.

"I'm in." Peter opened his car door.

"Me, too," said Keith. "What about you, Daniel?"

"I'd like to, but I have some business in town." Daniel placed his lunchbox in the backseat of the car and pulled out his dress coat.

"You seem to have a lot of business in town these days. What do you have going on anyway?" Keith paused as he was getting into the passenger seat of Ernest's car and frowned at Daniel.

"You don't go around asking people their business. Didn't your mother teach you anything?" Peter questioned.

Daniel looked over at Peter and gave him a look that said Be quiet! "Nothing serious," he said, instead. "I'm just looking for the best place to invest my millions." It was the best response Daniel could think of.

"You're so full of it, your eyes are brown. Come on, boys, let him keep his secrets. I bet he isn't going to be having the fun we will." Ernest put the key in the ignition and turned it.

Daniel stood and watched his workmates drive from the parking lot. How right Ernest was, and how he wished he was going to the pond with them, like he had since childhood. Instead, Daniel removed his work jacket and put on his good coat and climbed into his car.

At 3:50 pm, Daniel pulled up outside the Summerside law office of James Frederick Strong. Surprisingly, his father had suggested that Daniel see the lawyer, and James had agreed with the plan. Daniel waited a few minutes before climbing out of the car and walking up the pathway to the office in a lovely Queen Anne house. He was trying to time his entrance right: he didn't want to be too early, nor late. Daniel estimated that five minutes before the hour would be perfect and was pleasantly greeted by an older woman whose desk nameplate said Miss Olga Hogg, Secretary. She showed him into a small waiting room where Daniel sat alone, nervously twisting his hat in his hands well past the appointed meeting time. So much for appearing too eager, Daniel thought. Finally, at 4:15, Miss Hogg came into the room and told him Mr. Strong was ready to see him. She gestured for Daniel to follow her down the corridor, where she waved him into an office.

J. F. Strong, as he wished to be known, was standing behind a large oak desk. Daniel quickly noted the lawyer's appearance. Strong was somewhere in his sixties. It was hard to tell for certain as his well-trimmed hair was still jet black and the skin of his face was free of wrinkles. Strong appeared to be in excellent shape. It took only one glance for Daniel to be aware that the man's suit was tailor-made.

The lawyer held out a smooth, manicured hand to shake Daniel's, and motioned for him to sit down. "I'm sorry to keep you waiting. Something unexpected arose."

"It's fine, Mr. Strong. I appreciate you seeing me on short notice. I'm Daniel MacDougall." Daniel already liked the man. The apology suggested that the man was comfortable with himself. Daniel hoped Strong was a big man who didn't need to put on false airs.

"Yes, Daniel MacDougall of the Lot 16 Rangers. You're a talented young man on the ice." Strong placed his forearms on the desk.

“Thank you. I didn’t know you were a Rangers’ fan.” Daniel stirred in his chair. He had not expected the conversation to include hockey, or that a man like Strong would be aware of his existence.

The lawyer laughed and Daniel heard him tap his feet beneath his desk. “I’m not. At least not while the Freetown Royals are in the running. My grandson plays with the team. But I appreciate your skill and passion. So, what can I do for you?” Strong straightened up in his chair, ready to do business. For a lawyer, time was money.

“I need to borrow money. I’ve been told you could possibly set me up with an investor.” Daniel took a deep breath. He needed to score a win with this meeting, but there was no coach to advise on strategy. He was alone shooting the puck.

“I have a number of clients who are always seeking sound investments. What is it you’re wanting?” Strong tapped the fingers of his left hand on the desk.

He had returned the puck to Daniel’s end of the rink. With so many refusals under his belt, Daniel felt he should withhold certain facts, but when he looked into the shrewd eyes of the man seated across from him, he knew Strong’s help depended on everything being laid on the table.

Daniel moved to the edge of his chair. How he wished he could stand. Better still, tell the story while skating. He was graceful on skates. He launched into his situation: “I bought land a few years ago through a private mortgage with Charles Elliott, a storekeeper in Lot 16. No doubt you have heard of him, as Elliott has a number of business interests. Anyway, I have the mortgage four-fifths paid, well ahead of schedule, but Elliott is having a cash flow problem and is calling in my debt. The banks won’t deal with me and if I can’t get another lender, I’m going to lose everything I’ve worked for and hope to build upon. I recently moved a house onto the property and plan to plant a crop this spring."

Daniel felt as if he had played an entire shift by the time he finished the tale but was sure he hadn't come off as a sucker. He settled back in the chair and took in a deep calming breath like he did when returning to the Players Bench.

"I haven't heard of Elliott having any money problems, but then again I don't hear everything." Strong drummed his fingers on the desk.

Daniel took a risk with his next move. "Perhaps I am out of line in saying so, but I don't think he does have a cashflow problem. I think he is taking the opportunity to cash in on my stupidity of making extra payments, which will be a nice profit for him in addition to the land."

"It happens." Strong cupped his chin, and rubbed his fingers back and forth across the stubble that was starting to appear in the lateness of the day. The lawyer went silent, as though deep in thought. Daniel rubbed his chest and wondered if the game was over.

When Strong finally spoke, Daniel was surprised at the direction in which he went. "What I hear about you, Daniel, is that you can turn your hand to just about anything. So why choose the hard life of farming?"

"I didn't— it chose me." Daniel had been asked this question so many times, he didn't have to think about the answer.

"If that was the case, don't you think your path would be smoother?" The older man gnawed at his bottom lip with straight, even teeth. Another question he'd been asked more than once. Daniel leaned forward at the waist, intent in his answer. "Do you know any road without stones? If the way was always smooth, would you ever appreciate what you earn?'

"True enough. I like your thinking." Strong glanced over at the framed law certificate hanging on the wall, and at the family picture he kept on his desk. The lawyer lapsed once again into silent, deep thought. He then suddenly sat up straight, as if he had come to a conclusion.

"I'm thinking the best place for you to look for the money is with Malcolm MacDonald of the Island Potato Export Company. MacDonald understands the business of agriculture and will realize immediately this is a good investment," Strong said.

"In fact, I am going to suggest something very unusual for me, and certainly not profitable. I recommend you go directly to him and save yourself my fee for putting a deal together."

Caught off guard, Daniel didn't know what to think. "I get a lot of work with that company, but I've never dealt with Mr. MacDonald. He wouldn't know me."

Strong emitted a short laugh. "If you ever did a day's work for him, he knows you. I believe he will appreciate your situation, since he started from nothing himself. Malcolm MacDonald also knows a good deal when he sees one, and it's obvious by the rate you were paying back Charles Elliott, that you believe in living up to your end of a deal."

"But why cut yourself out?" Daniel was wary. Was there a play he wasn't seeing?

"Every now and again I feel compelled to give someone a break, like someone once gave me." Strong gave him a reassuring smile.

Strong was indeed telling the truth, but the gentleman lawyer didn't add that Daniel's father had called in a favour dated more than forty years. Duncan MacDougall had saved Strong's ass, and likely his life, in a street fight following a heavy night of youthful drinking and mouthing off. A sober Strong had given his thanks and promised a favour in return, if ever needed. When the call finally came, he wouldn't have had expected it to be so small or simple, or so polite: to please help MacDougall's son find an investor.

Strong drummed his fingers on the desk. "Take it quickly, before I change my mind. I'll call MacDonald's office and arrange an appointment for tomorrow morning," he said. "Wait for a few minutes in the waiting room until I get a time."

"I can't thank you enough for this." Still feeling a little unsure, Daniel put out his hand as he stood.

"I hope it works out for you, boy. I suppose there is no point asking you to take it easy on the Freetown team?" The lawyer placed his hand in Daniel's and felt the strength in his shake.

"That's how we tied the last game against them." Daniel tightened his grasp.

That evening, the mood was the lightest it had been in days around the MacArthur supper table. Even Jessie was uncharacteristically cheerful. "Imagine Strong waiving his fee. In all my years, I never heard of anyone getting a break from a lawyer," she said.

James, buttering another piece of bread, was contemplative. " I think he sent you in the right direction. I've always found MacDonald the fairest of any of the potato buyers."

"He'll still want more than what is fair. As it says in Proverbs, "The rich rule over the poor and the borrower is the slave of the lender." Jessie stood and walked to the stove to retrieve the teapot.

Isabel wished her mother wasn't always so practical or negative about such things. "Maybe so, but right now we'll be grateful to get MacDonald's money. Everything is riding on his answer." She looked over at her husband. "I'm glad it's you that's meeting with him, Daniel. I'd be so nervous I couldn't think," she said.

"Well, you just make sure to keep that helmet on tonight, so you can go in there in the morning with a clear head." Jessie lightly rapped Daniel's head as she filled his cup. The girls giggled.

"The way I feel right now, nobody will catch me on the ice tonight!" Chuckling, Daniel raised his cup to her.

"Daddy is faster than anybody else!" Mary shouted. Isabel smiled at her daughter's enthusiasm, then turned to Jessie.

"Mom, would you watch the girls so I can go and cheer my husband to victory?" Isabel rarely asked her mother to mind the girls even though they lived under the same roof. For once, a smile crossed Jessie's face. "Yes. Go enjoy the game." The family needed a taste of victory, even if it came from a hockey game.

CHAPTER 14

The Wellington Rink was packed to capacity. Fans were pressed right up against the boards, not the safest place to be, and seemed evenly split between the two teams. Children ran back and forth between the stands and the canteen. A few flasks were discreetly passed among friends, and even strangers. Everyone seemed eager to talk, which created a deafening hum in the wooden building. It was a night out and people were making the best of the time away from chores and responsibilities.

Isabel felt excited to be in the stands, for rarely did she get to the games now. Before the girls were born, she had never missed a game. She loved the excitement and community that came to life at the rink and on the trips back and forth to the various locations. Tonight, she was ready to cheer from the rooftop for she was sure this game belonged to Daniel and the Rangers.

"Good evening, Isabel." Reverend Mark Johnson sat down next to her. "It's great to see you at the game."

"It feels great to be here, Reverend Mark. I'm glad to see you here, too. I'm just sorry it has to be in the stands."

"It won't always be that way." The young minister tipped his hat and smiled at Charles Elliott who was just taking his seat two rows below.

"He doesn't seem happy to see us here." Isabel noted the scowl on Elliott's face before he turned his back on them.

"Don't let Mr. Elliott take away your joy in the game." Because I'm not, he thought to himself. "Want to see which one of us can cheer the loudest?"

"It's no contest, Reverend. It'll be me, especially when Daniel's on the ice," Isabel laughed.

In the Rangers' dressing room, the players listened to the chanting crowds while they waited for Coach Ramsay to outline the strategy for the night. He quickly got to the point. "Okay, boys, we all know why we're here tonight. It's the final game of the season and we're already in the playoffs, but. . ."

". . .but a win tonight keeps us in first place and Mount Pleasant second. Let's not waste time thinking we're not going to win, right boys?" Daniel finished the Coach's sentence.

"Yeah," agreed Peter. "We might be playing Wellington, but it's Mount Pleasant we're beating."

"Point taken. Just remember tonight is about the honour of the team." Coach Ramsay again took control of the pep talk. "Don't forget that you guys started on a patch of ice in the pasture field and now look at where you are. So, finish the job and make us proud."

"Hey, guys, just guess who is in the stands?" Percy burst into the room. "Ah, never mind, you'll never get it, and I can't wait to tell you. It's Chester Craig and some of the Mount Pleasant boys checking out first-hand how tonight's game goes!"

"Let's show them how the playoffs are going to go down!" Wendell hooted.

In an instant, the team was on their feet and through the door. Coach Ramsay motioned for Daniel to stay back.

"Tonight, I need you to show the leadership of a captain. Got it?" he said.

"You'll have no complaints tonight, Coach." Daniel jammed on his helmet and headed for the box.

The ice was perfect—smooth and crystal hard—which made for a fast-skating surface. As soon as the play started, everyone could see that Wellington was also in the game to win. However, Daniel was good to his word, and the Rangers dominated in keeping the play at the other end of the rink, where they pounded Wellington's goaltender with shot after shot on net.

"Score!" The Lot 16 fans went wild every time one of their beloved Rangers appeared to land a puck in the net. And then groaned just as loudly when the puck was deflected. Isabel was breathless from jumping up and screaming every time the puck was carried to the Wellington net. She couldn't recall the last time she had so much fun.

The Wellington fans showed their appreciation of their goaltender's skill by banging on the boards and rafters. An elderly gentleman was forced to remove his hearing aid. For most of the first period, the Rangers' defence lines were in the thick of the action and kept the puck from spending much time in their zone. Ivan was spending so much time on his that he felt nervous when the puck started coming his way, but the defencemen stayed with it and usually took it out before Wellington had a chance on net.

The trouble started when Daniel's line came on. Charlie chased his Wellington counterpart in control of the puck into the left Wellington corner. As they struggled against the boards Charlie felt a stabbing pain in his arm and conceded the puck to the other player.

Charlie stopped and looked at the boards to see if there was something sticking out of them, but saw nothing.

"Looking for something, honey?" An older woman pressed against the boards asked.

Charlie glared at her as he rubbed his arm and returned to the game, but precious moments had been lost. As Charlie skated off, he heard the fans in the corner laugh and pound the boards. When the puck came back down the ice to the Wellington end, it was Daniel who went into the corner. Just like Charlie, Daniel felt something plunge into his arm right through his sweater and shirt, and then be yanked out. He saw an older woman slip a darning needle into her purse.

"Stop the play!" Daniel shouted to the referee. The fans in the corner began to boo, and yell at him to get on with the game.

"What's the problem?" The ref blew the whistle and skated over to Daniel.

"That woman just stabbed me with a needle." Daniel pointed to where the motherly-looking woman stood. The referee turned to the woman, now sporting a look of pure shock.

"I never did no such thing," she said, looking indignant.

"Did you two see anything?" The referee turned to the linesmen.

"Nothing." The two men shook their heads.

By this time, both teams had gathered around the officials. Charlie spoke up. "I didn't see what it was, but I got jabbed in the corner with something sharp, too. You want to see the mark?"

The referee put up his hand to wave him off. "None of the officials saw anything, so there's nothing I can do. Let's play hockey! You fans move back from the boards."

The suspect lady stuck out her tongue at Daniel and Charlie, then moved back out of sight, but the crush in the rink made it impossible for everyone to move away from the boards. The fans had to fend for themselves when it came to flying pucks.

A face-off resumed the play, and Robert, assisted by Ernest, put the first goal on the scoreboard for the Rangers. They held Wellington scoreless in the first period.

The Rangers felt confident when the puck dropped for the start of the second period. Daniel passed the puck to Peter, who sheltered it in the curve of his stick and turned to carry it towards the Wellington net. He never saw a Wellington fan throw several pennies into his path on the ice, and when his skates hit them, he went down hard.

Flat out on the ice, Peter watched a Wellington player nab the puck. In the stands, an outraged Rangers' fan took a swing at the culprit, who ducked. The punch struck a poor innocent man next to him. Pandemonium broke out among the fans, while the play continued. Then Wellington's number ten forward scored, tying the game for two minutes on the clock, before Daniel set up Wendell who delivered the puck inside the Wellington net. The second period ended 2-1 for the Rangers.

Coach Ramsay made it clear he wanted a bigger lead on the scoreboard for the third period. What he got was Wellington, within seconds, tying up the game at 2-2. From there, the play got tense. Wellington tried to push the Rangers into taking penalties, but cool heads prevailed—no player wanted to be the one to put their team's chances of winning at risk. When Wellington saw the strategy wasn't working, the game became hockey at its best—fast skating, rapid passing of the puck from player to player, and shots on net that drove the breath from fans' bodies only to be sucked back in when a save was made.

Wellington made it 3-2 on the scoreboard with time running out. As the clock counted down to ten remaining seconds, Daniel set up Victor, who tied the game. The pounding of hands on the boards and the stomping of feet, along with the yelling in the rink, carried far out into the night air. Isabel had yelled herself hoarse, but still she didn't stop. Reverend Johnson saved his voice for preaching. Instead, he stamped his feet and clapped his hands until the skin felt raw.

Sudden death overtime would determine the winner. Without hesitation, Coach Ramsay put both Daniel and Peter's lines on. Peter moved to centre ice to take the faceoff. Every player tensed and coiled their muscles, ready to spring into action the moment the black rubber puck cracked against the ice. The referee moved to take his place between Peter and the Wellington player, the puck dangling from his fingers. Then, as Isabel would later recall the moment, it was as though time became suspended. The people, and yes, even the timbers of the rink, became silent. In what seemed like slow motion, the puck fell. Then all erupted in a fury of motion and sound. Movement on the ice was blurred as the players chased the puck with the primitive instinct of survival.

Daniel hung back in the Rangers' end to cover Ivan, but it was only minutes before he saw his chance to make a winning move. He allowed the Wellington centre to come in deep and line up his shot on net before he swooped in and stole the puck. In a burst of speed he carried it up the ice into the Wellington zone. Scanning, he saw Peter in the best position to receive the puck and hopefully deliver it in the net.

"Make it count, boys!" Daniel yelled as he released the puck. Peter caught the puck on the centre of his stick blade and sheltered it from the Wellington left winger. He carried it right to the net and slipped it between the goalie's legs. Realizing the puck was in, Peter skated away from the net with arms raised in victory. His teammates skated to him and surrounded him, delivering thumps to his back. The Rangers' players in the box jumped over the boards and skated to join their teammates for one massive group hug. "Way to go, Peter!" and "Perfect set-up, Daniel!" The Wellington players lined up to give their opponents a hearty handshake. It had been a hard-fought, but fun game to play with no reason to be sore about the outcome. The fans of both teams said "What a great game!" They would be talking for years about the darning needle and penny incidents.

In the dressing room, the Rangers were high on success, as they relived moments of the game.

"Great first goal, Robert. You were in the right place for Ernest to set you up with the puck. I don't think the goalie saw it coming," Daniel praised their youngest player.

"Hey, what about my goal?" asked Victor.

"Your delivery was pure artistry, Victor. Wendell's, too," Daniel responded. "And Peter's clinched the game. We couldn't have asked for more."

From there, Daniel let the others carry the conversation. He just wanted to let the joy of the win wash over him and absorb the pure pleasure of the night. So much of the match had been about the elegance of hockey when played in its truest sense. Tonight's game on the ice, and those shared moments in the dressing room were why he played. Why he loved the game. For the first time since Charles Elliott had delivered his devastating news, Daniel felt as though he had once again found himself. He felt centered, calm, and very much alive.

Coach Ramsay gave the players time to burn up their post-game high and then asked them to settle down so he could speak. He had to wait some time. Coach Ramsay cleared his throat several times before he spoke. "I am so proud of you guys for tonight's win and for finishing in first place for the year," he said. "However, it doesn't stop here. We are going to win the playoffs!"

Everyone cheered, but the Coach wasn't finished. He held up his hands to settle them down. "But," he paused for effect. "BUT. . . not only are we going to win the South Shore Championship, we are taking it in four straight games. Am I right, boys?"

"You have never been more right about anything, Coach Ramsay," the captain answered for the team. Complete pandemonium broke out in the dressing room.

Coach Ramsay put up his hand. "Other than a couple of recent games, you guys played your hearts out all season. It made my job easy, and I want to thank each of you. You should be proud of yourselves." He zeroed in on Daniel. "And Daniel as our captain was the leader we needed. When he was on, you were all on and when he was off, you were all off. Thank God he was on more than off," Coach Ramsay continued, amidst the laughter, "Now, like it or not, there is practice tomorrow night."

A groan of protest went up from the team.

"Who needs practice? We're hot!" Wendell quipped.

"Don't get cocky. Practice is at 7 pm sharp."

CHAPTER 15

When Isabel and Daniel arrived home, the house was quiet with the silence that comes from the slumber of its occupants. The fire still burned brightly, and a small lamp by the rocking chair cast a soft light over the room.

"Just let me check the children and then I'll massage your shoulders as a gift to my amazing man." Isabel blew a kiss to Daniel and slipped from the room.

Daniel smiled— this day just kept getting better and better. He loved when Isabel massaged the tightness from his muscles, her small smooth hands oiled to slip without friction across his skin. Daniel grabbed a chair from the table and placed it in front of the fire, removed his shirt and undershirt, and let them fall to the floor before straddling the chair, resting his arms and head on the back rungs to wait for her to return.

A small intake of breath announced Isabel's return. The scene was one of intimacy they were rarely able to share living as they did with her parents.

"You were great on the ice tonight." Isabel crossed the room to stand behind him and took the bottle of oil from the pocket of her dressing gown. She poured some into her hand and placed her palms together to warm it. Then, ever so gently, she placed her hands on his shoulders and began a circular motion.

"I was rather impressive, wasn't I?" Daniel turned his head slightly to catch a shadowed glimpse of his wife.

"There's no conceit in your family, because you have it all," she joked and pressed her thumbs into a knotted muscle above his shoulder.

"If you're good at something why isn't it okay to just say so?"

"I was taught it's vain to think too much of oneself and your achievements." Isabel slid her fingers across his trapezius muscles and frowned. "Don't tell me you weren't told many times not to get too big for your britches."

"It was a common theme in my childhood, but hiding your own ability doesn't increase someone else's. You don't rub your skill in people's faces, but you should feel okay to make all you can of a talent. Why else would it be given to you?" He exhaled deeply.

"I know, but often when I go after something I want, I will suddenly feel this guilt that I might be taking it from someone that needs it more." Isabel poured more oil on her hands and began to work her way to the depth of his back.

"We deserve good things, Isabel, and we're going to get them through hard work and honesty."

"I'm not sure that is how it is done these days."

"I know, but in the end, you have to live with yourself."

"I don't think Elliott is having a problem living with himself."

"Not yet, but who knows what's coming."

For a moment, they both felt Daniel's muscles tense then relax, as Isabel moved to his arms and worked her way down to the elbows, enjoying the sculpturing of his biceps "Do you ever wish you could have played in the big league?" she asked.

Daniel grew silent for a time. "It's fun to dream about sometimes, but I'm where I'm supposed to be."

"Do you really believe that?" Her hands paused.

"I do. I'm meant to be with you and the girls, and I'm supposed to be a farmer. Don't you think you're where you're supposed to be?" He turned to look at her.

"You and I work, and I wouldn't want to be without our girls, but was it fair for me to lose my teaching job because I got pregnant? I worked hard to become a teacher, and a good one. My parents sacrificed to make it happen. Then the trustees took it away in an instant. I disappointed and shamed my parents, and now I can't financially help my own family and carry some of the load." Isabel wiped away her tears.

Daniel felt her pain—her shame—because it was also his own. He took her hands.

"Life isn't fair, Isabel. Whether the rules make sense or not, we broke them. But you support this family in ways that money never could. You are a great mother, and wonderful wife, and daughter. When the time is right, you will be back in the classroom." He lifted her hands to his lips and gently kissed each palm. Then, in the gentle light of the kitchen, she leaned into him.

"Interested in scoring off the ice, Mr. MacDougall?" she whispered into his ear.

"I thought you'd never ask, Mrs. MacDougall," he replied and gently kissed her lips.

Once again Daniel arrived at the office of Malcolm MacDonald's Potato Export Company five minutes before his appointment. The secretary showed him right into the inner office. MacDonald was standing at the window behind his desk, looking out at the warehouses. He turned when his secretary and Daniel entered the room, but did not offer his hand for a handshake. Rather, MacDonald motioned for Daniel to be seated while he himself remained standing. The jacket of his tailored suit was thrown over the back of a chair, his tie was loosened at the neck, and the sleeves of the white dress shirt were rolled up past the elbows. MacDonald was a big man, but there was not an ounce of fat on his body. His face was lined from hours of working in the sun and wind. He looked how Daniel imagined a self-made man would look.

MacDonald spoke first. "I must extend my congratulations to you and the Rangers for your win last night. I enjoyed the calibre of the game."

Daniel was momentarily taken aback. Yet another conversation starting with hockey. "Thank you, sir," he said. "Now the plan is to win the playoffs against Mount Pleasant."

"I have often seen you at work on the railcars and the potato boats, but never around my warehouses and office. I understand Strong has arranged this meeting for you to discuss money." A faint smile crossed MacDonald's lips.

"I need to borrow money and Mr. Strong said you are the person to see."

"Then state your case." MacDonald finally took his seat.

"I need $1,200 to pay out a private mortgage." Daniel decided that MacDonald was a man who didn't waste time or words, so neither would he.

"With whom, might I ask?" MacDonald folded his arms across his chest.

Daniel was prepared for the question. "Charles Elliott. He runs the general store in Lot 16, along with other business interests. He would be the first to tell you how reliable I am. I paid the rest of the mortgage way ahead of schedule and I will pay you off just as quickly and—"

"—And how did you do that?" MacDonald interrupted.

"By working construction in Montreal. I can go back to Montreal this summer, if necessary." Daniel could feel his shoulders tense up and tried not to sound defensive.

"Your work ethic is one of the best I've seen." MacDonald leaned back in his chair as though deep in thought. "I am always looking for reliable men to work my own acreage, so I see little need for you to have to go to Montreal for work, although I doubt the wage I can pay matches Montreal."

"It would mean a lot to me to be able to stay put." Daniel leaned forward in his chair.

"Have you generated any income from your land yet?" MacDonald asked.

"Some rent income. This will be the first cropping season for me."

"So you're depending on your ability to do physical labour to pay back borrowed money?"

Daniel tried to think where MacDonald was going with the line of questioning. "Yes, until I have the farm up and running," he replied.

"If I loaned you money, your health would be of importance to me." MacDonald pursed his lips.

"I suppose." Daniel was confused.

"Investing in a farmer who would have no income if he was hurt playing hockey really wouldn't be in my best interest, now would it?" MacDonald gave him a hard look.

"I don't plan on getting hurt." Daniel shot back.

"No one ever does. I don't relish the thoughts of foreclosing on you. You are the kind of man I'd like to help if I can. So I'll make you an offer. I'll lend you the money at the same rate as

Elliott, but with the conditions attached that you expand your hours of work with my company and. . ." MacDonald paused. "Last night was your last hockey game."

Daniel could not have felt more stunned than if Malcolm MacDonald had punched him in the gut. "But the Rangers are in the playoffs. You can't ask that of me."

MacDonald stood and crossed to the window and looked out. He took his time turning back to Daniel. "I can, and if you want the money those are the terms. I need to protect my investment."

"I don't know what to say." Daniel simply stared at him.

MacDonald turned to look out the window and survey his holdings. "I can see you need some time to think it through, and maybe talk it over with your wife. I'll have my secretary draw up the papers and the cheque this afternoon. If you accept, you can sign in the morning. The offer stands until noon."

As Daniel got up to leave, MacDonald delivered another surprise. "Not that it makes a difference when it comes to my offer, but perhaps I should mention that Chester Craig, your Mount Pleasant nemesis, is my stepson. An idiot in my opinion, but the apple of his mother's eye, and she likes him to be happy. If he's happy, she's happy, and that means I'm happy. It would make Chester very happy for Mount Pleasant to win the playoffs." Again, MacDonald paused. "I expect to see you in the morning, Daniel—it's a good deal. Please close the door on your way out."

Daniel stood outside the inner office, hat in hand, in shock. It was only when the secretary asked him if he was okay that he placed it on his head and left.

CHAPTER 16

When Daniel arrived home, he found Isabel on her hands and knees, scrubbing the kitchen floor. She rose the moment Daniel came in from the porch.

Isabel didn't wait for him to close the door before she asked. "Did you get the money?"

Daniel took off his coat and hung it on the wall hook before turning back to her. It was only then that he spoke. "Yes. MacDonald will lend me the money."

"Oh, thank God! You did it, Daniel!" She threw her arms around him, so overcome with joy and relief that she failed to note his tense body language and dejected look.

"I haven't decided yet if I'll accept." Instead of hugging her back, Daniel stepped back to look her straight in the eye.

"What? What do you mean? How would you not say yes?" Bewilderment showed on her face.

"There are conditions attached to the money." He raked a hand through his hair.

"Such as?" she wanted to know.

"I would have to work more for him," he said.

The exchange then began to match that of a lawyer cross-examining a witness on the stand.

"How is that a problem?"

"It's not. But I must also agree not to play hockey again."

"Hockey? What does hockey have to do with anything?"

"He said a farmer playing hockey is a poor risk. But, in truth, he has a vested interest in Mount Pleasant winning the league championship. His stepson is Chester Craig, and I guess MacDonald thinks the odds are better for the Flyers if I don't play."

"Can he even do that?"

"It's his money. He can do what he wants."

Isabel paced across her freshly scrubbed floor, but Daniel did not move from the spot inside the door while he waited for her to speak. So much depended on her words.

"I'm truly sorry, Daniel, but you have to accept his terms. We can't lose everything we have worked for over hockey. Both of us have sacrificed too much."

His shoulders sagged. He knew that would be her answer. It was what made sense. It was practical. It was the right thing to do, but it wasn't what Daniel wanted to hear.

"I know it makes sense to accept his terms. But I don't appreciate being held over a barrel."

"The borrower is the slave of the lender," Isabel said, thinking of her mother. "You're in no position to dictate the terms."

"But I can refuse them, can't I. Am I that desperate for a piece of land that I can be bought?" Daniel's frustrated tone spoke volumes.

"So what? Stand on your principles and lose everything? This isn't just about you, Daniel."

"No, it isn't. What about loyalty to Coach Ramsay and the boys?"

"What about loyalty to your wife and kids?" Isaabel's voice hardened. "What about loyalty to your own dreams? I agree the whole thing stinks, but let's think about what really matters. You don't have a future in hockey. But you might have in farming. We could finally have a home of our own and build a future." Isabel fisted her hands and put them on her hips. She had never looked more like her mother. Husband and wife locked eyes.

Daniel hated that Isabel was right.

"Tonight, I'll tell the team I've played my last game."

He timed his arrival just before the practice began, when he knew his teammates would be busy getting dressed and talking a mile a minute about the previous night's win and the upcoming championship.

"Jabbing a needle into a player is something I could see a young person doing, but not an old lady. My arm is bruised today." Charlie was still ticked about the incident.

"She might have been fifty. That is hardly old," John snorted.

"It's old enough to know better," retorted Charlie. "As for the pennies, Wellington never does stuff like that."

"Not everyone in the rink was from Wellington." Robert looked up from where he was lacing his skates.

"True enough. It could have been another team's fan, just sour that we are number one." Charlie did a little jig. "Our revenge will be taking the championship in four straight games."

Daniel closed his eyes and listened to the voices of the men he knew so well:

"For a moment I felt kind of bad beating Wellington— but just for a moment." An unexpected softness from Peter.

"I didn't even have a moment of regret, and I definitely won't when we beat Mount Pleasant." Ernest was the scrapper.

"Think we can do it in four straight like coach wants?" John, the nervous one asked.

"We're the Rangers." Robert deflected the doubt.

"We'll need to double the width of Ivan's goalie pads, though." Wendell got his shot in at the goalie.

"Oh, it's happening." George, always with the last word, stated. "It's happening."

Daniel could feel tears pricking his eyelids. This was his team. His game. Was this place of camaraderie something he could really leave behind on terms that were not his? It was something he would have in common with Reverend Johnson, although that gave him no comfort.

"Get a move on, Daniel. What are you standing around for? I want everyone on the ice in the next five minutes." Coach Ramsay had entered the dressing room to tell the team this was a practice session not a trip down recent memory lane.

Daniel knew it was now or never. He moved into the centre of the room and stood facing his teammates. He cleared his throat, which caught their attention.

"I need to tell the team some bad news." He paused and wiped the sweat from his brow. "Something has come up, and I won't be able to play in the playoffs. I'm sorry, but I just can't."

A stunned silence filled the room. What seemed like a long time later, though it was mere seconds, Coach Ramsay spoke. "What the hell do you think you're playing at, Daniel? This is no time for jokes."

Daniel sighed. Why couldn't Coach Ramsay have just accepted what he said and left it there? But why would he? Daniel certainly wouldn't have.

"It's no joke," he said. "I don't like sharing my business, but I guess I owe an explanation. I just ask that what I tell you stays inside the dressing room. It is simple, yet complicated. Elliott has called in my mortgage. The only place I can get the money to pay him off is from Malcolm MacDonald, who as it happens, is my boss right now."

"And mine, George, Ernest, and Peter's," Keith interjected.

"That's right," Daniel said. "Anyhow, one of the terms MacDonald has attached to the money is that I can't play hockey. He says he can't risk my getting hurt and not being able to work for him and repay the loan. I've already put everything into the new place, and I have a family to care for, so I have to accept his terms."

"The weasel! He's lower than Elliott. I didn't think it was possible to be lower than him." Peter gave voice to the team's rage.

"There's more. He just happens to be Chester Craig's stepfather." Daniel gave a bitter laugh.

"You mean Chester Craig of the Mount Pleasant Flyers? Are you saying he is trying to keep you from playing hockey to help the Flyers win the championship?" Robert looked bewildered.

"It sounds like it to me. That is so wrong." Victor shook his fist in the air.

"I don't know if that is why MacDonald is attaching the terms to the money or if he really is concerned I could get hurt," Daniel shrugged. "But I'm starting to think if it weren't for bad luck, I would have no luck at all."

"Is there no other way, Daniel?" Charlie looked stunned.

"I've tried everywhere, and the story's the same. I don't have a credit rating thanks to paying cash and, before you ask, the banks don't care that I've kept up my private mortgage. That is not their world," Daniel said.

"My father is always ranting about the way the banks treat the common people of this country. I guess he might be right." John jabbed his hockey stick into the floor.

"I guess we're screwed. You've got no choice. Damn it all to hell! Mount Pleasant is laughing already." Victor was not a man to curse.

"No! You don't get to drop us. When you take on a commitment, you see it through." Coach Ramsay wasn't about to give up that easily.

Every set of eyes in the room turned to look at him, and then at Daniel who was seething. How dare Coach Ramsay talk about his commitment.

"That's what I'm doing—following through on the commitment I made to my family," Daniel almost shouted.

"So to hell with the team?" Coach Ramsay shot back. No one stirred on the benches. If they had been asked, the players would have said they were petrified to even breathe, let alone move.

"Maybe just once you could see beyond yourself and hockey." Daniel planted himself within inches of his beloved coach. "It's hard enough dealing with the guilt of letting the team down without you rubbing it in." His voice started to break. "You of all people know I always try my best. I always try my best."

But Coach Ramsay, blinded by the possibility of seeing his sacrifices and dreams lost to Mount Pleasant goals in the net, was beyond empathy. "Well, this time your best isn't good enough."

Daniel's shoulders sagged. "It seems it rarely is."

The air in the dressing room was charged. The coach and the captain remained standing, each silent, each accusatory, each bewildered by their own emotions, and perhaps worst of all, uncertain how to back down and move forward.

"I might have a solution for both Daniel and the team," Wendell quietly spoke.

"Well, then, man, spit it out!" Coach Ramsay thundered.

"Well...since we're a team, we could all chip in to raise the money to pay off Elliott, and then Daniel can play in the championship." Wendell gulped, his courage threatening to abandon him.

"Yeah. We could do that." Keith's voice was filled with excitement. "I say we go for it!"

"Yeah, let's do it! We're a team and we can do it together!" Everyone chimed in almost immediately.

"Wait a minute, just hold on a second." Peter plunged the room back into reality. "Let me get this right. You want Daniel to risk everything for you knuckleheads? I'm sorry, but that is a lot to ask of him." Peter stared at the now-silent group. "He owes $1,200. Do you guys even begin to realize how much money that is? And how little time we would have to raise it?" Peter paused for a moment to let the weight of his words sink in. "Well, do you? I highly doubt you do."

Peter stopped talking, although he had so much more he wanted to say. Like calling out the gall of Coach Ramsay who had inherited his farm, and the fact that other than George, the rest of them were responsible only to themselves and knew little about sacrifice.

"Sure, there's risk involved, but working as a team, we will be unstoppable. I have fifty dollars in the bank. That takes us down to $1,150 and I have a few pigs I can sell." Wendell wasn't about to give up on his plan.

"And I have firewood cut to sell," Ernest said.

Coach Ramsay slowly nodded, starting to see how the idea would be a win-win for everyone. "I have an Angus steer ready to go," he said.

"As long as the ice holds, Charlie and I can fish eels and sell them. Right, Charlie?" Victor looked over at Charlie, who nodded.

"I'll move some potatoes." Percy went next.

"And I have my trap line," Keith volunteered.

They turned to look at Peter, who shifted back and forth on the bench in discomfort. Wasn't he already doing enough, being there for his brother? Other than his car, which he needed, the only thing he had that was worth anything was the filly he had invested in and planned to break before going to Montreal. He stared at his teammates and heard himself say: "I guess I have my horse."

Daniel couldn't believe what he was hearing. He never could have imagined his teammates would be willing to help him. But their offer was really no different than what his in-laws had proposed, and handouts weren't Daniel's thing.

"No. I can't ask you guys to do that. It's way too much to expect. Besides, Peter loves that filly more than he will ever love any woman, and Wendell's been saving those fifty dollars since he was born," he said.

"You didn't ask us—we offered," Wendell jumped in.

"Besides, it's not like we're doing it out of the goodness of our hearts. We want the championship, and we need you to help us get it. You're our best bet," Charlie tried logic.

"Yeah, and you'd do it for any of us," added John. "If someone needs help in the community, you're one of the first there, and you don't even go to church."

Daniel's brain was churning. "I could sell the heifers I'm raising to get started with." He paused to think. "No. It's too big a risk for everyone, and there's not much time—not likely enough."

"If we get going tomorrow, we will have the time," Wendell argued.

"My father is always saying if you set your mind to something you can make it happen." Robert added his two cents.

Daniel was torn. Who knew better than him how much money $1,200 was. Success would depend on turning assets into cash and were there enough of those available was the question. No, the whole idea was sheer foolishness. He looked at the players looking at him. "I can't take that big a risk, boys." The voice Daniel heard coming out of his mouth was that of his father. The man who always played it safe. The man he promised himself he wouldn't be.

"Risk is what makes great men," responded Ivan, who had never risked anything in life other than putting on hockey pads.

"Do you really think we can do it?" Daniel wondered aloud.

"Yes!" Everyone minus Peter, responded in unison.

The sensible part of Daniel said no, but something other than the team was pushing him to say yes. Daniel didn't give himself any more time to ponder the immensity of what he was about to do. "Then let's do it. But it has to be our secret. Elliott can't find out."

The players gathered around him, pounding him on the back.

Wendell spoke for them. "We won't let you down, Daniel. That's a promise."

Coach Ramsay took control. "That's settled, then. Daniel, hurry up and change and let's get out there and practice. Then we can get down to work raising the money. Go Rangers go!" chanted Coach Ramsay as he left the dressing room.

Pumped up from their conversation, the players jostled out of the dressing room, leaving Daniel to change.

Peter hung back. "It would seem, Daniel, you forgot something really important in making your decision."

Daniel realized immediately what his brother was referring to. A mixture of emotions flitted across Daniel's face. "I never asked Isabel. She's going to be furious."

Peter walked to the door. "An understatement, if there ever was one."

Daniel stopped lacing up his skates. So caught up in the possibility of an answer that didn't make him MacDonald's slave, he had forgotten the most important person in his life. Isabel. When they married, Daniel had promised her that they would be partners in making all decisions in their life together. Not one to make waves, she had repeated the word "obey" in her vows, but she had made it clear to Daniel beforehand she would be an equal partner. She had embraced liberal ideas at Teacher's College that set her apart from other girls he knew. He loved that about her. They talked about everything, and they shared all accomplishments and worries. That was what he had missed so much when he was alone in Montreal. He couldn't put in a letter what he could tell her when they were curled up in their bed at night. She carried the majority of the parenting load, including the care of the girls when he was in Montreal, stretched their dollars, did the barn work to free him up, and ran the household alongside her mother so that it worked for them to live in her childhood home. He worked to make the money to support them, and to build a future. They were a good team, a strong team. And now, in the spur of the moment, Daniel had taken it upon himself to make the biggest decision of their joint lives without her. As Daniel resumed tying his laces, he prayed that his decision to try to save one thing did not cost him something of far greater importance.

CHAPTER 17

When Daniel arrived home after the practice, he found Isabel in bed reading. He knew he had to tell her right away, but how? He began to undress with his back to her, but by the time his shirt was unbuttoned, Daniel knew he owed her the courtesy of eye-to-eye contact when he told her.

"What did the team say when you told them your news?" Daniel turned to see Isabel looking at him, the closed book sitting on her lap.

Daniel felt his hands tremble as he tried to unbuckle his belt. Holding his head high, he looked at the woman he loved and, with quivering voice, spoke. "I accepted an offer from the team to raise the money for us," he said.

"You did what?" Isabel, with shock written all over her face, stared at him.

"You heard me right." Daniel would not—could not—repeat himself.

"Without talking to me?" Isabel stayed still in the bed and kept her voice low and steady, fully aware that her daughters and her parents were only steps away.

Daniel dropped his eyes. He wasn't about to admit he had forgotten her entirely in the moment. "There wasn't time." He made eye contact again. "And I knew what you would say."

"Really." Her voice was like cold steel. "So, you think for me now? How nice."

She paused to get a grip on her emotions. She picked the book up, and Daniel feared she was going to aim for his head, but Isabel put it back on the bed, and raised herself up onto her knees. When she spoke again, her voice was hard but tightly controlled. "How could you even think of trusting a bunch of brainless hockey players with our future?"

"They're not brainless." Daniel pulled off his shirt and undid the button and zipper of his pants.

"A bunch of boys that won't grow up and figure out their own lives, but you entrust them with ours just so you can play hockey." She barrelled on, ignoring him.

"You think this is about my playing hockey?" Daniel stepped out of his pants and angrily threw them across the room. The coins in his pockets fell out and noisily rolled across the plank floor.

"What else am I to think? Obviously, a chance at some championship means more to you than our land and home. Our children. More than our entire future." Isabel gave him a hard look.

"How about being true to myself and still getting what I want?" he demanded.

"Well, take it from someone with experience in that department. Good luck with that!" She laughed bitterly.

The comeback hit its mark. "Please don't be like this, Isabel. It'll be okay."

For the first time in their relationship, he could not read the expression on her face "Really. I find that hard to believe. And to think you refused my parents' offer to sign a bank note. It could have all been settled by now. But no, you had to do it your way."

She put her book on the bedside table, pounded the feather pillow into the shape she desired, and settled down in the bed with her face to the wall.

Daniel crossed over to the bed and climbed in. He went to reach for her, but the rigidness of her body changed his mind, so he turned the other way and settled in for a long, restless night.

The following morning dawned bright and clear. Daniel did not wake Isabel when he left their room. She was still turned towards the wall. He went through the usual motions: started the fire, got breakfast, and checked on the girls, being sure to pull the covers back up over them and kiss each little cheek. He paused. From the day they married, he had never left the house in the morning without kissing Isabel good-bye. But they had never had such a disagreement. Perhaps he should give her the day to cool down while he found the courage to apologize and ask for her forgiveness.

As Daniel drove to work, he replayed the conversation in the dressing room and his fight with Isabel. He knew it was stupid to put so much trust in the guys. To do so was to learn nothing from the Elliott deal. To gamble once was one thing, but to do so twice, when he had a viable solution was foolhardy. Daniel knew Coach Ramsay wasn't thinking about what was best for him, Isabel, and the girls. If he did, the Coach would have said forget the game. Take MacDonald's offer, pay off Elliott, have secure work, put Montreal in the rearview mirror, and build the farm. Daniel didn't want to dwell upon the coach's selfishness or motives. Why did the man's opinion matter so much?

Daniel fought to breathe. Peter was right that the guys didn't understand how much was at stake. And Isabel had every right to lose faith in him. He just couldn't bear it if she lost respect too. He didn't even want to think about the reaction of Jessie and James. Daniel would be lucky if they let him in the house again. Then there would be the disappointment of his parents. And what if MacDonald fired him? Daniel shook his head miserably to refocus on why his gut was telling him to take the offer of his teammates. But he couldn't get a clear answer. He just knew it was the right thing to do, and Reverend Johnson had once told him that your gut would never steer you in the wrong direction. Daniel pulled up to the rail station but let the car idle while he waited for something to tell him to drive immediately to Summerside and sign MacDonald's agreement. When the bell rang to start the workday, though, the message hadn't changed. So Daniel turned off the car, picked up his work gloves, and went to join the rest of the work crew.

From the door of his office, MacDonald told his secretary to hold all calls and make sure he was not disturbed until he told her otherwise. He closed the door and returned to his desk. Once seated, he looked at his watch to verify it was indeed an hour past the deadline he had set for Daniel.

"Well, it looks like the young fellow hasn't accepted my offer," he said to the man seated across from him.

"That was a big risk you took, but you don't seem surprised." Charles Elliott leaned forward and chuckled.

MacDonald returned the laugh. "Not really. I figure if Strong innocently sent him to me, then the land is meant to be mine. Besides, a man of integrity and loyalty won't be manipulated. So, either Strong got him another investor, which I highly doubt in this short time frame, or he is going to stand on his principles and forfeit."

"Hopefully, he is forfeiting and we can quickly settle up on the land." Elliott relaxed back into his chair.

MacDonald turned in his chair to look out the window. While he was doing business with Elliott, he felt contempt for the man . . . or maybe it was for himself? He would worry about that later. "I don't need it before spring cropping, and I think it best for both of us to put some distance between you repossessing it from MacDougall and reselling to me,"

"Yeah, but I'm anxious to get it done. I shouldn't have given him the extra time." Elliott did not sound pleased about a delay.

"It's rather too bad MacDougall's land butts onto the hundred acres I bought in the fall," MacDonald said. "If I rip out the tree lines that separate MacDougall's land from mine, that will be one hell of a field, plus I'll have extensive road frontage. The time has come to start increasing potato production in this province and I plan to be one of the leaders. Still, it's too bad about the young fellow. If he wasn't in the way of my business interests, I'd help him out."

But Elliott was only thinking of himself when he said, "I think it would be best if he went to Montreal for good, but I suppose you're likely still planning on employing him."

"Damn right. You don't find workers like Daniel MacDougall every day. He'll be a real asset in making me money." MacDonald stood to indicate the meeting was over.

"I certainly appreciate the way he is making me money," said Elliott as he rose from his chair.

CHAPTER 18

The playoffs were supposedly scheduled for neutral territory, which was the rink in Summerside. But the venue really had nothing to do with neutrality. The Summerside rink had more seating capacity for fans, which was a must in the playoffs. The diehard supporters of the league teams showed up all season, but there were many more who quietly followed the standings of their teams through the regular playing season and saved their cheering energy for the playoffs. As well, the Summerside rink was the only one in the county that had artificial ice, so regardless of the outdoor temperature, the show would go on, as it were.

When Percy pulled the truck up in front of the Summerside rink, the players could see a long line-up of fans already waiting to get in. It stretched well out across the parking lot.

"It's gonna be electric in there!" Robert enthused.

Even better, though was the large, lit sign outside the rink.

"Lot 16 Rangers versus Mount Pleasant Flyers," John reverently read aloud.

"This is what it must be like every night playing in the National Hockey League."

Ernest was in awe at the thought of the celebrity treatment.

The rest had to agree he might be right although Keith was quick to point out that he doubted teams like the Montreal Canadiens, Toronto Maple Leafs, and Boston Bruins were rolling up to the rink in the back of a potato truck. Just the thought of it gave everyone a good laugh.

The Rangers grabbed their hockey bags and headed inside. They immediately noticed the brightness of the lights and the sleekness of the artificial ice surface. They could hardly wait to try it out. The stands were filling quickly, with fans ranging from school age children to grandparents. Lot 16 fans were filling the seats on the side of the rink that had the Players Box assigned to the Rangers. Reverend Johnson scouted out where Charles Elliott was seated and walked by to say hello. He felt confident the Lord was okay with him having a little fun. After all, it was Elliott's problem that he felt it inappropriate for the minister to attend the Rangers games. Johnson saw the games as an opportunity to connect with his people, and he wasn't going to hide.

Every time the canteen door opened and shut, the mouth-watering smell of hot dogs and fries escaped. The noise of people talking and moving about was consistent and comforting. As the Rangers made their way to their dressing room, Daniel, as always, absorbed the surroundings. It felt good to be there. He was still excited for the game, although deep down he felt sad for the hurt he had caused Isabel with the betrayal of her trust. He wished she was in the stands. Never before had he minded her not being at a game, but tonight he felt her absence. She had kissed him good-bye and wished him luck, but the tone of her voice held a chill, and her smile did not reach her eyes.

In the dressing room, Coach Ramsay focused on strategy. "Mount Pleasant is going to try to provoke us into stupid penalties, so keep your heads on straight," he said. "We know that Chester Craig is going to be all over Daniel like a flea in a dog's ear, so the rest of you run interference when possible.

And keep it clean. I don't need to tell any of you that we want to come out of the first game on top. This is not going to be a come-from-behind series for the Rangers. Four is the magic number. Now let's play hockey."

As the Rangers filed into the Players Box, their fans began to chant: "No need to think twice, Lot 16 is here to melt the ice!"

From the moment the puck dropped, the Rangers played hungry for the win. The team kept their play clean and fast. As predicted, Craig was on the ice every time Daniel's line was on. He stuck to Daniel like glue, even though other Rangers ran interference. Finally, a Mount Pleasant line change delivered Daniel a breakaway. Craig stayed abreast of him, but rather than go for the puck, he slid his stick ahead of Daniel's skate and sent the Rangers' captain sprawling to the ice.

Rangers' fans were on their feet screaming for the referee to call a penalty, but the whistle never blew. Springing to his feet, Daniel was ready to give Craig the fight he wanted, but he caught sight of Coach Ramsay giving the signal to skate away. Daniel's revenge came with setting up a sweetheart of a goal for Peter, which gave the Rangers a 1-0 lead at the end of the first period.

"No need to think twice, Lot 16 is here to melt the ice!"

When both teams took to the ice for period two, the temperature in the stands rose in anticipation the play would only get better. The fans were not disappointed. If the puck had been moved from end to end any faster, heads would have spun. The Rangers outmaneuvered the Mount Pleasant Flyers until Ivan slipped up and dove for the puck instead of staying on his feet. In that moment, one of the Flyers flicked the puck a fraction to the left and tied the game.

Period three was hot and heavy, although still clean, as each team tried to take the lead. Both coaches were surprised and pleased that their respective players were all staying out of the penalty box. Chester Craig had grown tired and was losing speed, while Daniel was still playing hard, so their paths crossed fewer times. The shots on net were pretty even, but both goaltenders let nothing in. With one minute left to go in the game, Daniel set up a goal for Wendell.

The first match of the playoffs belonged to the Rangers. The boys were so busy on the ice congratulating themselves that the roar of their fans filtered through to them like the distant sound of the sea as heard through a conch shell.

"Mount Pleasant weep, Lot 16 will make it a sweep!"

Each Ranger treasured the win, but none more so than Daniel. Had he agreed to MacDonald's terms, he would never have experienced the euphoria of this moment. With adrenaline running high, he felt the confidence that comes with winning. Any doubt about the decision he had made evaporated.

The feeling of elation stayed with Daniel until he got home. Isabel was not waiting up to hear about the game. Nor was she in their bed. He opened the door to the girls' room. All three were asleep in the bed. For a moment he debated waking Isabel. Instead, he pulled the blankets over the three of them and kissed her lightly on the cheek. She didn't stir.

CHAPTER 19

Savouring the win of the hockey game paled in the dawn of the following morning. The cold reality hit the various men that they had made a huge commitment with high stakes attached.

What the hell had they been thinking? Keith wondered. Wound up from the game, and unable to sleep with the full moon shining in his window, he got up at 5 am and headed for his trapline. On snowshoes he travelled across the fields to the edge of the woods and entered. Even among the trees the moon guided him. Since November, he had supplied the Wellington butcher with a goodly number of rabbits, but could have sold more as the small animals were in demand for meat pies and stew meat. He had hidden the money he earned, totalling $35, under a floorboard in the bedroom for a rainy day. It had arrived.

Trapping was a sideline to Keith's day job, but as of today, it would have to play a larger role if Daniel's mortgage was to be paid off. Keith was determined it would be. He was big on keeping promises, since he had first-hand experience on losing a dream.

Keith allowed himself to think of Helen, the girl he had grown up with and planned on forever with. Mere weeks from the wedding Helen announced she was leaving him and the province for a young airman being transferred to the new

Cold Lake airbase in Alberta. Keith was devastated. He never had a clue Helen removed his diamond ring when she and her Summerside roommates went to base dances. The betrayal and broken engagement had happened over two years ago, and Keith was finally getting tired of letting it knock him down. Maybe helping Daniel get what he wanted would help him get out of himself and back into life. If it weren't for hockey and working with the crew, Keith didn't know where he would be, and he sure didn't want to lose either. At his first snare, a rabbit was trapped. Keith quickly removed the animal and reset the snare. He hoped his luck would hold down the line.

Keith had checked all his traps by the time Wendell sat down to breakfast. He looked at the food heaped on his breakfast plate. His mother often complained that his eyes were bigger than his stomach, which produced a precious waste of food at times. But maybe it wasn't just his eyes—maybe it was his whole thinking. In the hard light of day, Wendell wasn't so confident the team could raise the mortgage money. Worse still, he was the one who had come up with the idea and sold the others on it. Wendell pushed the bacon around on his plate. The deal with MacDonald was off the table. MacDonald had been at last night's game and he had looked none too pleased to see Daniel on the ice. But as Wendell chewed a slice of bacon, he decided that if a fellow couldn't think big, what was the point of life? Surely, you had to take a risk here or there. Except what if the risk wasn't yours to take?

Wendell shuddered when he thought of Isabel. She would give him the cold shoulder for this, and he hated the thought of that. Growing up, Wendell had a big crush on Isabel—not that he had ever told her about it—and she certainly had never looked at him, but she was a woman to admire and he wanted to look good in her eyes. Maybe Daniel wouldn't tell her the idea was his. Yeah, like that was going to happen.

Wendell finished his breakfast and wiped his mouth on a sleeve as he pushed his chair back from the table. Self-doubt wouldn't raise the money, only action would. He couldn't deny it was going to hurt to take his fifty dollars out of the bank. Wendell liked having that security, although against what, he couldn't say. Plus there were the pigs—six pregnant sows—and he would honour his word and sell half to put towards the mortgage fund. Of course, he hadn't intended on selling any of them as the plan was to raise the litters to weaner size and then sell the majority, while keeping back a few breeders to increase his herd. The sale of the sows would certainly hamper his expansion plans, but compared to what Daniel stood to lose, it was pretty small.

Wendell picked up the phone to call the buyer before he could change his mind, reassuring himself that it was going to be okay.

Wendell and Keith weren't the only Rangers who were having serious second thoughts about their agreement to help Daniel. Ernest left for work early so he could pick up George and Peter and see what they thought of the plan in the light of day. The two men were barely in the car before Ernest started in.

"Holy shit, boys, what if we've screwed Daniel's life?"

"Ease up on the gas, man," George said. "I'm as scared as you, but we didn't force him to take the deal with us."

Peter laughed from the backseat. "Didn't you? The team threw a drowning man a rope and he grabbed on, so there is no way we can let go. It's do or die boys, so let's just do."

"That appears to be the only choice now," Ernest said. "There is no going back to MacDonald."

"Unless that lawyer could quickly get another investor for Daniel. That could be a possibility," George proposed.

"Are you suggesting, George, that the team pull out of the agreement?" Peter asked, "because I'm sure that would leave Daniel in a really good place. Elliott has already diminished his trust in people. The team walking away on their deal would finish him."

"Shit. I never thought of that," George stuttered. "I was trying to think of regaining a safe deal for Daniel."

"And getting yourself off the hook?

"Hey, that is not fair," George protested. "I love Daniel like a brother. I'd never want to hurt him. We were impulsive the other night. Still all caught up in the high of the hockey win."

"Thinking we could do anything if we put our minds to it," Ernest slowed his speed. "And what if we can't?"

"Have you ever thought of how angry Isabel is right now that Daniel went with the team?" Peter threw the question out to the men. "He put their future in our hands."

"Shit. I never thought of Isabel." George rubbed the back of his neck. "I wouldn't want to be Daniel."

"She'll hunt us all down." Ernest gripped the wheel a little tighter. "We'll all feel her wrath. We made a commitment, and we have to keep it."

"We sure do," said George. "Let this be a lesson to do more thinking and less talking."

"We'll make it work." Ernest gripped the steering wheel even tighter. Peter hoped it was well bolted in place.

Percy's father had set aside two acres of the previous fall's potato crop for his son. He was a firm believer that the young man needed an extra incentive, along with the small wage he was able to scrape together to pay him, to keep him on the farm that would one day be his. Percy had chosen to hold a portion of the potatoes back in the hopes of a higher price on the early spring market. But the time had come and he hoped he could sell them on short notice. As soon as his morning chores were done, he opened the outside hatch to the farm-house cellar and headed down the steps. Wendell and John should be along anytime now.

Percy stepped off the rough wooden steps onto the firm clay floor of the cellar where the smell of potatoes, clay, and jute filled his nostrils. The young farmer looked to the far corner of the cellar where the dwindling pile sat. Percy had looked at that pile many times over the winter, relishing the cash each forkful out of it was placing in his pocket, and grimaced. This time it would be different, but he didn't begrudge the sacrifice. Percy knew what side his bread was buttered on. He had never known a hungry day or an unfilled need in his short life, and he knew he had an established farm coming to him. He never had and likely never would have to struggle for his dream the way Daniel did every day.

Percy pulled the small sturdy grader closer to the pile to save steps when forking the potatoes onto the grader, which was a low-tech, homemade setup that served the purpose. Built for the height of an average man, the grader table was narrow enough to allow one grader to be efficient, but worked even better with two. At one end, metal clamps jutted out for the fastening of two one-hundred-pound jute bags. A simple wooden chute directed the potatoes to one bag or the other. Usually, Percy graded alone or with his father, but having John and Wendell give him a hand would be a great help.

Just then, he heard the hatch lift and fall back into place as the two entered.

"Hey, Percy." John and Wendell hung their coats on hooks and stood still until their eyes adjusted from the bright light of the winter day to the dimness of the cellar.

"Wendell can fork, John can grade, and I'll bag. Sound good?" said Percy.

The men nodded and set to work. Percy was confident the grading would be light—the potatoes had kept well in the cool dark cellar and there had been no smell of rot since the crop was put in storage.

The three quickly fell into a rhythm. Wendell used the wide potato fork to scoop the potatoes from the edge of the pile and transferred them onto the grader bed. He was careful not to spear any potatoes with the prongs, which would render them cattle feed. John swiftly rotated the forkful beneath his hand to spread them out over the grader surface making it easy to see any rocks, undersized, or damaged potatoes. Two buckets sat at his feet for rocks and culls. Once John had finished grading a section, he pushed the potatoes along the grader bottom to allow them to fall into the waiting jute bag. When the first bag filled, Percy shifted the wooden divider to direct the potatoes into the second bag and then unclamped the first bag. He shook it to settle the potatoes and skilfully sewed the bag shut with a large needle threaded with fine jute. Breaking the thread, Percy picked up the bag and carried it to the bottom of the cellar steps and laid it flat on the floor, before swiftly moving back to the grader to fasten a new bag on the first clamp just in time to shift the divider and remove the second bag and repeat the process. At first, the three worked in silence.

"I've just been thinking that a potato gets handled a hell of a lot of times before it's eaten," Wendell said, an hour into their work. "Makes you wonder if it's worth it, but I've answered my own question. You really can't beat potatoes on the plate." He leaned on the fork to take a moment to rest his back. "Not when they're mashed and sit next to a thick slice of roast beef or pork and are covered in gravy." John stepped back from the grader and wiped his brow on the sleeve of his shirt.

"Yeah, but baked potatoes, fried potatoes, roasted potatoes, scalloped potatoes, or potato salad are just as good. Come to think of it, I've never met a potato I didn't like," Percy chuckled.

"Potatoes are good for more than eating," Wendell said. "I don't suppose, Percy, you know what Daniel, Peter, and I did one night to Ivan—using potatoes."

Percy, who figured he had heard all of Wendell's limited supply of stories more than once, had to admit he hadn't heard this one.

"If I tell, you can't ever breathe a word about it." Wendell was busting at the seams to tell the tale.

"You have my word." Percy wasn't going to deny Wendell his moment.

"You know how proud Ivan was of his first car," Wendell began. "You'd think it was the only car there ever was by the way he bragged about it. There was nothing he believed that car couldn't take on, 'Yeah, Wendell, the colder it is the better she starts.' 'Yeah, boys the deeper the snow. the better she goes through it.' It got to be enough to give us all heartburn. So anyways, on a night we knew Ivan had a date with a certain girl, the three of us armed ourselves with a half dozen potatoes and waited in the hedge along her parents' laneway." Wendell paused to make sure his audience was still with him. They were. "From our hiding spot we watched Ivan drive in and park by the house. When he stepped out of the car, we could see our boy was all dressed up, but still he had to slick back his hair one more time. We were laughing so hard we were scared he was going to hear us."

Wendell paused to put another forkful of potatoes on the grader. "Finally, Ivan walked up to the house and her father let him in the porch door. We knew if her father was there, we didn't have much time and it was likely too risky for all three of us to go near the car. I wanted to scuttle the plan, but Daniel and Peter said no way were we not going to finish what we had come to do. So while Peter and I kept watch, Daniel snuck up to the rear of the car and one by one pushed the potatoes into the tailpipe. He just made it back to the hedge when the house door opened and out came Ivan and his girl. Ivan was a real gentleman and held open the door for her. We heard him say how he had the car all cleaned up for the date." Wendell stopped and leaned on the fork. He wanted to give a strong finish to the story. "Then Ivan jumped in the driver's seat and started the car. She caught—and immediately stalled. He tried again, and the same thing happened. The third time she caught, Ivan floored her, and a potato flew out the pipe, and then she stalled again. He must have been ten or more minutes blowing out those potatoes and there we were in the hedge, killing ourselves laughing."

"Daniel doesn't have time for jokes like that anymore. I sure miss those days." Wendell shook his head sadly.

"The times are changing," John agreed. "But at least we still have him for hockey. I hope that doesn't change for a long time."

As soon as a load was graded, Percy called Ralph at the Miscouche railway office of MacDonald's Potato Export Company to ask about a possible sale. Ralph told him he was in luck as they were short to finish a load. If he could get there quickly the sale was his. Percy made the trip in record time. He even helped the crew unload.

"Your timing couldn't have been better," said Ralph when he came out of the office with the sale slip. "Any chance you could have another load by the first of the week?"

"It can be done," said Percy. With the crew quietly looking on, Percy thought he would try to push his luck a little, "Any chance of getting a few more cents out of MacDonald?"

Ralph heard that question several times a day, but the answer wasn't his standard line of "not much chance of that." He surprised everyone. "You never know because demand is staying high and the supply is getting scarce."

"Great, I'll be back." Percy grinned at the foreman.

"I suppose you have big plans for the money?" Ralph inquired.

"Sure do. It's expensive driving championship hockey teams to the games." Percy gave the crew a big wave, jumped in the truck and pulled out. The crew and foreman watched him go, but none made any comment.

CHAPTER 20

As the hands of the clock edged towards noon, Victor looked over at Charlie and raised his eyebrows. Time for Charlie to ask Johnny for an extended lunch hour. For some reason, Johnny was more inclined to grant a favor when Charlie asked. Victor claimed it was the baby face, while Charlie said it was because he asked nicely.

"Still alive?" Charlie asked his boss who had turned on the radio to listen to the dinner news and death announcements. Johnny, who had a fair number of decades under his belt, claimed the best programming on the radio was the death announcements, which he couldn't miss in case his name was read out. Every time Johnny told the story, he laughed as though it was the first time he had thought of the line. Charlie had the timing down for asking favours. Not too soon before the announcements and never during them.

"Appears so," the older man grinned.

"Glad to hear it," Charlie said. "Since we aren't heading to your funeral this afternoon, do you have a problem with Victor and me extending lunch to get in some eel fishing?

"Christ, there'll soon not be an eel left out there the way you boys are after them this winter," Johnny fiddled with the radio dial, trying for the best reception.

"Could be, but the fish mart in town is sold out and looking for another order. If we don't fill it first, they'll move on to someone else."

"Well, we can't have that, because then you two will be hitting me up for more money." Johnny settled into the old chair he kept by the fire and pulled out his lunch box. "Never! You're too good an employer for that," charmed Charlie. Victor rolled his eyes.

"No need to lick my boots, Charlie. You can have an extra half hour on the clock." Johnny cranked up the radio, signalling the end of the conversation.

Less than ten minutes later, Charlie and Victor had dressed and gathered their boots, axes, spears, and jute bags and were stepping onto the ice. They decided to skate out to the fishing ground, which would save time and also count as a practice in building speed. It was a good winter for ice on the Grand River, as the temperatures had been cold and remained steady, building a good thickness for ice fishing. Though the season was getting on, the ice would still be safe for at least another month. The wind had swept clear the ice, enabling them to travel at a good clip.

"I sure hope it is the truth that the fish mart needs another order," Victor said.

With other fisheries closed for the winter demand was high for the elongated fish. As a delicacy, eel meat fetched a better price than many other fish, especially from off-Island.

"If the fish mart can't take an order, we will just go door-to-door, liked we talked about," Charlie replied.

The two men lapsed into silence as they enjoyed the skate. They didn't notice the cold of the wind or the desolate look and feel of the frozen river. They were in their element. Both were sons of fishermen who had settled along the upper

Southwest banks of the Grand River and would have been hard pressed to name a time when they had not been either around, or on, the Grand River and Malpeque Bay. It could be said the salt water of the river and bay was their blood. They knew every inch of the river, and where the best grounds for each species were located. Now they headed for the inlet known as the quagmire, and soon were upon the eel grounds.

Putting the jute bags under them to protect their bottoms from the ice, they quickly removed their skates and pulled on cold boots.

"What do you say we chop the ice in the holes we used last trip out and give them another try?" Victor rubbed his hands together to get the blood moving in his fingers.

Charlie tucked the skates into one of the jute bags to protect them from the wind. It was wishful thinking that the bags could keep them warm for the trip back. "It's worth a try. The ice in them wouldn't be as thick and can be opened quicker, giving us more time to try our luck," he agreed.

Both men had learned the art of eel fishing as young boys joining their fathers out on the ice. Both Charlie and Victor chopped with their axes and the sound carried across the frozen river to the ducks swimming in the open water under the bridge. In fear of an unknown predator, the birds swam closer together. Soon Charlie and Victor cut through to the dark cold water below.

"Now all we need is a good number of eels burrowed in the mud below." Victor put down his axe and picked up his spear.

"Let's hope the river wants to give us a substantial number of eels. I mean, who more deserving than us?" Charlie lowered his spear into the water and moved it down into the depth until he felt the bottom.

"Yeah! Who better than the guys that need to raise $1,200 in no time at all. Have you ever seen $1,200, Charlie?" Victor worked his spear in the second hole a few feet away.

"Can't say that I have." Charlie gave a quick downward jab of the spear. "At least not in a single sum, but we will soon, Victor."

"We sure as hell better." With that, Victor gave his spear a quick downward jab, and trapped an eel between the tines of the spear. With a swift upward stroke, he caught the eel on one of the blunt upward points and pulled it from the water. "Bingo!" he shouted.

The eel didn't immediately yield, but flung itself about on the end of the spear. Victor let the eel go quiet before removing it from the spear, and reverently placing it inside a jute sack. Fishing was his life, yet Victor always felt that little sting of remorse for each creature he took from the sea. In truth, it was what made him a good fisher.

By the time Victor had the eel bagged, Charlie had made a catch. "Oh yeah, the river god is smiling on us, Victor!" he said.

"Us or Daniel?" asked Victor, as he pulled another eel from the mud.

"Us," answered Charlie. "We are the human hunters that she has cast her favour upon."

Victor pulled up a third eel. "Your eyes are brown."

Forty-five minutes later, they had a respectable number of eels in the jute bags. "We've taken our catch for the day, Charlie." Victor put down his spear.

Charlie whistled as he brought to the surface another one. "Are you thinking about what Johnny said about our catch this winter?"

"I'm thinking about what we can sell and the fact we need to get back to work." As he changed back into his skates, Victor reflected on what the sea had just given them. Unlike the land, which rested in winter, the sea was still giving. Fishers like him and Charlie needed to respect that fact and be thankful for every gift she gave them.

"Daniel should have thought about fishing over farming," Victor said. "At least we don't have to buy the river, other than get a license or a lease here or there, and look what it gives back."

Charlie thought for a moment. "Yeah, but you know how you feel about the water – it's part of you. That's how Daniel feels about the land, and there's no getting around it. Life's funny like that. I wonder what makes one fellow care for one thing and another fellow something else?"

"Not a clue," said Victor. "But its likely a good thing it is that way."

Victor looked at his watch. "Let's go. If we skate fast, we should still have ten minutes to warm up by the fire and eat our sandwiches."

The two of them started towards the small wharf that jutted out into the river. Smoke was rising from the chimney of Johnny's shed. Both his lobster boat and dory, as well as those of Victor and Charlie's fathers, were up on blocks on higher ground back from the shore. The sun reflected off the pure whiteness of the snow sheltering the land from the harshness of winter winds. The evergreen hedgerows were a sharp contrast to the snow. The sky was without clouds, casting its blueness on the frozen ice.

"Never gets old does it?" Charlie hollered out to Victor.

"Never," replied Victor.

As soon as they knocked off work, Victor and Charlie headed for town. The meat market couldn't handle anymore for another couple of days leaving the two young fishermen with no option but to try direct marketing. Both would be the first to admit they were not comfortable in sales. Being out on the river was where they felt in their element. It usually satisfied them to hand their catch over to a buyer and take whatever price was offered. But that couldn't happen today, so they were going to have to push themselves outside their comfort zone and go door to door.

"We're selling good eels and that's what we have to remember," Charlie said to Victor. "If someone doesn't want to buy, it's not personal. It's because they don't like or need eels. That what's we have to remember." Charlie was trying to convince himself more than Victor.

"I never thought of it that way," Victor said. "But yeah, we're not begging— we're offering an opportunity to buy a good fresh eel delivered right to the door. When you think of it that way, we're doing them a favour. That's really a service, and you're right. If they say no, it is about them, not us."

After thinking it over, Charlie and Victor decided they would price the eels higher than what they were getting from the market, but lower than what the market was selling them for. That way, housewives would think they were getting a great deal for fresh eels, and by cutting out the middleman, Charlie and Victor would have more in their pockets.

On the drive to Summerside, they debated their approach to selling.

"I think it would be best if we divided up," said Victor. "I can see a woman feeling nervous if the two of us are standing at the door when she opens it up."

"I can see a woman being nervous if it is just you standing there." Charlie laughed. "It will be my looks and charm that carry us."

"Well, let's find out," Victor grunted his annoyance. "We will each take one side of a street and see who has sold the most at the end. I'm pretty certain my hardy, honest look will secure more sales."

"You want to bet on it?" Charlie threw him a side glance.

Victor stopped the truck on one of the side streets, and parked. "We can't afford to bet. Not now."

As agreed, each of them took a side of the street. Their smiles were forced and their voices nervous when the first few doors they knocked on opened to them. But as their confidence grew with both sales and refusals, so did the naturalness of the smiles that showed white teeth in wind-burned, genuine faces. When successful with a sale, each went back to the truck with the housewife's basin and brought back her order. They moved the truck along the street every few houses. It only took them three streets to sell out. By the end of it they had lost track of who had sold what, but neither cared. By the interior light of the cab, they counted out the money. When the total was revealed, both men sat silent for a minute.

"Maybe we will conduct more of our business this way." Victor voiced what they were both thinking.

"Yeah," agreed Charlie. "I never thought about how big a slice of the pie the buyer on the shore and the retailer takes. Maybe fishermen need to be looking for a better way to sell their catch and even up the scales a little."

Victor put the cash in an envelope and sealed it. As proud as they were of their achievement, they both knew it was still a long way from $1,200.

"I guess it's back to the ice at lunch tomorrow," said Charlie.

CHAPTER 21

The thing about Isabel was that she didn't stay mad for long or hold a grudge. In that way she was like James, who liked to say, "If you can't fight and get over it, you're not much of a man." Or woman, Isabel would silently add to herself. Jessie took much longer to forgive, probably because she was too busy giving her all to people until it hurt, and of course stating her opinions on just about everything. But Isabel didn't have time to waste. If Daniel had turned their future over to the team, she wasn't going to stay in a snit until she could say she told him so. No way. She would take a hand in ensuring the outcome was positive.

Yesterday, she had gone to Elliott's General Store to post an ad to sell her wedding dress. Jessie had designed and sewn the timeless dress, which Isabel had intended to keep for her daughters. Yet the need of today had to come ahead of the sentiment of tomorrow. As Isabel pinned her ad to the notice board, Carol Ramsay stopped to read it. Carol made sure Elliott was not close enough to hear before she spoke.

"You were a beautiful bride, Isabel, and Daniel a handsome groom. I'm sorry to see you are selling your dress. It was definitely one of Jessie's masterpieces."

"My mother has an amazing talent," Isabel replied. "The dress is wasted in a cedar chest." She wasn't sure Carol knew of Daniel's deal with the Rangers. She couldn't give anything away. But there was little in the community Carol didn't know. She had learned to be a listener rather than a talker, and Roland couldn't keep a secret if he tried.

"Maybe, but I'm sorry for the reason behind your selling the dress, and my husband's part in it, not to mention the jackass behind the counter." The two women stole a look at Charles Elliott arranging the tobacco products. "I'd like to give him a piece of my mind, but then the plot would be revealed and we can't have that." Carol gave a quick laugh. "Just remember, Isabel, lots of people are working for you, including me." The older woman placed her hand on Isabel's arm and gave it a light squeeze before walking to the counter.

"So, Charles, where do you hide the women products? It's a natural thing, you know, and they should be up where they can be seen." Isabel watched the red rise in Elliott's face as he mumbled and pointed to a corner shelf. Carol flashed Isabel a big smile as she walked over to the shelf and brought a box of sanitary napkins to the counter.

"It's just good business, Charles, to display the obvious," Carol finished off the now-mute Elliott, as he hastily stuffed her purchase in a paper bag. If anyone could toy with Elliott, it was Carol Ramsay.

Isabel looked back at the bulletin board to make sure her ad was clearly visible, but her eye caught on something else: a request for a tutor. Her interest piqued until she saw that Miss Catherine Wall was the contact name. Frowning, Isabel turned and left.

On the way home, Isabel wrestled with emotions she had long kept buried. When the trustees had dismissed her five years ago, they hired a male teacher to replace her. When Irwin Barlow had moved on a year ago, Isabel had not been considered for an interview. She blamed the board chair, Charles

Elliott, who had seen her fired in the first place. Instead, Catherine Wall had been hired. Isabel felt doubly betrayed, and rightly or wrongly, had kept her distance from the young woman. Isabel acknowledged Catherine was a nice enough woman, but just seeing her name triggered feelings that Isabel worked so hard to suppress. Except now was not the time to let feelings or stubbornness get in the way of her family's future. There was no sense cutting off her nose to spite her face.

Over the course of the day and well into the night, Isabel allowed her feelings to surface, and felt the pain behind them. Yet, when the sun rose the next morning and Isabel realized she felt far from defeated, she knew she had to act. Isabel dressed Jeannie and Mary for outside and told them they were going for a sleigh ride. This always excited them. The girls were content to be pulled through the snow for what seemed to Isabel as aimless hours on end. But today, the one-room schoolhouse that housed grades one to eight was the destination. She timed the trip to arrive at the recess break. The students were just coming out of the school as Isabel pulled into the short school lane, and the older ones, whom she had taught, ran to greet her. After appointing two of the girls to mind Jeannie and Mary while she had a quick word with Miss Wall, Isabel crossed the schoolyard, her stomach full of butterflies. What if Miss Wall had already hired someone else for the tutor position? Or what if she felt Isabel lacked the right qualifications? Isabel shook her head at her panicked thoughts. If the job was filled, so be it. But Isabel was more than qualified, which she wanted Miss Catherine Wall to know.

Isabel entered the school porch, stomped the snow from her boots, and knocked on the classroom door, waiting to be invited in.

"Come in," she heard from inside. She opened the door and stepped into the space that had once been under her control.

Miss Wall was seated at the desk on the raised platform at the front of the room. Upon seeing Isabel, she gave a welcoming smile, rose from her chair, and started down the aisle with her hand outstretched.

"Mrs. MacDougall, how nice to see you, especially here at the school. You left a lasting impression on this place," Miss Wall said. "When I first came here, the older children talked about you constantly. Mr. Barlow couldn't fill your shoes, and I doubt I ever will. And now you have those two adorable little girls. How fortunate you are. So, how can I help you?"

Isabel said nothing for a moment, only offered her hand, processing Miss Wall's words. Never had she imagined her life as enviable.

"I'm here about your ad for tutoring services. I would like to know more about it, and if it is still available," she said.

"How wonderful! I have three students who will be writing the provincial exams this year. As you well know, the exams are challenging, and so their parents have offered me money on top of my pay for extra tutoring. But with teaching so many grades, I don't have the time to give them extra help. I suggested that we first try to find someone qualified who could work with the three. You, I believe, are the perfect answer. It would be an hour a day after school, and two hours on Saturday. What do you think, Mrs. MacDougall? How soon could you start?" Miss Wall clapped her hands together.

Isabel felt a familiar excitement course through her. Preparing the students for the exams would be a real challenge, and yet would not overly interfere with her family responsibilities. It could be the best of both worlds, plus she would be financially contributing to her family's future.

But she had to play it calm. "You know, Miss Wall, I believe I am the person for the job, but I would have one condition before I said yes. I would need half of the money up-front."

Miss Wall smiled. "I see that as no problem at all: half up front, and then monthly payments until the exam. Then, depending on the results, maybe even a little bonus. What do you say, Mrs. MacDougall?"

"I will start tomorrow." Isabel gave the teacher a genuine smile.

"Tomorrow it is, then," the teacher agreed. And with that, Isabel turned and left, feeling more hopeful about her family's future than she had in weeks.

Jeannie and Mary might well have wondered about their mother on the trip home. She ran with the sleigh and zigzagged it from side to side to increase the excitement of the ride. She joined in their laughter. And when they reached the house, she made snow angels with them, and then a family of snowmen. Jessie looked out at them from her pantry window and smiled. It had been a long time since she had seen the lighter side of her daughter.

Later that evening, Isabel told Daniel about her new job and when she whipped from her dress pocket the up-front payment she had demanded, Daniel was stunned and amazed at the size of the bills. Hearing the happiness in her voice, Daniel wisely kept his mixed feelings about the tutoring to himself. Isabel needed him to be proud of her and appreciative of her financial help. She didn't need his anxiety around his breadwinning abilities getting in the way. When it came right down to it, neither did Daniel.

CHAPTER 22

The night of the second playoff game sported a bright moon high in the night sky. The fields were well lit as Daniel snowshoed to the school to meet the truck. A fox was ahead of him heading for its den with a small animal in its mouth. He wondered if the fox worried about where its next meal was coming from. If not, Daniel concluded, the fox already knew heaven. He supposed Reverend Johnson would argue with him about the notion that animals had souls that lived on, but if humans did, then why not animals? In Daniel's opinion, they were the worthier species. He smiled, finding it hard to believe that as a youngster, he had planned on being a preacher. Daniel hardly knew when that dream had died, but had no regrets. Though his faith was strong, Daniel rarely entered the doors of the church anymore, although Isabel often asked him to join her and the children in the pew on Sunday morning. He felt connected to God when he was out in nature. Daniel looked up at the vast sky filled with shimmering stars and felt that one of them was looking down on him tonight.

He was pumped for the game. Having cleared the air with Isabel, Daniel felt lighter, and able to breathe, and no longer a total louse. It hadn't been easy to apology to his wife, because for several days, Isabel had made it impossible to find a moment alone. Finally, Daniel took action. He apologized at the supper table with James, Jessie, and the girls as an audience. It wasn't an ideal setting for the discussion, but Daniel was willing to offer an apology in front of the MacArthurs if it meant healing the hurt he had caused. Putting himself in Isabel's shoes gave him an appreciation of what he had done. After five and a half years of marriage, he should have respected the fact that he wasn't a solo act.

He'd waited until everyone was served and quietly eating, then dove in.

"Isabel, I know I have hurt you deeply and I am sorry." He finally had her attention.

"Do you really know, Daniel?" Isabel asked. James shrank in his chair. Daniel felt Jessie's eyes bore into him, but he forced himself to keep talking.

"Yes, I think I do. I betrayed our deal to be partners in all things. And there is no bigger thing than our future. It would rip my heart out if you had done what I did."

"You forgot about me." Isabel's lip quivered.

"Yes, I did," he admitted. "I so badly wanted another way out that I forgot everything but the offer in front of me. It was stupid and selfish. I realize the land and the house have little value without you. It is the working together to achieve them that really matters. I can't do it without you Isabel."

Accept the apology, thought James. This boy has guts, thought Jessie.

"Well lucky for you, because you don't have to. I am hurt, Daniel," Isabel said. "But I can understand where you're coming from. I don't like what you did, but your apology helps. I believe it is real."

"It is real, Isabel. Please don't ever doubt that," Daniel said.

"Just don't ever again forget that I am an equal partner in our endeavours." Isabel pointed her finger at him. The fight was over.

Charles Elliott was standing just inside the entrance of the rink, waiting for his wife and girls to return from the canteen, when he saw Malcolm and Mrs. MacDonald at the admission booth. Elliott quickly turned his back, but had been spotted. MacDonald spoke quietly to his wife and waved her towards the stands before making his way over to Elliott and casually tipped his hat in greeting.

"Evening, Charles. Anything new happening in your world these days?" MacDonald looked about to make sure no one was paying attention or close enough to hear.

Sure that MacDonald was playing with him, Elliott was curt in answering. "It's business as usual, Malcolm," he said. "Pretty quiet with the time of year, but I expect things will pick up shortly with the coming of spring. I imagine it's much like that for you as well."

"Oh, I have a lot of irons in the fire. One or two of them are always red hot, but you're right, more of them will heat up with the coming of spring—one in particular, I hope."

The message was delivered and received that neither man had any information on what was happening with Daniel. They would have to wait for the mortgage due date. Neither liked waiting for what they wanted, especially if the bugger was going to drag it out on principle.

"I see the rink is packed to capacity again tonight." Elliott decided to take the conversation in a different direction. "Summerside must like the business the championship is bringing in. Let's hope the Rangers don't wrap it up too quickly."

"I doubt there is much worry of that." MacDonald then turned and walked away to find his wife in the stands.

When Elliott was finally joined by his family, he directed them to the opposite side of the packed rink. Even though the game hadn't started, Elliott's enjoyment in the evening was already significantly depleted. Suddenly, Reverend Johnson was passing in front of the family to reach a seat further down the bench. He stopped to talk.

"Good evening, Mr. and Mrs. Elliott." He tipped his hat and smiled. "What a grand night for a hockey game." He then turned to the Elliott girls. "Who do you think is going to win the game?"

The girls giggled. "You know, Reverend Johnson, it will be the Rangers."

"Well, I don't know that for sure, but I hope, you are right girls. Except winning isn't everything. More important is how you play the game, wouldn't you agree, Mr. Elliott?" The Reverend turned to Charles Elliott.

"Charles would certainly agree with that statement, wouldn't you, dear?" Mrs. Elliott patted her husband's arm and gave him a generous smile.

"It is an honourable thought, Reverend," Elliott agreed. "Not always profitable, though."

Judging by the vibe in the rink, Elliott was the only one feeling deflated. Fans were scrambling to get seats, with the Flyers' fans gong to the right side of the rink, and the Rangers' fans going to the left. People knew that with the heightened emotions around the playoffs, it was best to be seated by a known face.

"Hey, can you folks push down some and make room for a couple more?" Elliott's wife nudged him as a handful of fans stood at the end of their row. Irritated, he slid over a few inches.

In the dressing room, the Rangers were jovial. The conversation never strayed from hockey and the strategy for the game. As usual, Coach Ramsay stressed they keep the game clean, stay out of the penalty box, and focus on out-skating and out-scoring Mount Pleasant. He then looked at Daniel. "Hard as it will be, don't let Craig get to you. Understand?"

"You will have no complaints about your captain's performance tonight," Daniel agreed.

It was apparent within the first minutes of play that Mount Pleasant was cutting back on intimidation tactics and stepping up their skills. In the first period, Chester Craig was given little ice time, so the level of play that unfolded was worthy of big-league teams. It was the kind of hockey game Daniel loved, with the emphasis on skating and stick-handling the puck. He was totally immersed in the game and having fun. Time and again, he took the puck from Mount Pleasant players with only a skillful flick of his wrist, and then enjoyed watching the forwards do their job when he passed it to them.

Halfway through the period, Daniel carried the puck out of his own end and, seeing no opportune pass, kept going with it towards the Flyers' goalie. He could have taken the shot further back than he did, but felt like playing cat and mouse with the goalie and so continued to skate forward forcing him from the net. Just when it appeared the two would collide, Daniel veered sharply to the right and shot the puck into the net just inside the goal post. The Rangers' captain usually made it a point not to be showy on the ice after a goal or assist, but just for once, he allowed himself to raise his arms in victory as he skated away from the net.

"Now Mount Pleasant knows, he skates like a pro, he shoots like a pro, he's our captain you know!" The Rangers' fans took to their feet and raised a cheer. Daniel laughed to himself. The MacKinnon twins, dedicated Rangers' fans, had obviously composed a few new chants for the playoffs, and Reverend Johnson was conducting his seat section to ensure they were the loudest in the rink.

The Rangers kept on top of the puck, but Mount Pleasant never let up in forcing the play back into the Rangers' end. Daniel's defence line was in the box when the Flyers evened up the game to end the first period. Fans could be seen rubbing their jaws to relax the muscles. No one doubted there was a lot more tension coming.

The second period of the game played out much like the first, in that the concentration was on the play. Even the fans who had come hoping for some good fights were satisfied with seeing good hockey instead. Daniel set Victor up for the only goal of the period, giving the Rangers a 2-1 lead.

Again, the Rangers' fans rose to their feet and sang out, "Now Mount Pleasant knows, he skates like a pro, he shoots like a pro, he assists like a pro, he's our captain you know! And Victor, well, he scores like a pro."

Victor felt heat rising in his face and knew it wasn't from physical activity. Being the focus of attention felt great. Made a guy want to score more often.

Chester Craig's line started the third period. Mount Pleasant Flyers were changing strategy. The atmosphere became charged both on and off the ice. Craig managed to force a couple of small run-ins, but no penalties were called much to the distress of the Rangers' fans. It didn't matter because the Rangers' defence lines succeeded in frustrating Mount Pleasant players by keeping them away from Ivan and their net. The Rangers' forward lines kept the Flyers' goalie busy, but could not get past his defences.

Both sets of fans shouted plays to their respective teams, which were being ignored, leading to more fan frustration and insults.

Behind the bench, a displeased Coach Ramsay raised his hands in frustration. "It's easy to play the game sitting on one's ass in the stands," he growled.

With ten seconds left on the clock, the game appeared to belong to the Rangers. Daniel should have been satisfied, but he wanted one more goal on his team's side of the scoreboard, one more goal just for Malcolm MacDonald. Daniel glanced at MacDonald, who was seated above the Mount Pleasant Flyers' box, and fueled by a sense of injustice, stole the puck from Chester Craig, and pounded it over to Peter. The puck was a blur moving across the ice until Peter harnessed it with his stick and hammered it into the Flyers' net.

"Now Mount Pleasant knows, Daniel skates like a pro, he shoots like a pro, he assists like a pro, he's our captain you know. And Peter, well, he scores like a pro." The fans went wild, and this time, a very satisfied Coach Ramsay chanted with them. His boys were delivering the goods.

When the Rangers walked out of the Summerside rink after their second win, they were both relieved and anxious about the coming break in the series. It was an intentional delay, by the league, of several days. With the artificial ice, the season could be lengthened out, so the delay was a good tactic to build suspense, as well as give people the time to scrape together the next entrance fee.

As he watched the players and some fans crawl into the back of the truck, Percy felt envious about missing out on the game chatter that would carry on until they unloaded back at the schoolhouse in Southwest. But just then Ellen and Jane crawled into the cab with him, and he forgot the boys in the back. Neither girl was related to him, both were pretty and single. Percy had already seen the game. This was a new opportunity. Giving the girls his biggest smile, Percy put the truck in gear and headed out of the parking lot.

"Good game, team," Daniel said once they got underway.

"Yeah, but what if we lose our edge in the down time?" George figured others were thinking the same thing.

"It's just a couple of days, George. No different than the spacing of our weekly games." Daniel wasn't worried.

"Yeah, but our weekly games aren't the playoffs." George pulled a few packages of gum from his pocket and passed them around.

"Really?" Wendell looked at him, wanting to question the unnecessary expense of gum, when they should have been saving every extra cent they had. George caught the look as they passed under a streetlight. "It's gum, Wendell, just cheap gum."

"It all hinges on your thinking, boys," Coach Ramsay interjected. "If you remain relaxed off the ice, you will perform with confidence on the ice." Silently, he hoped he was right. He wished he believed his own pep talks.

"Relax you say? How can we do that when...." Remembering the fans, Keith caught himself as he folded a stick of gum in his mouth. "Yes, just relax with confidence, boys, just like Coach Ramsay says. Yes indeed."

The players broke into laughter. The fans wondered what the inside joke was.

CHAPTER 23

The following morning John got up extra early. He had completed his chores, eaten breakfast, and was washed and dressed in town clothing and outside Elliott's store five minutes after it opened. John parked his father's old car right next to the door and took a wire basket half full of white eggs from the trunk. John couldn't help but feel proud. Against his father's advice, John was pretty sure he wanted to stay on the family farm, but he didn't want to just do what had been done for decades. John was always looking for a way to make farm work a little easier, and to push productivity a little further. He had experimented over the winter with ways to keep his flock of hens laying productively over the season and was already seeing results. It had taken some convincing to get his father to invest in wiring the henhouse in the fall to lengthen daylight hours, but the results of increased production made the old man a believer. A little extra feed had also improved the quality of the eggs, and John had taken to asking a higher price per dozen when he sold to the Summerside stores.

Today, he had Elliott in his sights. John hadn't previously approached the storekeeper, knowing that many of the local housewives depended on trading the eggs from their small flocks with Elliott for groceries. But their numbers would be low this time of year, so John believed he would not be hurting anyone. Besides, he relished the thought of Elliott unknowingly donating to Daniel's mortgage.

John walked to the door and grinned. He was going to enjoy this transaction. He sauntered into the store and up to the handsome maple counter where Elliott was reviewing a ledger. They were the only two in the store.

"Good morning, Charles. I was just on my way to town with a delivery, when it struck me you might be interested in buying some of my eggs." John set his basket down on the counter. "They're top quality, and we all know you only sell the best."

The storekeeper, not wishing to appear overly eager, continued what he was doing for a few seconds before joining John, who removed the cloth from the basket to reveal the snowy white eggs.

"I've only been stocking brown since the fall, so some white in the showcase would be a treat." Elliott reached for one and held it up to the light. "Are they fresh?"

"When have I ever sold you anything other than fresh?" John asked.

"Since you have never sold me eggs, I guess it would be never," Elliott laughed. "I imagine you're looking for a pretty penny for them."

"For you, Charles, and if the order is big enough, I'm willing to take a cent less than I'm getting in Summerside. That would be fifty cents a dozen. I figure you will have no trouble selling them for a tidy profit, as I hear housewives these days are eager for white eggs and white flour." John kept his tone light, but businesslike.

"Fine. I'll take what you have in the basket, and likely more in the coming days," Elliott said.

"Thanks. I appreciate the sale. I'll make you out a bill right now." John grinned.

"But your mother owes on her account. I'll put the eggs against it." Elliott frowned.

"Charles, you know my folks are good for their bills, and since the eggs are my business, I'll be keeping it separate." John didn't waver. "I'm looking for a cash sale only."

Elliott took his time replying. What John said was true—his parents were good for the bill, but it was always to Elliott's advantage to try and take a trade. The young fellow had him. If he didn't take the eggs for cash, John would take them to town or peddle them door to door, and that could cut down housewife traffic in the store and the probability of additional sales when they were tempted with other products. It was good business to buy the eggs. He looked intently at the young man he had watched grow up over the years. "Do up your bill then, boy."

"Will do. Isn't it a good thing when community businesses can support each other?" John quickly wrote out a bill of sale and handed it over to the shopkeeper, smiling to himself.

"As the saying goes, you line my pocket and I'll line yours. You drive a hard bargain, young man. Business might be your calling." Elliott reached into the till for seven dollars, which he gave to John.

"I'm of the mind, sir, that a farmer needs to be a good businessman like you as well as a good farmer," John said. Once outside, he stood for a moment on the sidewalk, fingering the bills in his pocket. Elliott would have been taken aback had he known what was going through the young man's mind. It surprised him how much he had enjoyed putting one over on Elliott. John didn't suppose his mother would approve, although he hadn't done anything wrong. He couldn't believe how satisfied he felt, but he was also worried. Selling eggs wasn't going to raise $1,200 in a hurry. He needed to think of a way to make a bigger contribution. Elliott also got him thinking about what his father had been telling him—that John should take a commercial course. John guessed maybe his old man knew something after all. It was one thing to know how to produce eggs, but another to know how to market them.

CHAPTER 24

Robert opened the floor hatch to the cellar of the big cattle barn and carefully walked down the stairs into the darkness below. While the rest of the barn had electric lights, the cellar didn't, which contributed to his unease. He held the lantern high and shone it around the walls and corners before stepping off the stairs, relieved when no eyes shone back at him and he heard no movement. If rats were in the barn, they would likely be in the cellar. Robert wasn't necessarily afraid of the creatures, but their sudden scurrying movements unsettled him.

He hung the lantern from the centre beam and surveyed the pile of firm, plump turnips he had harvested in late fall. It always amazed him how the tiny specks of black seed he planted in the spring had grown into a harvest of food for both humans and cattle. The crop had been plentiful, which Robert was now extra grateful for.

The timing of the wholesaler couldn't have been better. He had called in the morning to place the biggest order of the winter, which would enable Robert to contribute the kind of cash he wanted to Daniel's mortgage fund. As Robert worked alone, grading and bagging the turnips, he thought about the risk Daniel had taken in believing the team could raise the money. Selecting a turnip the size of his head and holding it eye level, Robert began a conversation.

"I was all for Daniel taking our offer, but I doubt I would have done so myself," he confided to the vegetable. He felt a strange sadness. "I'm twenty-one and play life safe like an old man, Turnie."

Robert went to place the turnip in the bag, but then set the vegetable at the edge of the grader. He removed the full jute bag, tied it shut, and placed another one on the grader hooks, checking that Turnie was still sitting.

"I've no commitments other than to Dad, who is still a young, healthy man with plenty of years of work in him yet," Robert said. "If I'm ever going to try something different, now is the time. I don't want to end up with regrets that I missed out on something, although I have no idea what that might be."

Robert removed the full bag and repeated the process. Under the guidance of his father, Robert had never thought to do anything other than farm and play hockey.

"But it's complicated, Turnie. After that talk with Daniel, I just don't know if I'm doing what I'm doing because I want to . . . or because I never thought to do something else. He paused. "Maybe I'm just afraid to try something different."

It was okay for people like Daniel to tell Robert he had it made, but he needed to know that for himself. Working alone in the semi-darkness, Robert muddled an idea over in his mind, and made a decision.

"You know what, Turnie? I'm going to ask Peter to get me on with the construction crew in Montreal for the summer. That way I'll know what this place means to me."

Robert stopped grading and looked over at the turnip as though expecting a response. He wondered how his father would take the news that his son wanted to head out to Montreal. Robert doubted it would be an easy conversation. He filled another bag before turning back to the turnip.

“You know what else, Turnie? I think I’ll just go whole-hog and ask Sadie to a dance. I’ve liked her since grade school and never had the nerve to do anything about it. The worst that can happen is she says no, and what is that in comparison to the rejection Daniel got at the banks?” Robert removed another bag from the grader. “Maybe I should ask her skating. I’m more graceful on ice than on the dance floor.”

By the end of the afternoon, Robert had the order filled and piled by the cellar door. He would make the delivery in the morning, and see if he could secure a second order, but right now, he had the evening barn chores to do. Since there was no time like the present, Robert decided to walk over to Peter’s after the work and make his request.

“You are a great listener, Turnie.” Robert patted the turnip still sitting at the edge of the grader. He took the lantern down from the beam. “I’ll give you an update tomorrow.”

CHAPTER 25

Isabel unpacked her books and set them on the teacher's desk in the schoolroom. She inhaled the smells of the room that were once so familiar to her: chalk dust, pencil shavings, wet boots, and mittens drying by the coal pot belly stove, and apple cores in the garbage pail. Catherine Wall emerged from the cloakroom dressed in her winter coat and boots ready to return to her boarding house next door at the MacLean farm. The two women had agreed that it made more sense for Isabel to tutor in the classroom and for Catherine to do her marking and class preparation at the boarding house. It kept the tutoring students in familiar surroundings and gave Catherine an opportunity to put her feet up while she worked. An extra bonus was having the luxury of Mrs. MacLean serve her tea and freshly baked cookies.

Isabel and Catherine were now on a first-name basis, which made Isabel ashamed of her initial feelings towards the woman. Though Catherine was slightly older, Isabel was discovering they had much in common. She was also surprised at how the tutoring job was enabling her to enjoy her two daughters so much more. Isabel had never fully admitted that she held a little of herself back from them because her unplanned pregnancy had cost her the teaching job. She hated thinking that she blamed them in some way for the loss. It wasn't their fault. She was the one who had gambled with the rules and got burnt. Nothing was of their doing. The truth was, they were two amazing gifts that were growing quickly and would slip away from her if she wasn't careful.

"I thought you might want to know that your students are putting their extra grammar tutoring into practice. It came across in their latest assignment. Good work, Isabel." Catherine picked up her overflowing satchel and slung it over her shoulder.

"That's wonderful news! I can't wait until they get back from their snack break to get started. It feels good to be teaching again." Isabel could not keep the look of delight from her face.

"I'm sure it is, but it must also be nice to leave here and go home to your own family." Catherine inquired.

On impulse, Isabel looked up from her lesson plan, hesitated for a moment, and then plowed ahead. "Would you ever be interested in a date with a hockey player?" she asked.

Catherine stopped pulling on her gloves.

"I believe you know Keith? He's good-looking, witty, and an honest hardworking man." Isabel could have named more of his attributes, but didn't want to appear to be overselling. "I think the two of you would have a lot in common."

Catherine shyly looked at her. "You think so? I have to admit I think he is attractive, but he has never looked my way."

"Then maybe it's time he had some help getting his head turned. Leave it with me." Isabel snapped shut her book.

"Sure. I guess a little help in the love department never hurts, especially since I'm not making much progress on my own," Catherine laughed.

The three students returned to the school, revived from the break and good food in their stomachs. They were eager to learn and the time flew by. Isabel has broken it down so that one afternoon they covered algebra, science, and English, with geometry, literature, history, and geography the next. She was a little suspicious that perhaps they were so co-operative because she was married to the captain of the Lot 16 Rangers. Every opportunity they got, they talked about the team and the playoffs and wanted to know her opinion. She indulged them because it made her feel good that they wanted to know what she thought, and she had to admit she was proud to be married to the captain.

CHAPTER 26

On the date of the third game, the sun shone down on a perfect winter day. It was crisp and clear with little wind, a rarity on Prince Edward Island. Players and fans alike rushed about their work as if they hoped they could speed up the day and the arrival of game time. When Percy pulled into the school parking lot, he was met by a staggering line-up of fans. As he wondered how he would fit everyone in the truck, a few cars drove up. Some of the community men had got to talking after church on Sunday, and planned a procession of cars loaded with fans, to travel ahead of the truck as a fine show of support for the Rangers, and perhaps a little snub to Mount Pleasant. Thankfully, the cars were able to handle the overflow of fans.

With everyone loaded, car windows down so fans could shout slogans, and horns blowing, the procession pulled away from the school right on time. As they waited at the stop sign to pull out from the side road onto the main road to town, they watched a parade of cars and trucks coming from Mount Pleasant sail past. The Lot 16 group suddenly looked small in comparison.

At the Summerside rink, it appeared all rules around capacity were forgotten. Spectators were scrambling for seats and places to stand. A few enterprising young boys even made their way into the rafters. Usually, the rink manager would put the run to them, but not tonight. They needed the seats. Twenty minutes before game time, the ticket saleslady called the rink manager over.

"Should I stop selling tickets?" she asked, despite knowing the answer.

"Technically yes, but do you want a riot on our hands, woman?" The manager went to the door to look out. "Holy shit!" He blurted. The lineup still wound out into the parking lot. It would be a hefty admission take, and worth the possible fine if the fire chief happened to show. He went back inside and summoned his two assistants. "Boys, fit as many spectators per row as you can," he instructed them.

The canteen door never stopped swinging. After watching it go back and forth for a couple of minutes, the manager felt like he might have a seizure from the effects of the rapid movement. He hoped to God they had gotten in enough potatoes for making fries. He had taken a risk and bought half a truck load from some young man called Percy, who said he would take a cent less per pound for a cash sale.

The manager used his hands to push his way through the crowd into the canteen, and into the back room where staff were busy on the fries assembly line. After the potatoes went through a wash and the mechanical peeler, a few young women put them through the fry slicer and into a brine of salt water before landing them in fryer baskets. Cooked fries were dumped on large metal pans and salted, before being scooped into paper holders and passed over to customers who doused them in vinegar and ketchup and more salt. Hot dogs and onions sizzled on the grill, while the buns warmed in the steamer. If the cook snuck a drag of his cigarette every few minutes, he didn't break stride with the work. The manager paused for a moment to savour the smells and the efficiency before moving on to inspect the storage room. The bags of potatoes were quickly dwindling, but there would be enough for the night. The manager frowned, though, wishing he had got Percy's phone number. Wherever the young man was getting his spuds, they were superior quality.

The manager climbed the backstairs to his office that overlooked the ice surface and stands. Gazing out over the crowd, he wondered if the police should be put on notice of potential trouble, but then figured there was no point in being a worrywart. He just had to hope for the best. He turned away when he spotted some discreet betting in the corners, well out of the sightline of wives and several members of the clergy who were present. What people did with their money wasn't his business. He wished he could place a bet of his own.

Charlie had also noticed the betting activity as the Rangers made their way to the dressing room. For a brief moment, he had considered asking Percy to place a bet on both teams as a way to raise money for the cause, but quickly decided that perhaps there was a rule against such behaviour and it might be too risky. He would have to find other ways to make quick money.

In the Flyers' dressing room, the excitement had a tense edge to it. They needed a win.

"The Flyers are no quitters," Coach Dyment started his pep talk. "You went easy on the Rangers for the first two games, lulling them into false confidence, but tonight that generosity is behind you. Tonight, every one of you is a tracking hound that will chase your prey on the ice until you can smell their fear, and then take them down one goal at a time." He struck a fist into his hand.

"You know whose scent I want you tracking." The Coach zoomed in on Chester Craig. "But no one gets themselves thrown out of the game or takes unnecessary penalties, you got that? Now, let's play hockey."

The atmosphere in the Rangers' dressing room had a different tone. If the team was equally as excited as their opponents, they were also feeling a bit apprehensive. Coach Ramsay and the players were certain that winning the first two games was likely a piece of cake compared to what was coming tonight. The Rangers weren't afraid of dirty play. They just couldn't afford a penalty and the possible loss it might cause.

"Let's get one thing straight, boys. I need you to play both defensively and aggressively, yet cleanly. I want everyone to give their all," Coach Ramsay said, making his expectations clear.

"I'll have no problem giving my all tonight, Coach Ramsay. Like always, I'm wearing my lucky socks." Ivan held up his foot. "Sometime they work, but sometimes they don't."

"If they don't work all the time, they are not lucky socks, Ivan," Ernest said.

"The odds are good for them." Ivan held to his theory. "Arlene knit them for me while we were dating."

"You bonehead! Arlene dumped you and you think the socks are lucky." John said in disgust as he pulled on his jersey. "I bet you think the moon is made of cheese."

Ivan wiggled a sock-clad foot into his skate. "As a matter of fact, I have a nibble every night." Ivan's smile was ear to ear, and suddenly everyone realized he was having them on to lighten the mood.

Even Coach Ramsay laughed before he carried on with his pre-game talk. "We are the leaders in the series and we can't let our guard down." He looked hard at Daniel as he spoke. "Not for a single moment. Because tonight, we are going to claim our third victory.

CHAPTER 27

Coach Dyment had, without doubt, lit a fire under the Flyers. When the puck dropped, they moved for a quick offensive attack and head-manned the puck. They hit hard and often with clean moves. For their efforts, they scored the first goal. The cheering of their fans, combined with the booing of the Rangers' fans, mixed in with the dramatic sound of the organ, was deafening even on the ice surface. The Flyers had scored the first goal on Daniel and Peter's shift, a bad sign with the best Rangers' lines on the ice.

This fact undoubtedly added to the cocky confidence of the Flyers, but Peter quickly wiped the grins from their faces by tying the game. It was one of those beautiful unlikely goals. Daniel had taken the puck off the Flyers' winger in his own end and faked moving it up the ice himself before suddenly flipping it to Ernest, who with a powerful shot, transferred it to Peter who, through pure luck, caught it on his stick and delivered it to the right upper corner of the Flyers' net.

"Mount Pleasant weep, Lot 16 sweep!" chanted the Rangers' fans. Mount Pleasant Flyers' fans had a few choice words, but they didn't rhyme.

In the next minute, John was the play maker for Robert, who roofed the puck into the Flyers' net for a 2-1 lead for the Rangers. Again the Rangers' fans were on their feet, "Mount Pleasant weep, Lot 16 sweep."

When play resumed, Ernest unintentionally tripped a Mount Pleasant player in the chase for the puck. For once, the referee was on the ball and called the first penalty of the game.

"Thank the lord! An amazing miracle," hollered Reverend Johnson jumping up from his seat. Realizing his loss of control he sheepishly sat down, only to see Charles Elliott glaring at him.

The noise coming from the fans was deafening while the Rangers played short. Both teams were moving the puck end to end with lightning speed. Daniel, shadowed by Craig, managed to cover Ivan, which kept Mount Pleasant's shots on goal to a minimum until the penalty ended. Both the Rangers and their fans breathed a sigh of relief. Then, to the shock of everyone, the Flyers' left wing forward scored unassisted to tie the score at 2-2. As the clock ran out on the first period, Daniel and Wendell put the Rangers' third goal on the board.

The second period was gut-wrenching for the fans of both teams. Tempers in the stands flared and ebbed. It seemed certain that George's drive of the puck towards the Flyers' net was a sure goal, but it caught just enough of the goal post to spin it back out. Robert took a perfect shot from a distance, which the Flyers' goalie came out to meet and jam with the blade of his skate. The Flyers managed to return the puck time and again to the Rangers' end, which kept the defence lines back covering Ivan. It took until the end of the period for Keith to set up the Rangers next goal for George, giving the Rangers a 4-2 lead. Coach Ramsay knew it was still anyone's game. He wanted that two-goal lead widened.

In the third period, things got rough when Robert was ploughed into the boards and Wendell took a shot to his shoulder. After a particularly hard hit, Charlie saw stars for a few seconds, but the play went on and the scoreboard remained unchanged. Craig tantalized Daniel at every opportunity by cornering, unnecessary shoving, and interfering, but Daniel refused to take the bait. It wasn't that he didn't want to, but the stakes were too high in the game. He would beat Craig with skill, not a fist to the face. That would hurt the big goon a lot worse. His stepdaddy too.

Rough as it was, the Rangers were holding their lead. Then Keith and John both got caught too far up in their own end, when a Flyer's forward broke free and took a slap shot that Ivan should have easily deflected, but didn't. It totally rattled him and a minute later he let another goal through to tie the game at 4-4. In the box, Daniel had to grab onto Coach Ramsay's coattail to keep him from going over the boards, crossing the ice and choking Ivan on the spot. He had never seen the man that furious. Though they played hard, the Rangers gave up another goal giving Mount Pleasant a 5-4 win. Gone was the dream of the championship win in four straight games. The Lot 16 Rangers' fans were no longer chanting.

CHAPTER 28

After the game, Coach Ramsay didn't join the players in the dressing room. That was a first for him. Unease filled the room. An angry Coach Ramsay beat a silent, absent Coach Ramsay any day. The players got changed in near silence. When it came time to leave the dressing room and Coach Ramsay still hadn't made an appearance, Daniel decided he needed to say something. He was, after all, the team captain.

"Listen guys, it was a great game. Both teams were on the ball."

"But John and I got caught too far up the ice. I've never seen Jacob Sanders skate that fast. There must have been liniment in his drawers." Keith lamented.

Ivan jumped in. "I wish there had been some in mine. I wasn't quick enough to make the save."

"Well, my line let the first goal happen," Daniel said. "We've all made mistakes at times. It's part of the game. The fact is we played a great game, but so did they."

"They got lucky. It could just have easily been us. There's no point in beating ourselves up." Charlie swung the hockey bag over his shoulder.

"I don't think Coach Ramsay is going to see it that way." John pulled on his coat.

“Coach Ramsay has put a lot of pressure on us, expecting we take the championship in four straight, especially now.” Peter let his voice trail off.

“Especially now that you are trying to raise money for me, right?” Daniel completed his brother’s thoughts.

“Don’t get pissed, Daniel.” Peter put his hands up. “We are still going to take the trophy. It’s just going to take five games.”

Daniel turned to the rest of the team. “So how do the rest of you feel?” he asked. “Are you finding out raising money isn’t that easy? Are you angry now that you made the deal?”

“We’re not angry, Daniel. We’re just worried and tired.” Wendell looked at his teammates before answering.

“It’s hard work. How do you carry such a load, Daniel?” Victor asked.

“It’s not the work that is hard,” John disagreed. “It’s the worry. I guess you know that, though, Daniel. We just don’t want to disappoint you or Coach Ramsay.”

“Or ourselves,” George cut in. “This is a new game for us, Daniel. The stakes are a lot higher than putting the puck in the net.”

“Or keeping it out of the net.” A gloomy Ivan added. The despondent team looked to their captain.

“I’m sorry, guys. We are all stressed and tired. I shouldn’t have accepted the team’s offer to help me.” Daniel pushed up from the bench.

“Yeah, you should have,” said Robert. “Somebody had to help us grow up.”

“I don’t have enough years on earth to make that happen for you birds.” Daniel snorted.

Outside seated in the truck, Percy watched Coach Ramsay stride back and forth along the side of the rink. Several times he put a fist to the wall. Even at a distance Percy could see the rigidness of his body. Coach Ramsay was steaming. Finally, he walked the short distance to the truck and opened the passenger door. He stood looking up at Percy, who silently returned the stare. After a moment he slammed the door shut and headed for the rink. Percy resumed breathing. Coach Ramsay threw open the door of the dressing room, and slammed it behind him. He walked to the centre of the room.

"I should've been here right after the game, but I couldn't trust myself." Coach Ramsay started pacing the room.

"It's okay, Coach. The captain took over for you," Ivan made the mistake of saying.

"Did he now?" Coach Ramsay stopped pacing to focus on the goalie. "Well, Ivan, did he tell you that your goaltending cost us the game? Those last two goals were entirely preventable. You handed Mount Pleasant the win." The heat in the coach's voice was replaced with pure frost. "Next game, take an afternoon nap so you won't need one on the ice."

Ivan pulled his shoulders in towards his chest as though trying to protect himself from the barbs, angry and embarrassed that the coach was dumping the loss entirely on his shoulders. However, Ivan was not the only Ranger in Coach Ramsay's crosshairs.

"As for you, John and Keith, obviously neither of you were paying attention to where the other one was on the ice," Coach Ramsay raged on. "For both of you to get too far up the ice is unacceptable. How many times do you have to be told that one of you must always cover Ivan?"

Seeing what happened to Ivan when he spoke up, John and Keith wisely kept their mouths shut.

"Not that you were alone leaving Ivan uncovered. Daniel and Ernest did no better. You both know to protect the net."

George jumped into the fray. "Yes, Coach Ramsay, mistakes were made, but you can't deny we played one hell of a game. Maybe you could mention one or two good plays we made."

"You did play well, and you would have played even better if your minds were fully on the championship." The coach turned on George. "You are allowing yourselves to be distracted. The Flyers are only thinking about hockey."

The sucking in of breath was heard throughout the room.

"Don't blame the guys for that." Anger stirred in Daniel's gut. "You were the one who was determined I stay with the team. And yeah, maybe we are distracted a little, but we have two wins to one loss. So, considering everything, I think we're doing well." He pointed his finger at Coach Ramsay. "Remember the championship isn't just your dream."

The captain's words hit their mark. Heat rose in Coach Ramsay's face as he suddenly felt the shame of his behaviour.

"I'm sorry, boys." Wearily, Coach Ramsay rubbed his forehead. "We have two different games to win in a short time frame and we'll do it together. But for now let's just go home."

Percy watched the parking lot empty out, including the Mount Pleasant parade with horns blaring. When it appeared that even the rink staff would be leaving ahead of the Rangers, the team finally exited the building and made their way across the parking lot. No one seemed to notice that the procession of cars that had led them to the rink was not leading them home. Still, the fans travelling with them were elated about the game and did a better job analyzing it than either Coach Ramsay or the players, who listened intently.

When there was nothing more to be said, a comfortable silence settled in the truck. Some of the fans drifted to sleep. The players retreated to their own thoughts about what tomorrow might bring.

CHAPTER 29

Wendell was up extra early the next morning. Half of his breeding sows were leaving the barn and he wanted them well fed and their pens cleaned and bedded before the buyer and truck arrived. He mixed crushed grain with water to make a slop, realizing that come the evening feeding, he would only be mixing half the amount.

Filling the buckets, he left the feed room and entered the piggery with its rows of pens. As soon as the sows heard him coming, they got to their feet and starting squealing. Wendell liked to think they were telling him to get a move on—didn't he know they were hungry?

"Patience, ladies! I'm coming, I'm coming," he chuckled. It didn't take him long to go down the line, pouring the breakfast into their troughs. He put down the buckets and stood watching them eat.

"You ladies sure enjoy your food. We have a lot in common." Wendell reached down to scratch Daisy's ears. "Selling you three is nothing personal. I would much rather keep you, Betsy, and Sally, but you are helping with an important cause. Sometimes a fellow has to think beyond himself." He watched Besty polish off her breakfast. "Or learn to keep his mouth shut."

The transport truck arrived at the arranged time. The buyer helped ease Wendell's distress by commenting on what a nice efficient and clean setup he had. As the pigs were loaded on the truck, Wendell consoled himself with the thought that he wasn't starting from scratch to rebuild the herd for half the sows were left, and the litter born yesterday would make excellent replacements. He was down, but he wasn't out. There would be another Daisy, Betsy, and Sally. When the loading was finished, the buyer handed him ninety dollars. Wendell double checked the count and as he placed it in his pocket, he thanked the man for doing business. In amidst the sadness, he felt a flicker of joy about the tidy sum he could contribute to Daniel's mortgage.

Wendell was not alone in making a difficult good-bye. At the MacDougall farm, Peter stood outside his father's small barn for what seemed like a long time. He saw nothing of the natural beauty that surrounded him as he fought to hold back tears. Finally, he pushed open the door, registering that the track needed oiling. Instantly, he heard the familiar whinny of welcome. Peter shut the door and stood still to let his eyes adjust to the dimness of the barn's interior. This time, the whinny sounded impatient. The beautiful two-year-old filly he had raised from birth was waiting.

"Good morning to you, too, Nell," he said.

Peter could honestly say that Nell was the only Island girl he missed when in Montreal. He liked the freedom to date whoever he wanted in the city, and there were plenty of girls willing to spend time with him. But whether it was PEI or Montreal, Nell was the only girl he shared any secrets with. The only girl who was always in his thoughts.

"Such a little beauty you are." Peter paused at the door of the box stall as Nell came directly to him. Her chestnut coat gleamed in the sunlight coming through the window, a coat that Peter spent hours brushing. He opened the door to join

Nell in the stall, and she immediately began to nuzzle at his chest and sides, searching for a treat.

"Of course I have something for you. When did I ever forget?" Peter pulled a carrot out of his jacket pocket and held it in the palm of his hand. He felt the tickle of Nell's soft muzzle as she ate it and then looked for more. This had been their game from the time she had been weaned from her mother, Peter's way of making up for that separation. He stroked Nell's mane, feeling his heart rip apart and barely able to see through the tears. Nell, sensing Peter's distress, turned her head and nuzzled into his neck. It tickled and made Peter laugh. Nell whinnied as though proud she had lifted his spirits.

Peter began to run his hands over the smoothness of Nell's back in an effort to calm himself.

"You know I would never let you go if I didn't have to. But I've made sure it's a good place you're going." Peter whispered as the little horse leaned into him. "They have had their eye on you for a time now. They'll take care of you, Nell. They will treat you like the queen you are."

At the sound of a truck engine, Peter hastily wiped his eyes and reached for the rope halter hanging on the stall door to place on Nell's head. The filly began her usual little dance of anticipation for going outdoors.

"Oh, Nell." Peter again buried his head in her neck and breathed in the smell of her. "You can be sure I'll never forget you."

Peter finally led the filly out to the walkway, listening to the clip-clop sound of her hooves on the hemlock floor for the last time. Outside, the driver had already lowered the truck's tailgate and was on his way to the barn. "Morning, Peter," he said, reaching for the rope. Peter shook his head no.

"I've got it. Nell isn't used to being loaded. I want to do it myself."

The driver dropped his hand. He knew from experience that the parting between a beloved animal and its owner was hard for both. He stood back and watched Peter lead the trusting filly up the tailgate and into the truck box.

"Such a good girl." The fact that Nell followed him with no complaint or apparent fear, made Peter feel worse than had she panicked and pulled back. He tied her in place and ran his hands along her back before exiting the truck. He helped the driver put up the tailgate and chain it in place.

"MacGregor sent the money along and said to be sure to tell you to drop by any time you want to check on the filly." The driver handed Peter an envelope. It held eighty-nine dollars.

Peter reached out and took the envelope and turned it over and over as though looking at something he had never seen before. "Tell him I appreciate that, but I don't think it will be anytime soon."

Nell began to whinny from inside the truck box. Peter almost lost his nerve but then quickly stuffed the envelope into the pocket the carrot had come from. The driver tipped his hat and quickly moved to the cab. He started up the truck, put it in gear, and slowly rolled down the lane. Peter watched until the truck was out of sight. He had never felt like such a traitor. He struggled to convince himself that he cared for Daniel a little more than he cared for Nell. Reverend Johnson liked to remind people the only way over loss was through it. He would let himself think about Nell and the pleasure she had brought into his life. Someday. But today it hurt too much.

Daniel was at that moment preparing to make a different deal. He sat in his father-in-law's barn, avoiding looking at the two heifers contently chewing their cuds. Daniel had brushed and curried them until not a speck of dirt could be found on them, and their coats glistened.

Daniel didn't have to wait long for the cattle buyer to arrive. Jack Birt was a large bulk of a man and well-known across Prince County. Some farmers said he was fair, while others called him a scoundrel. Daniel figured Birt was pretty good at playing both roles for his own gain. Still Birt was the best of the lot of buyers out there. Something Daniel failed to understand was why the farmers didn't come together and open their own sale barn to force the buyers into a bidding system. It was something he planned to push for if he ever got a foot in the door. But Daniel had learned a thing or two about the game of cattle trading from James, and considering what was at stake, he planned to hold his own.

When Birt arrived, he walked down the alleyway taking in the look of every animal. Daniel knew the buyer had the eyes of an eagle and missed nothing.

"Well now, boy, that's a cold day out there, but spring will come one of these days." Birt laughed as though he had truly said something funny. "You and your father in-law have the cattle looking not too bad for the time of year."

Daniel opened his mouth to reply, but Birt didn't give him time to speak. "Of course, you know it's not a good time of year to sell, what with a long time between now and grass. What did you have in mind, boy?" the large man said.

Daniel gave a half smile. He understood the underlying implication in the word "boy"—that he wasn't to think he knew too much about the game of selling and buying cattle. He walked a little further down the alleyway to where his two young purebred heifers stood in their stalls. They were bred to calve in the spring just when the grass would be at its best and the demand for milk would be at its highest with the cheese factory.

"What will you give me for the two of them?" Daniel walked between the two animals and ran his hands down their backs while he looked directly at Birt.

The buyer pushed his hat back and scratched his head. He recognized the animals, and he could certainly see the effort Daniel had put into raising them. Birt felt a tinge of disappointment in the young fellow. "Now what are you thinking, boy? I sold you these animals as calves for foundation breeding stock. What's changed here?" The buyer had believed Daniel had a good head on his shoulders and would stick with building a purebred herd.

"I need the money for another investment, and of my few livestock, these two will bring the best price." Daniel didn't bother hiding the truth.

"True, but is it worth the setback?" The buyer spit tobacco juice from the side of his mouth and assessed the steady way Daniel was gazing back at him.

"This wasn't an easy decision, so let's get to it," was all Daniel said.

"It sure seems a shame to let them go." But Birt shrugged. A deal was a deal, after all.

"Sometimes you don't get to choose what you let go," Daniel said.

"Alright, then. You know I can't give you as much for them now as I could in the spring, closer to calving. Someone's going to have to feed them a month or two longer than they would ideally want," Birt calculated out loud.

Daniel was surprised and shocked when the buyer named a price of seventy dollars per animal. So was Birt. He knew he could have gotten the heifers cheaper—in fact he should have—but something in the young fellow's eyes held him back. God, Birt sure hoped he wasn't going soft. If he did this too many times, he would be out of business. Before Birt could change his mind, he took an impressive roll of bills from his pocket. Daniel envied the easy way the man peeled bill after bill from the roll, certain the entire handful of money was more than the balance on his mortgage. There was no doubt about it—life wasn't fair at times. He stepped aside to watch Birt and the driver load the cattle and raised a half-hearted wave as they pulled away from the barn.

"We'll make a quick stop at Roland Ramsay's place," Birt told his driver. "He called yesterday to say he has a beef steer he wants a price on, so we might as well check it out while we're in the area."

"Not often you get two calls from the same area in a day."

"Every now and again it happens, but the timing is usually later in the winter when farmers are getting down on feed." Birt frowned. "But Roland Ramsay's not one of those guys. He'd have the feed calculated out to the mouthful. No . . . I suspect something is up."

Birt looked forward to sparring with Roland Ramsay. It was like a hockey match with words. Ramsay was a sharp opponent. Birt rehearsed his strategy. He would start with asking Ramsay if the steer was on the liften. That would get Ramsay's dander up.

Only after Birt left the yard did Daniel return to the barn and start scraping down the stalls. It wasn't until the tears touched his lips that he realized he was crying. Surprisingly, the young man allowed the tears to come with no attempt to wipe them away. James, who had quietly entered the barn, left as silently as he had come. When the tears were spent, Daniel seated himself on a sack of grain and wiped his face with his sleeve. He looked at the vacant stalls. The upside was there would be less work for Isabel to handle on the mornings he was working.

For George, the sacrifice was of a different kind. He stood at the back of the trailer looking at the sawed lumber weighing it down. It was the first of his logs to go through the sawmill. George had cut timber on the halves with his uncle the previous spring, planning to use them for an addition on the small house he had inherited from his grandmother, which was getting cramped for his young family. George and his wife, Ruby, also dreamed of building a veranda across the front of the house that overlooked the river so they could enjoy sitting out during the warm nights of summer. They had debated the pros and cons between screening in the veranda to keep out the bugs or fully closing it in with windows he had salvaged from an old house to utilize the space all year round.

The plan had changed because of the deal made with Daniel. George would keep enough lumber to build the two bedrooms, but the veranda would have to wait another year. The lumber for that part of the project would be sold for the fundraising effort. It equalled the lumber that would go into the bedrooms, so George didn't feel he was shortchanging the cause. Besides, if he didn't deliver on the bedrooms, he likely wouldn't be playing hockey ever again. Caught between two intense promises, George knew he still had it good. He wasn't living with his in-laws and the gift from his grandmother put him ahead of the game. George could wait for the veranda to sit on and look at the beauty of the river, which wasn't going anywhere.

John looked at the tidy sum of money in his hand, placed there by the machinery dealer who had driven out of the yard with John's tractor loaded on a trailer. John didn't watch, but rather concentrated on the money. Knowing egg sales alone couldn't do what needed to be done, John had studied his options. He only had one: the old tractor he had bought a year ago and restored to running order. Having invested hours into getting the tractor in sound working order, John had struggled with the decision to sell, but in the end had made the call. Besides, the tractor wasn't a necessity, but rather an investment he had turned into a hobby.

Now looking at the money the dealer had paid, John calculated the difference between what he had put into the tractor and what he had sold it for. He had made a good profit. In the coming days, he would find another cheap tractor in need of restoration. John smiled. When a man put his mind to it, there were ways to make money. The thing he was learning was that one shouldn't put all their eggs in one basket. Charles Elliott had taught him that business and life tip.

Keith checked his trapline, which he had extended, every morning. For him, there wasn't the possibility of one or two transactions that could raise substantial money. It was one rabbit at a time. Fortunately, for the past week he had found a rabbit in every snare, every morning, making it worth the pain of getting up dirt early each day to check the line and prepare the rabbits for sale. He was now supplying both the Wellington Meat Shop and Alfred's Butcher Shop, and both were telling him to keep the meat coming. Keith was beginning to think winning the playoffs would be a breeze in comparison to raising the mortgage money. Still, it felt good early in the morning to be alone with nature as she shared her bounty. Keith was starting to wonder if there was more than luck to his recent good trapping results. He hoped so.

CHAPTER 30

The time to the fourth game had flown by thanks to the urgency of raising mortgage money, completing daily work chores, and fulfilling family obligations. If asked, most of the players might have said they were both tired and energised at the same time.

On the day of the game, Coach Ramsay was on a rip-tear to get everything taken care of before leaving for the rink. He wanted to get to the rink well ahead of the team, but the milk cow that went into labour late afternoon wasn't worried about his schedule. Still, when he had looked at the calf wobble to its feet only minutes after birth and instinctively make its way to its mother's udder to feed, he felt the pleasure of witnessing new life. He took it as a sign there would be new life on the ice tonight.

Coach Ramsay rushed through supper and left Carol to wrap up the chores, enabling him to meet his planned departure time. He sailed past the school just as Percy pulled into the parking area. He looked straight ahead in case anyone was trying to flag him down for a ride.

"Just because we're not going to take the championship in four straight doesn't mean we aren't going to take that trophy home, right boys?" Daniel asked the team as they travelled in the truck box.

"Damn right we're taking the trophy home," Ernest said. "I think the setback might have done us some good. Now we're twice as determined, aren't we boys?"

Suddenly, there was the same excitement among the players that had been there the first night of the playoffs. There was no doubt the championship belonged to the Rangers.

"I wonder if Coach Ramsay sees it the same way, though." George, ever the realist, had to get his two cents in.

Silence settled over the group as the team considered what he said.

"Of course, he does. Isn't he the one that is always preaching something worth having doesn't come easy? By the time we get to the dressing room, he will be over being sore about us losing the last game," Daniel said.

As much as they wanted to believe their Captain, the team felt some trepidation. After all, the coach had decided to travel to the game on his own.

The Rangers were thankful to see a line-up outside the rink. Victor and John had worried that the Rangers' fans might not show for the game, since no procession of cars had appeared, but as Peter pointed out, why wouldn't they be there?

"Without a doubt, they will get their money's worth tonight," Peter said as he surveyed the long line of fans waiting to get in.

As soon as they unloaded, the players quickly made their way to the dressing room where Coach Ramsay was waiting for them. He appeared calm and relaxed, which meant they could relax, at least inside the dressing room. Everyone quickly set about dressing for the game while keeping a lively banter going.

"Have a look, boys! I'm sporting my lucky underwear tonight, so the game is ours." Charlie dropped his pants to show his flaming red long johns. He pulled his cup on over the top of them and reached for his hockey pants. "Mom washed them before the last game, and I had to wear my grey ones. That's why we lost."

"Get real, Charlie," George smirked.

"I am really, really good in my red underwear. I'm not taking them off again until the playoffs are over." Charlie was adamant.

"That is just vile, Charlie." Peter stopped lacing his skates. "You trying to kill everyone?"

"No wonder you can't get a date," tormented George. "Women don't want to smell you before they see you."

"Aw, you arses know what I mean. I'll be wearing them for the games only." Charlie rose to the bait. "I can get a date anytime I want."

"Your cousin doesn't count," said George.

"And you'd know all about that, right?" Victor taunted. "Didn't you marry your cousin, George?"

Everyone hooted. Coach Ramsay rolled his eyes.

George, in the midst of tying his hockey pants, turned to Victor. "Look weasel face, you leave my Ruby out of this."

Victor laughed. "So it is true then?"

George shook his fist at Victor. "No it's not, and you know it."

The banter put the players at ease.

When ready, the players looked to Coach Ramsay for his pre-game talk, but he appeared in no hurry to get started. Instead, he was pacing back and forth across the floor periodically removing his right hand from his pants pocket to glance at his watch. Each time, he shoved the hand back in the pocket and continued pacing. Suddenly, the dressing room door opened and an unfamiliar man carrying a hockey bag walked in and stood by the door. All eyes turned to look at him, trying to place the unfamiliar face, but with no luck. The newcomer looked at the Rangers as silently as they looked back at him.

Coach Ramsay walked over to the door and took the young man by the arm and led him into the centre of the room. Though there was still not a sound in the dressing room, he held up a hand to call everyone to attention. "Boys, I'd like you to meet Archie Ellis. He'll be playing nets tonight."

If possible, the depth of the silence deepened in the dressing room. The players looked at Coach Ramsay and Archie Ellis and then they looked at Ivan. No one moved or spoke a word.

"What the hell? You can't replace me. I've been in nets all season!" When the Coach's intention finally registered with him, Ivan shot to his feet, outraged.

"You wouldn't know it by the way you played the other night," was all the Coach said back.

"I'm not allowed an off night?" Ivan could barely choke out the words.

"Not in the playoffs. You screwed up our chance of winning in four straight." Coach Ramsay pointed his finger and spoke slowly as though Ivan couldn't comprehend.

"I wasn't playing alone. I get to take the fall for the whole team? Thanks." The anger that coursed through him gave Ivan courage to speak to the older man in a way he never would have otherwise. "I have a good notion to go home right now and leave you stranded."

Daniel sprung to his feet before anyone said something that could not be taken back. He turned to Coach Ramsay. "Coach, Ivan's been there for us all season," he said. "Defence has to take some of the responsibility for the other night. Can't you start Ivan tonight and see how it goes? Then if you have to, you can put Archie in."

Coach Ramsay looked back and forth between the two goalies. He placed hands on hips and paced a short distance across the dressing room. Finally, he turned and looked at Ivan. "Okay, you can start, but mess up, and Archie is in. Get dressed, Archie, in case we need you at a moment's notice. Come out to the bench as soon as you're ready."

"The nerve of trying to replace me." Ivan grabbed his gloves and stick and headed for the door, muttering under his breath. Archie dropped his bag on the bench and opened it to take out his gear. Coach Ramsay walked to the door and held it open while looking back at the rest of the team. "Boys, it's time to head for the box. Make sure it's a good game."

The men wasted no time heading for the players' box, except Daniel, who hung back.

"You better hope this little stunt doesn't backfire, Captain," Coach Ramsay said. "You never would have agreed to it if you thought it could." Daniel smiled as he slipped on his helmet. Together, the two men followed the team to the box.

No one was surprised to see the rink was packed. Even the standing room area was full. Even before they got to the players' box, the Rangers could tell by the deafening noise that the fans of both teams were wired. Which could prove good or bad. Only time would tell. As Daniel scanned the rink, he hoped that at the end of the night, both the rink and everyone in it would still be standing.

The players on both teams felt the pure energy of the crowd penetrate their muscles and bones. When the puck dropped, everyone was ready and waiting. Daniel intentionally stayed back at the start of the game to cover Ivan, but the goalie, fueled with a sense of injustice, stopped everything that came his way. Daniel's plan to motivate Ivan by dangling the threat of Archie was working. It sure beat the coach's plan to replace Ivan.

Mount Pleasant was still high on their last win, and they moved quickly to dominate the play. But the Rangers were fired with the desire to regain control and matched their opponents play for play. With Daniel staying close to his own end, Craig was coming down the ice more than necessary. But it wasn't hard to see that the Flyers were attempting to draw Daniel into a penalty play.

Much to the disappointment of the fans, both teams steered clear of the penalty box. Nevertheless, the spectators got great hockey for their entrance fee. The game was fast and smooth. The puck didn't stay with one player for any length of time. People were dizzy trying to keep track of it. Well into the game, the scoreboard remained empty: fans forgot about the anticipation of a fight-now they just wanted to see their team on the board.

When the puck dropped to start the play in the third period, Daniel knew the Rangers had to make their move early. A Rangers goal would rattle the Flyers. He moved his play further up the ice and when the opportunity presented itself, Daniel set up the puck for Peter, who delivered by placing it ever so neatly in the left lower corner of the net. The puck scraped the post as it went in.

"Don't think twice, Lot 16 melt the ice!" Reverend Johnson, seated behind Charles Elliott, jumped to his feet and chanted. He waved his arms at the fans to join him. The sound of the united voices filled the building. Reluctantly, Elliott did as well, making his daughters very happy. While the Lot 16 Rangers' fans shouted in jubilation, the Mount Pleasant fans littered the air with colourful curse words. But it didn't intimidate the Rangers. If anything, the words empowered them.

As Daniel anticipated, the goal unsettled the Flyers. Halfway through the period, Craig made the mistake of holding the puck and carrying it down into the Rangers' end. Daniel let him come in deep, giving Craig the confidence of being in control. Then, just as Craig got ready to deliver the puck to the net, Daniel skated forward and stole it and was long gone before Craig could react. But Daniel knew it was no time to be a lone wolf. Skating towards the centre line, he scanned the ice, found Charlie in the best position for a pass, and directed the puck his way. It flew with ease and speed across the ice, and cracked against Charlie's stick. Charlie had only a moment to debate his move. Did he shoot from where he was, or did he skate in towards the net hoping to retain control?

"Lucky reds, do your magic," he muttered, as one of the Flyers' best forwards bore down on him. Charlie made his choice and shot the puck towards the Flyers' net with all the strength he could muster. No one expected the move, least of all the Flyers' goalie. The puck sailed past his glove. Charlie spotted George and pulled up his jersey to flash his special long red underwear. George gave him a thumbs up. The scoreboard lit up 2-0 for the Rangers.

Now the Rangers had to hold the lead, if not widen it. Mental exertion mattered as much physical exertion. The players scanned the ice looking for surprises from their opponents, such as a hit from the side; they watched where their own players were, too, so they didn't lose precious moments setting up a play. Coach Ramsay made shift changes in under a minute to keep everyone fresh and fierce, repeating his instruction to "Cover Ivan" every time the defense line changed. He needn't have bothered, though, because Ivan shone.

The score did not change for the remainder of the game. The night belonged to the Rangers and it certainly belonged to Ivan, who had delivered a shutout. Mount Pleasant showed their frustration by throwing their gloves and sticks to the ice surface, but few fans paid them any attention. Most eyes were on Ivan doing a little dance in front of his net, followed by a celebratory skate around the rink waving to the crowd as he went.

"IVAN, IVAN, IVAN!" The fans screamed his name and pounded the boards. The rest of the team stood back, giving their teammate his well-earned moment in the limelight.

In the dressing room, the noise was almost as loud, as one player after another tried to put their spin on the game. Archie Ellis listened to Ivan brag, secretly glad that the ruse had worked so well. Archie, though an excellent defenceman with a down-east team, had never played nets in his life, and he had no interest in starting in the midst of a high stakes play-off series. No sir, he was much more comfortable as a spectator in the box.

When the Summerside rink manager turned out the last of the lights, he paused for a moment to soak in the silence and gave a sigh of relief. The rink was still standing. He bent and picked up a chocolate bar wrapper, crunched it up, and aimed for the distant garbage can. When the wrapper landed in the centre of the can and fell out of sight, the manager imagined he had just scored the winning goal. With a spring in his step, he walked out the door and put the key in the lock.

CHAPTER 31

Come morning, Keith was in the shed preparing rabbits for drop-off on the way to work. Alfred's Butcher Shop had placed another order. Keith was going full out supplying two shops, playing hockey, and working. He yawned. Yes, he was plenty busy these days, maybe too busy. Yet he felt the best he had in a long time. He had a sense of purpose. He now grimaced, thinking about Daniel's question after the game.

"Interested in a date with Catherine Wall?" Daniel had said, far too casually. "Isabel thinks you two would get along." Keith didn't know what to make of the idea. His engagement to Helen was long over, so it wasn't guilt that held him back. He realized he was just plain terrified to put himself back out there. It would be just a date, he reminded himself. It wasn't like he had to marry the woman.

Daniel's father-in-law James MacArthur inhaled what he knew was the first smell of spring in the air. If asked, James couldn't have said exactly how one smelled the coming of a season. A farmer just knew he did. Although the calendar said spring arrived in March, there were few actual signs in Prince Edward Island, but James had the smell, the lengthening of the days, and warmer temperatures to tell him spring was slowly, but surely, on its way.

On this day in March, James was conducting a spring chore usually reserved for late April. He was selling a load of seed barley. He walked to the centre of the granary and picked up the last burlap bag of grain and carried it to Henry Rankin's parked sleigh. As Henry loaded the sack, James stood back and looked at the piled bags. It pained him to sell such a large load, but it had to be done so there was no point whining.

Henry jumped to the snow-covered ground and gained his footing before speaking. "I'm surprised you're willing to sell this much barley seed. I figured after taking first place with it at the exhibition last fall, you would refuse to part with any."

James wasn't about to admit he hadn't wanted to sell the award-winning seed for at least another year. The plan had been to plant it all in his own fields to increase the yield yet again and send an entry to the Royal Winter Fair in Toronto in hopes of another award that could launch a lucrative seed business. James had been working on the project for a number of years after he realized Island farmers needed good quality grain seed grown in the province, rather than shipping it in from elsewhere.

But, in order to contribute to the mortgage fund, James would have to sell some of the precious seed this spring. Henry was more than willing to pay the extra money for the seed, and perhaps it was a good thing James' hand was being forced. James had put a lot of years into bringing the seed to this level and was always trying to do better. He had no more excuses about why this wasn't the year.

"I seriously debated it, but the yield per acre in the harvest was so good that I felt selling to you would be a good move. You know how to get a good crop, and if you are successful, there'll be more demand out there next year," James said, as he tipped back his hat to scratch his forehead.

"Well, I sincerely thank you, James. I'm mighty glad to get it. I expect good results from this seed." Henry reached into his back pocket for the wallet chained to his belt and pulled out several substantial bank notes.

James took the money in his hand and did a count before answering. "So do I. Hopefully, neither of us will be disappointed."

As Henry drove off, he thought of his luck in getting the seed. He had tried the past several years, but James had always refused him. Henry had to wonder if there was more to the story than James was telling. Henry would bet money there was. One day he would find out the whole story. But in the meantime he gently slapped the reins on the little mare's back, and she slowly ambled along the lane.

Daniel's mother-in-law Jessie was also working to contribute to the mortgage fund. Seated at her Singer sewing machine, she operated the foot pedal with both feet at full speed while guiding the material under the needle to form a perfectly straight seam. Jessie couldn't remember a time that she hadn't sewn. She had learned at the knees of her grandmother and mother, and like them, she had become an excellent seamstress. Jessie came to the end of the seam and broke the thread to remove the fabric. She felt a tug on her leg and looked down.

"All done, Grannie. See?" Mary, seated on the floor, held up the small piece of fabric Jessie had given her to practice stitches on.

Jessie reached for her granddaughter's handiwork. She looked at the uneven stitches and offered praise.

"This is beautiful work, Mary. You are a good little sewer. Would you like more thread?"

"Yes, Grannie." Mary was pleased at her grandmother's words. "Can I have red this time?"

Jessie took the needle from the small hand and threaded it with bright red thread from the spool. "Here you go, sweetie."

Mary took it and began to sew. As she concentrated, her tongue curled outside her lips. Jessie watched her for a moment before going back to work. Would Mary be like her Grannie who provided all the clothing for her family, and for years had sewn for most of the community? On Sundays, Jessie's mind often wandered from the church sermon to scan the pews and count the number of dresses, coats, and suits she had created. People came to her with a picture from the catalogue to ask for an outfit just like it, and she could—and she would—make it for them. She had the talent to look at that very picture and then draw a pattern using the measurements of the person in question onto a newspaper, which she then transposed onto material. It would be the perfect fit.

She looked down at Mary. The little dress the child was wearing had been made from the material in a dress that Jessie's sister had sent from Boston. And each wedding outfit Jessie made included the silent prayers she added with every stitch. She pressed her lips together when she thought of bridal fittings. She was always the first to know if the bride was expecting. She had let out many a seam. Isabel was the only one she had missed. And that, she supposed, was because she hadn't wanted to see.

Only last week, Jessie had taken the silk material of her own simple wedding dress to make the burial gown for a six-month-old baby. She had also fashioned the child's little pine coffin and lined it with the remaining soft silk. Jessie received no pay, nor had she asked for any. She had made the gesture to help the family, who lived in poverty, give the child a decent burial and maintain some dignity. Well, she hadn't done it for the entire family. No, she had done it for the deceased infant—tiny angel—and grieving mother. She hadn't done it for the father whose drunken behaviour put little food on the family table. Try as she might, Jessie couldn't extend her generosity that far.

Jessie pinned together the second side seam of the dress and lined it up with the machine needle, and began to pedal, slowly at first, and then with increased speed. She often wondered if she had gone to Montreal or Boston, like her sisters, might there have been greater opportunity for her talent. Maybe she could have designed those very dresses that appeared in the catalogue and have had the finest in materials to work with. She thought of the sale of Isabel's dress to a Toronto bride.

And maybe her sewing wouldn't have had to wait until after all the other farm and household chores were done, which often required her to sew into the wee hours of the morning. Maybe she could have had a name in the fashion industry. Then again, maybe she would have been just another small fish in a big pond. Jessie knew she had much to be thankful for in her situation. Though the prices she could charge in the farming community didn't truly represent her time and talent, people appreciated her work and wore it with pride. Plus, James was a decent man who knew the meaning of love. She had a good family, and her health, yet she couldn't help on occasion dreaming of something more. She and her son-in-law had more in common than he would ever know.

Isabel's unplanned pregnancy and loss of her teaching position had disappointed Jessie greatly. What she would have given to have had the educational opportunities of her daughter. For years, she had directed many of her sewing dollars into Isabel's educational fund with the hope of laying down an easier path in life for her daughter than she herself had known. At first, it had been easier to be angry than to feel the extent of her sorrow for what was lost. But with time, she had come to respect that Daniel was an honourable man doing his best to make a good life for her daughter. She looked down at Mary and watched her work. She had two granddaughters she adored. Still, Jessie couldn't entirely let down the wall she had built against Daniel, although seeing Isabel teaching again was helping.

Jessie came to the end of the seam and cut the thread free then rose from the sewing machine and walked to the ironing board to press out the seams. She had promised Thelma MacLean the dress would be ready by the end of the day, and she was expecting Edith MacLeod at any moment to collect her order. She called out to Isabel who was working in the kitchen to tell her she would have to look after getting the noon meal ready.

Jessie had just finished pinning the hem of Thelma's dress when she heard Edith arrive. She went to the door and invited her in through to the dining room, which was the perfect spot for sewing for the public. The family used it only on special occasions, so the large dining table was ideal for cutting out patterns and the wood stove kept it warm and comfortable for working. An extra bedroom lay just off the dining room and was perfect for fittings.

Jessie held up the dress for Edith's final inspection. Edith clapped her hands together as she said, "It is beautiful, Jessie. I never thought you would have it ready so quickly."

"I'm putting in some extra hours lately. I have a little something I'm saving for. Do you want to try it on before you pay?"

Edith reached for her pocketbook. "I don't think there is any need. It fit perfectly when I tried it for you to measure the hem." She handed over the three dollar payment they'd agreed on and Jessie carefully folded the dress and placed it on the table.

Edith picked the conversation up where Jessie had left off. "Well, don't be pushing yourself too hard with the sewing, on top of all your other work." Edith reached into a large bag and withdrew a pair of suit pants. "But do you think you could hem Walter's pants in the next day? His uncle could pass any time now and I want us to be prepared."

"It shouldn't be a problem. Come about four in the afternoon tomorrow and I will have them ready."

Edith gushed her thanks as she packed up her dress. "I have marked them for you. I suppose I could hem them, but I could never do the job you will, and I want Walter looking his best at the funeral." She lowered her voice and leaned in towards Jessie. "Between you and me, I think Walter is going to come into a nice little inheritance when his uncle dies. Of course, we will miss the old fellow, but where there is life there must be death."

Yes, thought Jessie, an inheritance from an old uncle would come in handy right now. Still, the three dollars meant she now had twenty dollars towards Daniel and Isabel's mortgage. By the end of the week, she hoped to make it thirty if her back held out.

Jessie would do what she could to help them, for they were trying to help themselves. She wanted Isabel to have her own home, which she could run as she saw fit. When Jessie married James, they had moved into the farmhouse with his parents, whom she had cared for until their deaths. Then her father had moved in, and then it was Isabel and Daniel and their girls. Jessie could count on one hand the nights she and James had spent alone. They had been good nights.

Jessie closed the porch door behind Edith, added wood to the kitchen and dining room stoves, and began to cut out the pattern pinned to the wool material on the dining room table. She handed Mary a small pair of scissors and material so she wouldn't feel left out. As Jessie expertly guided the scissors through the material, she wondered why such a hard-working young man like Daniel was struggling so hard. But the answer was simple. He had thrown his lot in with a snake and gotten bit.

"I think that will be all for today," Isabel said, as she closed the reader on her kitchen table and handed it to the young student next to her. Since word had gotten out that Isabel was tutoring the older students for the provincial exam, another parent had approached her to help her young son get a better grasp on his reading skills. The boy came to the house after supper two days a week, and Jeannie and Mary listened to him read while they sat at the table next to him with their colouring books. Isabel actually liked that Jeannie constantly interrupted the boy with questions about the story, for when he answered them, she knew he understood what he had read. The youngster also enjoyed being the centre of attention and a leader, rather that being at the bottom of the reading line, which was helping build his self-confidence.

As the boy reached into his pocket for the coins for the hour of tutoring, Isabel almost felt guilty taking them. All the child really needed to improve his reading was a bit of extra attention. Isabel knew he frequently got overlooked as a middle child in a big, busy family. The mother was often exhausted, and the father cared more about making money than investing time in his children. Isabel looked at the coins in her hand. She had given the boy far more than what the money covered, so she had no reason to feel guilty. She had earned this money. Isabel closed her hand around the coins and slipped them into her apron pocket.

It was going to take more than coins to pay off the mortgage, though, and that was where she had some good news for Daniel. Catherine Wall had sold Isabel's wedding dress to a friend from Toronto for five dollars more than the asking price. Jessie was thrilled when she heard the news. A wedding dress she had envisioned and then sewed was going to be worn by a bride walking down the aisle of a large Toronto church. Now that, Jessie never could have imagined.

And so it was, that Daniel's family and friends passed along every spare coin or bill they could to Wendell, who was in charge of keeping a running tally.

"Peter, do you know how close we are?" Daniel asked as he pulled what he could spare out of his Friday pay packet and handed it over to his brother.

"No." Peter placed the bills inside his wallet. "Wendell was cagey when I asked. He would only say he was expecting an impressive amount to come in this weekend."

As the two brothers headed for their cars, Daniel wondered about Wendell's words. He told himself not to read anything into it, and to just be thankful for how things were going. Orders continued to be placed for potatoes, thus providing him with a steady job, and MacDonald hadn't ordered him fired for not taking the deal. He tried not to think about the new shoes his children would need in spring, or the materials he needed for the house. That was the future, and he had to worry about today first. Besides, Daniel had often experienced waking in the morning without a cent in his pocket, and through some unexpected occurrence, having a few dollars by nightfall. The shoes would happen. His grandmother had always preached that the Lord provided in the most mysterious of ways.

CHAPTER 32

The Rangers' dressing room was unusually quiet before the start of the fifth game. Everyone was dressed and ready. No one even had a snide remark about Charlie's red long johns. Each player appeared to be gathering his strength in preparation for what should be the final game. There would be plenty of time for noise following the win as they paraded the cup around the ice surface of the rink.

Coach Ramsay seemed to be of the same mind. He kept his talk short and concise. "Okay, boys, we can wrap it up tonight. Let's do what we came to do."

Daniel couldn't have agreed more. The Rangers were going into the game with a 3-1 lead. They couldn't afford to make mistakes tonight. He couldn't afford to make mistakes. Through example, he had to show the other players they were winners and balance it all with Coach Ramsay's directives. Like never before, Daniel felt the tightness in his shoulders from the tension of the expectations. He gave himself both a mental and physical shake.

Daniel had always loved the game and tonight he was right where he had always wanted to be, where he had worked to be, and somehow he had to embrace it, and let the joy and excitement of the challenge back in. Looking around at the faces of the other players, Daniel was one of them – at least for tonight. As he pulled on the leather helmet he imagined skating by the

Flyers' box holding high the trophy. They were so close. Then he remembered the land and the little house. He had been so close there, too. He quickly shut the thought down. Now was not the time for doubt.

As they walked from the dressing room to the box, Daniel absorbed the sights and sounds of his surroundings. As expected, the rink was packed. The stands were a sea of tightly-packed colour, and the sound of voices filled the air. And tonight, there was an extra bonus. The local radio station had decided to broadcast the game, so he knew Isabel would be listening at home. Daniel wanted her to hear his name over and over again on the radio. He imagined what the Rangers and Flyers were feeling in the moment was no different than what the players in the national league felt when they faced their fans. Dreams could come true even here, he thought. It was a combination of luck, skill, and determination. Daniel knew he had proven he had the skill and determination. Now, he really needed Lady Luck. Not just for the fifth game, but in his life. Especially his life.

As expected, Mount Pleasant made it clear from the moment the puck dropped they planned to stay in the game. They started the play rough and dirty, and the crowd ate it up. Daniel felt his excitement start to build. He had always seen a dirty player as a lesser opponent and took great pleasure in outwitting him with skill and speed, and his own brand of mind game. Hanging back to read the plays, and attempting to control an opponent's moves were two of the things he liked best about playing defence. Mount Pleasant's strategy ignited the fire in his gut and took him fully into the game. It surprised him how much fun he was suddenly having, and it showed in every play. His teammates quickly caught his spirit and dug in. The Rangers scored early in the first period. Keith set up the goal for Charlie. The Rangers were outskating and outshooting the Flyers, but then Peter took a penalty for high sticking, and while the Rangers were short-handed, the Flyers scored. What made it worse than the score itself was that Craig got the assist.

Coach Ramsay came close to losing it behind the bench. If there was one thing he wanted, it was for the Rangers to stay out of the penalty box. The tie changed everything. Players were suddenly taking risks everywhere on the ice, and while both teams were getting plenty of shots on goal, the goalies blocked each one. Daniel knew for Ivan it was the fact that Archie was dressed and sitting in the box, but he couldn't explain what had come over the Mount Pleasant goaltender who seemed unusually aware and agile. He wondered what threat was being held over him. The thought made Daniel laugh and more determined than ever to score, but no matter how many goals he set up or tried to directly deliver into the Mount Pleasant net, the goalie kept them out.

The radio sports announcers sent every play across the airwaves:

"MacDougall takes the puck off Ballum behind the Rangers' net, sending it over to Birch, who is unable to get by Craig. Birch shoots straight across the front of the net to a waiting MacDougall. Ballum is trying to gain control of the puck, but MacDougall is holding on with some pretty fancy stick- handling. Yes! MacDougall has broken free of Ballum and is moving the puck up the ice. He shoots it over to Yeo. Craig intercepts and is carrying the puck back to the Rangers' end! Campbell is staying in the net where both defensemen are covering him. MacDougall takes the puck off Craig, passes it back to

Birch, who moves it over to Cann. Cann carries it across the centre line, and passes it to Peter MacDougall! Yes! Colvin of the Flyers takes it from the Rangers' centre, but not for long. Smith, playing left wing, has laid claim to the puck. He shoots! Yes! Enman makes an impressive save with his right glove. So close to a goal for the Rangers."

Back home in the MacArthurs' kitchen, Isabel paced back and forth while Jessie and James listened from their chairs by the stove. Jessie was knitting her husband a pair of socks, and though a fast knitter at any time, her hands were flying in time to the game. It made James smile.

There was no doubt the fans were getting exceptional value for their admission. People in the stands forgot their feet were cold, and no one left their seats during the game to venture to the bathroom or the canteen. That created long waits at the bathroom stalls and in the canteen between periods, and since the canteen was doing such a brisk business, the officials were persuaded to lengthen the break. This only heightened the tension in the rink and the dressing rooms.

When the siren ended the play of the third period, the game was still tied. The officials determined there would be a five-minute overtime period. If that didn't decide the game, sudden death overtime would determine the winner. In the office, the rink manager wisely notified the police department of the situation. When he placed the call, he told the officer on the other end that the steam from the heat in the rink was rising to the rafters and instantly turning to frost. He wanted it to stay cold. The officer understood and put a call out over the radio. But the men in the squad cars already knew as they were tuned into the game as well.

As he waited for the play to start, Daniel scanned the third row of seats until he found Reverend Johnson's face. The minister was looking back at him and tipped his hat slightly. It was their private signal to stay focused, shut out everything but the play on the ice, and deliver the goal.

Coach Ramsay put on his first lines to start the overtime period. “Listen, boys, you can outskate and outshoot the Flyers—so let’s see you do it. We are going home with the trophy.”

He stressed each word. The whistle blew to resume play, and the fans of both teams sat with bated breath, not wanting to distract their players, yet waiting for the moment they could erupt in the sounds of victory.

Daniel and Ernest knew the importance of keeping Ivan covered. He alone had played the entire game and was getting tired. When the puck dropped, forwards on both teams started moving it up and down the ice with lightning speed. In their defence zone, Daniel and Ernest quickly moved the puck out and, for the most part managed to stay between the Flyers’ puck carrier and their own net. With thirty seconds left on the clock, Daniel made a good shot from a distance—sending the puck well up the ice to George who passed to Charlie, who in turn sent it on to Peter, but the Flyer centreman intercepted the pass and moved back into the Rangers’ zone. Skating backwards, Daniel moved to block his progress towards the Rangers’ net and at the opportune time remove the puck from him.

A Flyer wingman was shadowing Daniel from the side, but he wasn’t worried because he could see his teammates had him covered. The next moment, he was down, sprawled on the ice, a wad of bubble gum on his blade. The Flyers’ centreman skirted round him and passed the puck to Craig, who shot at the net. The Flyers’ left wingman’s stick tripped up Ernest, and though he stayed on his feet, his focus came off the play.

Ivan panicked and made a dive for the puck. He missed. Craig scored. The rink went wild.

When people talked of the win afterwards, they said it was hard to know who was the most shocked about the outcome of the game—the fans, the Rangers, or the Flyers. Coach Ramsay demanded the referee disqualify the goal because of the gum thrown on the ice. He said it was nothing short of sabotage by the Flyers. Ivan reported seeing the Flyers' centre, wearing the number 10 jersey, spit it out just before Daniel fell. Coach Dyment argued that the Flyers didn't have to stoop to such tactics to win the game, and the Rangers could prove nothing. The referee and linesmen agreed. Whether the gum had been there or not, the outcome might have been the same they said. It was a clean win for the Flyers. Coach Dyment was all smiles, while Coach Ramsay looked ready to spit nails.

If the Rangers' dressing room had been quiet before the game, it was now like a tomb. An honest loss would have hurt badly enough, but sabotage was something else again. Coach Ramsay had few words as he battled to hold back the tears. "We will not stoop to their level," he told the silent players. "You boys will win the championship. And you'll do it fair and square."

CHAPTER 33

The Rangers woke to a sober dawn. None of them had much get up and go, but they couldn't afford to slack off. They had another game ahead of them. Plus, the deadline for the mortgage payment was drawing ever closer on the calendar.

Ernest had lined up good sales for firewood, thanks to the increased need for fuel during such a cold winter. There wasn't a lot of seasoned wood to be had so he upped the price seventy-five cents per cord. Ernest knew he could have gone higher, but he didn't want to be thought of as someone who would gouge people when they were in need. Ernest reasoned that getting greedy could backfire on him come fall. People had a long memory around money and Ernest didn't want to risk any of his customers looking for new suppliers. He would take only a little extra now, and hope it paid off for him in the long run.

Walking out of the house into the crisp morning air, Ernest knew he had a long day ahead of him. Every last stick of firewood had to be loaded by hand onto the truck, and once he arrived at his delivery points, they would have to be thrown off again. Yet Ernest had no complaints. Today, he was his own boss, and though the work was hard, he enjoyed nothing more than the firewood and lumber business. Ernest's grandfather had taught him from the time he was a small boy how to work in the woods and respect its dangers, while appreciating its beauty and resources. Ernest knew every species, and that softwoods gave a quick hot fire to warm a room, while hardwoods produced a slow steady heat for ovens that produced the perfect loaf of bread or cookies. The most valuable lesson his grandfather had taught, was that if Ernest took care of his woodlot, the woodlot would take care of him.

Ernest understood Daniel's dream, and also understood there were people who would think it as foolish as his own. His father was one. Ernest Senior had counted the days as a boy until he could escape his father's farm and woodlot and make his way in town. He blamed Ernest's grandfather for giving Ernest a love of the place during summer holidays. But Ernest was grateful to his grandfather. Maybe it suited his father to be a shoe salesman, but it suited Ernest to be a woodsman and a farmer and he felt no less for it. If donating a few loads of wood helped give Daniel the opportunity his grandfather had given him, Ernest was more than willing to put in the effort. As Ernest worked at loading the first of many loads of firewood, he knew that by nightfall the sound and feel of money would be in his pocket. It would be a substantial contribution towards the mortgage.

Ivan also planned to have his contribution to the mortgage by nightfall. He pulled himself up into the massive loft of the barn that had been one of his favourite places on the farm growing up. He and his two sisters had spent hours up there playing hide and seek, searching for kittens, and reading on rainy days, while chasing sunbeams on sunny ones. The storage space was a great place to curl up and listen to a thunderstorm or have sleepovers in the freshly stored hay on hot summer nights. But those days had flown by and his sisters were now married with homes of their own. Only Ivan came to the loft now. Twice daily, his job was to throw down the hay to feed the livestock and the straw to bed them. It was still a pleasant place to be with the sweet smell of the timothy and clover feed.

Today, Ivan was throwing down more hay than usual. After feeding the farm's livestock, he loaded Percy's truck with hay to sell at the racetrack in Summerside. The hay was the best of their feed. His father was a progressive farmer who was always reading the material written by the Department of Agriculture and farm magazines on how to do things better. Mr. Campbell had taken to harvesting the hay crop earlier than other farmers to capture all of the nutrients. The venture was paying off, as the racehorse owners had a hankering for the quality product and were willing to pay top dollar. They were even willing to come up with more money for delivery to the race barns. Since Ivan did most of the work loading and delivering the hay, his father was generous with his compensation.

Ivan had intended to use the pay he received for the next three loads for a chrome exhaust system on his car, but now the money was going to something even more important.

CHAPTER 34

Carol Ramsay had the idea to hold a team fundraiser and booster rally in the community hall. It would be a great time for the whole community and the team didn't have to say what the raised funds would actually be used for. When Carol put the idea to her husband and the team, they immediately said yes, since there was need of something that could raise a substantial amount of money in one go. Also, their spirits needed something fun. Fear was taking hold that they may have gotten in over their heads. When the men stopped to think about it, perhaps there was a reason they hadn't taken the series four straight, because the way things stood they had a reason to justify the fundraiser. Roland Ramsay often joked that his wife would be a perfect military general, and the players were happy to let her take charge.

Carol was excited to be heading the fundraiser. While she was rarely able to attend a game in person, she was an avid fan. Carol also loved that coaching hockey gave Roland a much-needed outlet from the stress of farming. She had been disappointed, but not surprised, to learn that her husband had asked the young captain to put the team ahead of his own welfare. He had tunnel vision when it came to the Rangers. Carol knew she needed to help make her husband's actions right.

One quick meeting around her kitchen table had the night planned. The schoolteacher, Catherine Wall, had also joined them. Isabel had asked Daniel to ask Carol to make Catherine a part of the planning committee and to tell her why. Although Daniel had told Isabel that Keith was receptive to going on a date with Catherine, she was doubtful he would act on it without a little help. Daniel had not been fond of the idea of bringing Carol into the mix, but he wasn't going to risk being back on Isabel's blacklist, so he had followed through.

Carol had welcomed the suggestion and wondered why she hadn't thought of the plan herself. She was one of few to know that Catherine and Keith both had been jilted. Unfortunately for Catherine, her breakup had taken place on her wedding day. Carol's sister had been one of the hundred guests seated in a Charlottetown church waiting for the ceremony to start. After Catherine had recovered from the devastating humiliation, she had put a great distance between herself and home by coming to Lot 16 to teach. She was a beautiful young woman with a lot to offer. Keith, on the other hand, had gotten off lightly in Carol's opinion. She felt Keith suffered from hurt pride more than anything else and the schoolteacher would be a major catch for him. Much better than the spoiled brat he thought he wanted.

At the planning meeting, Carol had skilfully seated Catherine and Keith next to each other and made sure they wound up on the games committee. Daniel was amazed at how smoothly Carol had carried out her matchmaking plan. Keith never had a clue anything was up, so remained fairly relaxed. When Catherine smiled at him, he seemed startled that she noticed his presence. He had shyly smiled back, while wondering to himself if he had the courage to ask her out. One thing he realized sitting that close to her was that she sure had pretty eyes.

Carol envisioned the fundraiser as a family event with something for all ages. She laid out everyone's tasks. The players were responsible for spreading the word about the event. Their female family members and the Women's Institute would help Carol organize the food and cakes for the auction sale. The players would do the heavy lifting in setting up the hall and Roland would make sure the fire was on early in the day to have the large building comfortable for the evening. Carol put herself in charge of the entertainment. Early in the evening, there would be games, followed by a cake auction, lunch, then dancing to music provided by a fiddler and piano player.

Catherine and Keith were given the job of rounding up the games to ensure they would have to get together another time on their own to source them. When Carol checked the last to-do-item off her list, she marvelled at how fast and efficiently they had put the fundraiser together. She wondered why governments couldn't manage themselves in the same manner, but since competent women didn't hold many legislative seats, there was no surprise it took forever to get anything done.

On the night of the fundraiser, as Carol stood waiting for the crowd to arrive, pride filled her. The boys had polished the hardwood floor of the old country hall until it shone. The big stove provided a comfortable even heat. Tables, covered with gingham tablecloths, awaited plates of sandwiches and sweets, and large porcelain jugs of tea, coffee, and juice. More tables lined the stage waiting for the cakes that would arrive for the auction. Tables set up for cards, checkers, and crokinole occupied the centre of the floor. The admission table was by the door. Daniel, as team captain, had been given the job of collecting the entrance fee of thirty cents per person, or a dollar per family of five or more. Carol realized that meant Isabel and the girls would be on their own for the first part of the evening, but Isabel was totally capable of handling herself in a crowd.

Coach Ramsay and Carol would greet people as they arrived. She just knew the evening was going to be great.

At the appointed time, the first footsteps stomped snow from boots in the outer porch and people opened the door into the hall itself. For the next half-hour, it was a flurry of activity at the entrance.

"Thanks for coming out tonight to support the team," Carol said to each person as they arrived.

"I wouldn't miss supporting the boys and their coach. You must be pretty proud of them, Coach Ramsay," was the standard reply.

"I certainly am. They're a fine bunch of players," Coach Ramsay would answer, giving the boyish grin that had first endeared him to Carol.

Much to Carol and Isabel's delight, Catherine and Keith arrived together, accompanied by his mother. By the time the couple had completed their assigned tasks for the fundraiser, they had fallen into easy conversation with each other. Keith had been dubious that he could make paper flowers with his big hands, but she had skilfully shown him how. Keith was surprised that when the job was done, he had effortlessly offered to pick Catherine up and take her to the hall the night of the fundraiser. He was even more surprised when Catherine accepted the offer. Since Keith had extended the invitation, he paid admission for both her and his mother. After all, the money was going on the mortgage.

Daniel wondered, as he took the money, if Keith realized what was happening with Catherine. That the two were definitely on a date. Daniel watched as Catherine asked Keith to hold her cake so she could remove her winter coat. Daniel noted she was wearing a pretty dress that likely had never seen the inside of a classroom.

"Thank you," Catherine said, turning to retrieve the cake. "Mrs. MacLean let me use her kitchen to make my upside-down coconut cake. I think it turned out splendidly."

"It's Keith's favourite," said his mother, winking at Catherine.

When they walked away, Carol smiled at Daniel. "It appears we did well."

"He has no chance, does he?" said Daniel, as he and Carol watched the group move into the room.

"No chance at all," she said.

A moment of tension filled the air when Charles Elliott and his family entered the hall. Carol had known friction was a possibility when putting Daniel on the door, because there was no doubt Elliott, as the biggest businessman in the community, and an avid Rangers' fan, would attend the evening.

But as Carol expected, Daniel rose to the situation. "Well, good evening to the Elliott family." Daniel kept his tone upbeat. "You and your daughters are looking especially fine tonight, Mrs. Elliott."

It was the truth. Mrs. Elliott was a handsome woman, and, if asked, no one could have recounted a time of seeing her with a hair out of place, or not clothed in a stylish dress and heels. Fortunately, her young daughters had her looks rather than their father's.

"That will be one dollar and twenty cents, please, Charles." Without speaking, Charles handed Daniel the money, and the young man passed him tickets.

"I sure am glad to see you cheering for us at the games. I hope you are going to help us take the championship." Daniel turned back to the Elliott girls.

The two young girls gave him an adoring look, but it was Mrs. Elliott who answered. "You can count on all of us being there. Right, Charles?"

"I'll be in the stands when you take the championship." Charles glanced at his wife, then focused on Coach Ramsay, who had joined them and was now holding out a hand to the storekeeper.

"It means a lot to have your support, Charles." Coach Ramsay held Charles's hand longer than necessary and propelled the two men away from the entrance.

"Winners are always easy to support." Elliott withdrew his hand and gave a slight laugh.

"I hope you and the family enjoy the evening. I have a feeling there will be a few bids on that cake Mrs. Elliott is holding," Coach Ramsay replied.

Carol had given Ivan and Ernest the job of taking coats and hanging them in the cloakroom. Ivan smartly stepped up behind Mrs. Elliott and placed his hands on her shoulders. "May I take your coat, Mrs. Elliott?"

"Certainly, Ivan. You are such a gentleman." Turning only her elegant head, Mrs. Elliott looked at the handsome young goaltender and for a moment wished she were twenty again.

Ivan flashed her his biggest grin as he slipped the coat from her shoulders. Ernest, in the process of taking the rest of the family's coats rolled his eyes and muttered under his breath. "Right." He had noted that since the start of their coat duty Ivan was beelining for the women leaving him with the men.

George arrived with Ruby and their two boys, who scampered off the moment they saw school friends. Daniel felt uneasy taking their admission fee. George had told him about forgoing the veranda to raise mortgage money, so Daniel imagined Ruby was angry. She set her cake on the table beside

Daniel, and waving Ivan aside, removed her coat, which she then handed to Ivan. Then she leaned in close and lowered her voice.

"Don't worry. George and I can wait to sit on the veranda to view the river. Skinny dipping in the warm water after dark when the boys are asleep is more fun for us right now."

Ruby straightened, picked up her cake, and walked off laughing at the colour rising in Daniel's face. He looked up to see George watching him with a foolish smile on his face.

Wendell and John came out of the kitchen where they had been assigned the job of collecting and numbering the cakes before handing them off to Victor and Charlie. The two stood by the kitchen door and looked at the number of people in the hall.

"This is a far bigger crowd than I expected." Wendell tried to imagine how much money the tickets would bring in. "Look, there are people here from Grand River, Arlington, and Port Hill. How come? They are Tyne Valley fans."

"Everybody loves a good time, and with Tyne Valley out of the running they can easily support us." John looked around the room. "Look in the back corner. There are people from Miscouche and down from Wellington."

"Holy Mackerel! Those are die-hard Wellington fans. Can you believe it?" Wendell shook his head.

But John was looking at who had just walked through the door. "Good grief! It's Robert with Sadie. How did he ever get the balls to ask her to come with him?"

The hall quickly heated up with the crush of bodies. The sound of laughter and conversation carried in the air.

Coach Ramsay turned to Carol and took her hand. "It's a great night, Carol. Thank you."

"We're a team," Carol said and hurried off to make sure everything was going perfectly.

CHAPTER 35

After a couple of hours, Carol announced that the game portion of the evening was over and the cake auction would soon begin. Everyone could see that many of the community women had gone to a great deal of trouble with their donations. The decorating on the cakes was truly creative. Hockey players, hockey sticks, and skates were piped on the top of white icing. Isabel had produced a delicious-looking chocolate cake that she decorated with maple icing and small flowers made from red and green gumdrops. She hoped it would fetch a good price.

"Which one are you bidding on?" Charlie quizzed Victor as they organized the cakes on tables as directed by Carol. Victor pulled a face.

"We can't buy cake—we need money for the mortgage," he said.

"Yes, but since the money raised by the cakes is going to the mortgage..." Charlie shook his head as he explained the obvious. "We'd have our cake and eat it, too, right?"

"In that case, I'm going for Ruby's marble cake!" Victor decided.

When Carol gave the signal, Coach Ramsay stepped onto the stage as the auctioneer. Holding up his arms he called out. "Attention, everyone. Can I please have your attention?"

He waited for a good minute or two for everyone to settle down so he could begin.

"As you know, tonight is all about supporting the Rangers," he said. "That championship is almost ours." A long, loud cheer went up from the audience.

Time passed before Coach Ramsay could speak again. "Some of the finest cooks in the community have donated cakes in support of the team. So, gentlemen, I expect you to open your wallets wide and take home a real treat." He turned to Ernest.

"What's up first?"

Coach Ramsay held up the cake that Ernest passed to him and consulted the attached note. "I have here Mrs. Ethel Thompson's prize-winning chiffon cake with lemon butter icing," he said. "That's lemon butter icing, everyone, so do I hear fifty cents to start the bidding? Frank Barnes, did I see a hand? Yes? Do I hear seventy-five cents. Yes. Now do I hear a dollar?"

By the time the bidding ended on the chiffon cake, a sizeable price of two dollars and fifty cents had been paid by Mrs. Thompson's son, Alex. The crowd roared with laughter as Alex stepped forward to claim his prize. "Mom always sends her best baking away from home, so I'm here to bring some back," he said and grinned.

Catherine's cake was the second one on the auction block. Several single men, including Peter and Percy, placed bids, just to torment their teammate, but Keith came away the winner at two dollars and seventy-five cents.

"Go get 'er, Keithy boy!" The rest of the team began to hoot and holler when he went up to the stage to collect the cake, causing him to blush ear to ear. The crowd laughed once again, enjoying the auction immensely.

"Keith has bit the dust." Wendell nudged John.

John agreed. "It could be worse, I guess."

The auctioning of the cakes proceeded quickly. People were eager to place a bid, with the cakes going for an average price of two dollars. Isabel's cake was the final one to come up for auction, and for only the second time that evening, Charles Elliott bid. He had claimed his wife's cake, but he knew more would be expected of him. The storekeeper was standing right at the front of the hall where he could easily be seen by both the auctioneer and the audience. He expected to take the cake at a price just a little higher than the average and come away looking like the big spender of the evening, but someone at the back of the hall kept countering his bid. Before Elliott knew it, the price was over four dollars and climbing. Elliott was cornered. There was no way he could back down without looking unsupportive or worse still, cheap. Every eye in the room knew if anyone could pay a good price for Isabel's cake, it should be him. Elliott had a whole lot more than a cake riding on the bid.

"I have five twenty-five. Do I hear five fifty?" called Coach Ramsay. "Yes, five fifty it is." Elliott turned several times to try and see who was bidding against him, but in the crush of people, he couldn't get a clear view. Since Coach Ramsay wasn't identifying either bidder, Elliott didn't feel he could demand to know his opponent.

"Six dollars!" Elliott felt a sweat break out on his brow when he raised the bid by fifty cents.

Coach Ramsay paused. "I have six dollars. Do I hear six-fifty?" he said, in his best auctioneer's voice. No one spoke.

"Going once at six dollars," he said. "Going twice at six dollars." He paused one final time, his eye on the back of the room and then: "Gone—at six dollars to our esteemed storekeeper, Charles Elliott, highest bidder of the night!"

The crowd put their hands together and gave Elliott a resounding round of applause. The eleven hockey players, plus Percy, whistled and chanted their thanks. When the noise finally quietened, Coach Ramsay continued.

"The Rangers and I really appreciate all the support here tonight," he said, in his booming voice. "Now we'd all like to see you dig into that lovely lunch and then hit the dance floor."

The crowd now hooted their approval. At the back of the hall, Percy, a silly grin on his face, turned to look at Peter, the mystery bidder, and gave him the thumbs-up sign.

"That was close!" Peter wiped his brow. He sure didn't have six dollars in his pocket, but had counted on Elliott's pride going for the win. He felt a tap on his shoulder and saw Percy's grin disappear. He turned.

"Nice one, boys," said Reverend Johnson. He looked at the two men, knowingly. "I expect to see the two of you in church in the morning." All three broke into laughter. People nearby turned to looked at the young men and wondered what the joke was.

The lunch would have done any community proud. Carol was pleased to see all the empty platters, for the success of an Island event was always judged by the food served. There was neither a sandwich nor sweet left when the plates were cleared away, and jug after jug of tea, coffee, and juice had washed them down. If stomachs rumbled, it was in protest of being stuffed, rather than being hungry.

A night lunch was part of the rural culture and didn't slow anyone down from heading to the dance floor when the musicians took to the stage. Ella on piano, Calvin on fiddle, and Raymond on the harmonica quickly made people light on their feet. There was a lot of dancing to be done before midnight announced the arrival of the Sabbath. Women spread out coats at the back of the hall for the younger children to lie down on. The music would lull them into sleep. Isabel stayed with the girls until they drifted off, and then she searched out Daniel. He was in the far corner chatting to several elderly women whose faces reflected their pleasure of his time and attention.

Isabel felt a swell of pride in her chest as she took in his good looks. She waited for a break in the conversation to move forward. She placed her hand in Daniel's and said to the women. "I hate to interrupt, ladies, but might I claim my husband for a dance?"

"Certainly. I wish young women could have been that forward in my day. I would have had a lot more fun!" Jane declared with a wink.

"Do I not have a say in this?" Daniel asked the women.

"If you are a smart young man, you will accept the lady's invitation. Be off with you," Helen ordered.

The dance was a waltz and Daniel pulled Isabel close to him. It felt good to hold her and sway to the soothing sound of the music. He allowed himself to relax and enjoy the moment. Daniel couldn't remember the last time they had danced, and that was not a good thing. They needed more moments like this, and he promised himself he would make them happen.

"Have I told you how handsome you are tonight?" Isabel asked, interrupting his thoughts.

He looked down into her upturned face. "Not in words. I am not sure a lady should be casting such looks about, but I can tell you, I like it very much."

"Ah, you noticed. I wasn't sure you would." Isabel laughed and snuggled a little closer.

"And have I told you that I consider myself the luckiest man here tonight to have a woman of your beauty and brains claim me?" Daniel whispered into her ear.

"You're okay with being claimed?" Isabel whispered back.

"As long as it's for a lifetime. When our hair is silver, and our gait slow, I still want us to be waltzing together." Daniel looked at her soft lips. How he would love to have kissed her right then, but knew it was not the place. As it was, they were dancing too close together.

"Now where does a farmer, hockey player, construction worker, and labourer learn to talk like that?" Isabel looked at him with admiration and sighed contentedly. She hoped the dance would never end.

CHAPTER 36

"Just over a hundred dollars!" Carol turned to Wendell, triumphant after sitting at the Ramsays' kitchen table to roll coins and stack bills early the next morning.

"The cakes must've put us over what I thought we'd get." Wendell was impressed and relieved. He added the money to the 'contribution can' and took it home to hide in his closet. He crossed his fingers. Surely more would be added in the next couple of days. He planned to say a few extra prayers in church later that morning.

Peter went to church with his parents. He didn't dare miss. He had been worried Reverend Johnson would say something from the pulpit about misleading others, but the message was about following your heart and blooming where you're planted. Peter felt Daniel might have been the inspiration for the message, but Reverend Johnson didn't know what was happening with Daniel. Peter did know the message spoke to him.

When the MacDougalls returned home, they were greeted by the smells of a pot roast cooking in the oven. Peter was surprised until he saw Reverend Johnson's car pull into the lane. The roast made sense now. Families in the congregation took turns inviting the single minister to Sunday dinner and did their best to serve a good meal.

Reverend Johnson bounded up the steps and into the small front entrance of the house where Peter greeted him.

"Please take the Reverend's coat and bring him along to the table, Peter, while your father and I get the meal on the table," Allison MacDougall called from the kitchen.

"It's good to see you, Reverend Mark," Peter said. But when he reached for the Reverend's coat, he felt a packet of paper put into his hand, not a jacket. He looked down to see an envelope in his palm.

"My contribution to the cause." Reverend Johnson lowered his voice. "Sorry it can't be more."

"How do you know about the cause, Reverend Mark?" Peter glanced behind him to make sure neither parent was near before he whispered back.

"A man of the cloth never tells his sources," the young minister whispered back. "I am so proud of the team, and what they are doing for Daniel." This time, he handed his coat to Peter and waited to be ushered down the hall. Peter slipped the envelope into his pocket. As he hung up Reverend Johnson's coat, he noticed the threadbare cuffs and sighed. Peter was well aware of the small salary the Reverend was expected to live on, and yet he had given to the cause. He wondered if the money had been saved for a new coat.

The MacDougalls shared a lovely meal with the minister. When they had finished dessert, Duncan told his son to take their visitor to the parlour, while he helped his wife clear the table. Peter followed his father's instructions, knowing that Duncan was more comfortable pretending to help in the kitchen than carrying on a conversation with the "whippersnapper Reverend" as he called him.

Peter was glad for the opportunity. He had enjoyed the time Mark Johnson had spent with the team a few years back, and was sour the church elders, under the chairmanship of Charles Elliott, had put a stop to his coaching. Peter was sure

God wasn't as opposed to people having fun as were some of the so-called pillars of the faith. When they were seated in front of the parlour stove, Peter asked the clergyman to expand more on his morning message.

"Does following your heart really make life easier?" Peter wanted to know.

"It depends what you mean by easier, Peter. If I had joined my family business, as my father and brother wanted, my life would be much easier financially and materially, but not mentally. I doubt I would be as content and satisfied as I am now. I don't think following your heart is all about easy. It takes a lot of work to get where your heart wants to go." Reverend Johnson took a drink of water from the glass he had carried through to the front room.

Peter thought of Daniel, and then himself. "I have been struggling to figure out what my heart wants, and where," he confided. "I love the Island, but I like Montreal, and it has more opportunities."

"There is nothing to say you can only love one place, Peter. If the Island holds your roots, maybe Montreal holds your wings." Reverend Johnson thought of leaving his own beloved home.

"I've made good money in Montreal, but I've nothing to show for it. I talk about not wanting to financially struggle like my parents and Daniel, yet my brother is way ahead of me." Peter put another stick in the stove.

"And why is that?" Reverend Johnson questioned.

"Fear that if I try, I might fail. I've never seen myself doing anything other than working for someone else, but even then, I could have been smarter with my money."

"And now?" The minister asked.

"Watching Daniel go for what he wants has taught me a lot. I've made a plan, Reverend Mark. I'm going to Montreal to work construction until I have learned everything there is to know to make me a master craftsman. My mentor tells me I am a natural when it comes to the trades. Then I'm coming home to start my own company. I think I can make a living here. If not, I'll go back to Montreal, but I don't think I will have to."

"I'm impressed. Sounds like you have it all figured out, Peter." Reverend Mark settled deeper into the soft chair.

"Far from it, but making a decision is a big start." Peter smiled.

"I agree that the first step is the big one. The second is accepting it won't always be easy. It will take determination, and sacrifice," Mark Johnson added.

"Hockey is also teaching me that. When I get back to Montreal I'm in for fewer nights out and more trips to the bank to deposit money, so that when the time comes, I can borrow money." Peter had figured out what he would bank weekly. He knew he had to find a balance between saving and enjoying life so as not to fail in the endeavour.

Reverend Johnson chuckled. "It also means you can play hockey in the winters for another couple of years and build muscle loading railcars." He paused. "Any romance in the offing?" Reverend Johnson knew that one of the things Peter enjoyed about Montreal was a variety of girlfriends.

"I think I'll keep it light. I had to sell my filly Nell, which nearly broke me." Peter grimaced. "I'm not ready for a serious relationship. Daniel's life could have been much easier if he'd stayed single another few years."

After Reverend Johnson left, Duncan and Allison asked Peter to join them for a chat. In Peter's memory, his parents wanting to talk wasn't a good thing. He was greatly surprised when his father pushed an envelope across the table towards him. Was this the day of envelopes?

"Your mother and I want to contribute," Duncan said. "Daniel can't lose that land and his dream. The boy has guts I never had, and I don't want to see his spirit broken."

"The deal is supposed to be a secret so Elliott doesn't find out. How do you know?" Peter was taken aback.

"The best way to get the right information is to ask the right person." Duncan leaned back in his chair. "I asked Daniel if he got the money from MacDonald. That boy could never lie."

"How did you get the money?" Peter was impressed by what he saw when he looked inside the envelope.

"We were putting the money aside for our funerals. We don't want to be a burden. However, we have decided we like living and will have time to save up again," Allison answered.

"And if we don't, bury us out behind the barn wrapped in a wool blanket." Duncan gently squeezed his wife's hand.

Allison laughed. "I rather like the idea. As long as we're side by side."

Peter had to wonder if he was hearing right. His fearful, uptight parents were laughing, holding hands, and talking about just living. These truly were strange days.

CHAPTER 37

There was no question that stomachs churned the entire day of the next championship game for both the Mount Pleasant and Lot 16 players. Fans couldn't seem to concentrate on their work. Everyone just wanted the magic hour to arrive, when they could leave for the rink. Daniel worked at the rail station, but was careful to pace himself to prevent exhaustion. He ate a big breakfast and a good lunch, and drank lots of water. Ralph even let them go an hour early so they wouldn't be rushed. When Daniel arrived home expecting to start his barn chores, Isabel and James told him they were all done, and Jessie had his favourite supper ready to put on the table.

Everyone arrived early to board the truck and Percy pulled out of the parking lot right on time. There was a line of traffic ahead and behind him on the road heading into town. No one on the truck doubted where the traffic was heading. The parking lot of the rink was full when they arrived, and people were parking on the street. Percy had to take the truck to the back of the rink near the rear entrance. Maybe that was a good thing. The players wouldn't have to face the hubbub of coming through the main entrance. By entering through the back, they could stay calmer.

Coach Ramsay and Archie were already waiting for the Rangers in the dressing room. Archie was dressed in full goalie gear and sweating, not that Coach Ramsay seemed to notice.

"No wasting time," Coach Ramsay said. "I have asked Reverend Johnson to lead us in prayer before I give my talk." The players just looked at each other. Was this really their coach? Even when Reverend Johnson had been an assistant coach to the team, Coach Ramsay had never asked him to pray in the dressing room before a game. Had the coach lost all faith in them? Nevertheless, they did as they were told.

The players were seated on the benches when Reverend Johnson entered the dressing room. He instantly felt at home. Mark Johnson had been a stellar hockey player through high school and business college.

"How I have missed this place." He drew in a deep breath to reacquaint himself with the smell of the sport.

"Let's get this done before I lose my seat out there and have to stand against the boards," Reverend Johnson said then indicated the players should bow their heads.

Archie looked around. "Please God, keep me out of the net tonight," he silently prayed, before Reverend Johnson could start.

"God, if only you were my direct boss, I'd be behind the Rangers' bench tonight," Reverend Johnson began. "You know, and I know, that the Rangers are a talented team. Tonight, they need to believe in themselves and the gifts you have bestowed upon them. Give them confidence out there on the ice and let them feel the heat of the devil on their tails as they play." Wendell snorted. Peter gave him a jab in the ribs. Reverend Johnson continued: "Please, Lord, guide them in using their abilities wisely." He paused and looked at the players. "That sums it up, other than let's make sure this doesn't get back to the elders. Amen."

"Amen," responded the Rangers.

Coach Ramsay thanked Reverend Johnson and saw him to the door. The Reverend abruptly turned, a twinkle in his eyes. "Speaking as a former coach, rather than a man of the cloth, I say this championship belongs to the Rangers. So go play some good hockey!"

Everyone laughed as Ramsay let the door swing shut and turned to deliver his own message. "You heard what the man said. This championship is ours because we are the better team and we have worked hard to be here. We deserve to be here. You all have talent, so use it tonight so we can have a victory celebration," Ramsay said. "Let's stay focused and take what's ours."

As he walked along the bench looking at their faces, he knew they believed his and the Reverend's words. The series would be over tonight. But for all his confidence in them, he couldn't quiet the uneasy feeling in the pit of his gut.

The mood inside the Flyers' dressing room was charged with tension. Coach Dyment looked at his players who were seated and waiting. He didn't try to persuade himself that they had the skills of their opponents, but they had proven that with the right strategy and breaks in the game they had what it took. He wanted the win as much as the players.

"We have to win tonight to stay alive." Coach Dyment got right to the point and then looked at Chester Craig.

"Everyone knows what needs to be done. So get out there and force a seventh game."

The fans were as jittery as the players. The bets had gone in favour of the Rangers wrapping the series up tonight. Though it was what the Rangers' fans wanted, the thought also disappointed them a little. Once the series was over, a long spring lay ahead of them, one filled with melting snow, dreary days of rain, and mud to the axles. It would be weeks before they could stand on the sidelines of the ball fields and cheer their favourite team on. But they had tonight.

The stands were jam-packed. Joining the old faces like Elliott and MacDonald were some fresh ones. Carol had informed her husband that if this was the night the championship was won, she and the boys would be in the stands to witness the victory. It meant disrupting the timing of the chore schedule, but for one night that was the way it was going to be. Coach Ramsay had agreed. He didn't dare say otherwise. Now sitting in the stands Carol didn't know who was more excited, she or the children. The boys were stuffing themselves with the rare treat of french fries and orange pop, while Carol was chewing gum a mile a minute. Tonight, she didn't care that her mother would say it was not ladylike, because tonight she was a fan of the Lot 16 Rangers whose handsome coach just happened to be her husband. She snapped her gum and blew a massive bubble. George's wife, Ruby, sat to Carol's left. Her parents were looking after the boys and all of them would be listening on the radio. Ruby was ready to make a racket for the Lot 16 Rangers. She had two kitchen pots in her oversized purse ready to bang together. Carol hoped her hearing would be intact at the end of the game.

Catherine Wall sat on Carol's right. This was her first game as a spectator. Keith had asked her to come and to travel in the truck with the team and fans. She had thought about saying no as she had done in the past. Catherine had never felt comfortable being in social settings with her students, but she figured if she were going to date a hockey player, then she would have to get over that. Much to her surprise, she had enjoyed the drive in the back of the packed truck, cozy from the cold with the heat of all the bodies. She listened intently to the chatter and learned a lot of things about people she had not known before.

Catherine wondered how her parents were going to react to learning their daughter was dating a hockey player who loaded potatoes on railcars and trapped rabbits. She laughed to herself to think of the look on her Supreme Court Judge father's face when she told him, but she was sure it would be nothing in comparison to the look on her proper society mother's face. Catherine was going home to Charlottetown for Easter and would break it to them then. But in truth, she didn't really give a damn what they thought. They had been all for the young up-and-coming lawyer that left her standing at the alter. And look how that had turned out.

Tonight, Catherine was going to follow Carol and Ruby's lead about how to behave at a hockey game. She wished Isabel had come, but the captain's wife said her nerves couldn't stand it, but she'd be by the radio.

It was game time when the clock struck eight. The starting lines of both teams came out of their respective boxes and skated to their positions on ice. The referee dropped the puck at centre ice and the play began. The Rangers concentrated on moving the puck into the Flyers' end and staying in front of their net zone. The Mount Pleasant players, struggling to move the puck out of their end, concentrated on hitting hard.

It didn't take long for the Rangers to put the first goal on the board. Daniel had moved the puck up from his end and passed it to George, who had moved it over to Charlie, who delivered it into the net. The crowd went wild with their favourite chant "Don't think twice. Lot 16 melt the ice!" but the Rangers didn't celebrate yet. They were a long way from the finish line.

The goal seemed to ignite the Flyers. Suddenly, they wanted to skate rather than hit. They successfully moved the puck out into the open and into the Rangers' end. The Rangers' defencemen stayed on it and made crisp, clean outlet passes. The forwards carried the puck back to the Flyers' end, but their defence managed to block the shots and guide it back out. It was on a breakaway that Mount Pleasant scored their first goal to tie the game just as the period ended.

"Tire them out with the speed of your skating. You know they don't have the same skating skills. Play cat and mouse with them. Jerk them around," Coach Ramsay told his players.

The Rangers, when they took to the ice, did just that. They passed the puck when obviously not necessary, causing the Mount Pleasant Flyers to be constantly changing directions, which was a killer for their ankle benders. Defence was communicating with the forward line and vice versa. At the halfway mark, Ernest stayed in the Rangers' end while Daniel initiated a breakout from the defensive zone. He carried the puck well up into the Flyers' end and gave the signal he was going to take it right to the net. Every opponent came for him, and just as they closed in, he slipped the puck to the left where George was in position to catch it on the edge of his stick. Meanwhile, Daniel skated backwards a short distance from the net, and George shot the puck straight across the net to the right where it was claimed by Wendell, who barely let it contact his stick before he moved it off to Peter in centre.

The Flyers were starting to scramble. The centreman and right winger came in on Peter, who did not aim for the net, but instead flipped the puck to Daniel, waiting behind them. Then he dodged to the right and zipped it between the goalie's skates, just like they'd practiced on Mick's Creek so many times.

They continued to skate circles around the Flyers throughout the rest of the period. The Lot 16 fans were on their feet, adding fuel to the fire, as they screamed the latest chant by the MacKinnon girls:

"He's our captain, don't you know? You're never sure where he'll go!"

The score was 2-1 for the Rangers at the start of the third period. Near the boards close to centre ice, Daniel saw a chance for a breakaway into the Mount Pleasant end. He eyed the puck which proved a mistake. He never saw Chester Craig come from the side. In an instant, the Mount Pleasant player cross-checked Daniel headfirst into the boards. Daniel's helmet flew off as he fell face first, bounced and fell again, his head making contact with the ice. The sickening sound of the thud put an instant end to the action. The crowd went silent as he lay there. The moments ticked by. Panic flooded Craig's body as shock registered on his face. Throughout the game, he had carried out his coach's wishes with pleasure, but this was far more than even he had planned. Willing him to get up Craig started towards Daniel's prone body, but quickly backed away.

"Daniel!" Peter threw his gloves on the ice and raced to his downed brother as loud Booos for the dirty play came from the stands. Dropping to his knees, he shook Daniel's shoulder.

"Daniel? Are you okay? Can you hear me?" Peter's voice shook as he sensed the referee and linesmen gathering close behind.

"Is he breathing?" The referee looked to Peter as the two men turned Daniel over. "I think he's just stunned," Peter said, seeing his brother's eyes flutter open. After several minutes, they helped Daniel to his knees, but that's as far as he could rise.

"You big lout, Chester Craig! I'll kick your behind!" An outraged Ethel Thompson had jumped to her feet, and against all odds, made herself heard over the crowd.

"Sit down, Ethel, for Pete's sake!" implored her dismayed husband.

"I'll sit when I want." Ethel pushed his hand away and pointed to the ice. "Get to the penalty box right now, boy," she shouted, triumphant when Chester Craig slunk off to the box.

"Forget the penalty box! Throw him out of the game!" yelled Carol, shaking her fists. The crowd took up the call. "Throw Craig out, throw Craig out!" they chanted, in unison, to the beat of the pots that Ruby vigorously pounded together. Catherine covered her ears.

"Leave our boy alone. He was playing the game!" Mount Pleasant fans had heard enough. The Flyers' players shouted in agreement, "Yeah, Chester was just playing the game." The Rangers dropped their gloves. Both coaches immediately called their players to their respective boxes to prevent a brawl. The linesmen breathed a sigh of relief as did the rink manager. Fists on the ice could mean fists in the stands.

With the support of Peter and Ernest, Daniel finally got to his feet and skated off the ice to the dressing room. It was obvious to all he was gone for the night but he was up. Surely that was a good sign. Isabel and her parents, glued to the radio, resumed breathing. The referee suspended Chester Craig for the rest of the game, and Coach Ramsay sent in Keith and Robert as replacements. The referee quickly called for the play to resume; he didn't want a delay giving the crowd an opportunity to become unruly.

Doctor Edward McNeil was waiting in the dressing room when Peter and Ernest lowered Daniel down onto the bench. He groaned from the pain, but still Daniel's thoughts were on the game. "Get back on the ice, guys. Quick!" he said and winced.

Peter looked over to Doctor McNeil. He signalled Peter to stay.

"I'm not leaving you, Daniel. Not until Doctor McNeil looks you over."

Ernest returned to the ice where it was quickly becoming apparent the distracted Rangers were losing their edge and the game was becoming Mount Pleasant's. The Flyers scored at the five minute mark of the resumed play, thus tying the game.

In the dressing room, Doctor McNeil looked in Daniel's eyes, felt over his head and neck, and asked a number of questions, including, "What's your wife's name?

"Isabel." Daniel's head cleared enough to realize she knew from listening to the radio. "Upset Isabel," he corrected himself.

Doctor McNeil turned to Peter. "Get Coach Ramsay's car and get him home and into bed as quickly as possible. He's going to have one hell of a headache and sore muscles and bruising for a few days."

"No, finish the game," Daniel said to Peter. "They need you to win. I can wait. Besides, I don't want to miss the celebration."

"You heard the Doctor. I need to get you home." Anger rose in Peter's chest. This wasn't the way the final game was supposed to go. Nothing was going right, and now Daniel was hurt. Percy was waiting for news outside the dressing room door, and on hearing the need to get Daniel home, brought the car to the back door of the rink. It took both men to get Daniel in the car as his legs refused to hold him. Shutting the door on Daniel, Peter turned to Percy, "What's happening on the ice?"

"The Flyers have tied the game." Percy kept it simple.

Peter got behind the wheel and looked across at his brother with his head back against the seat, eyes closed, his face pale and drawn with pain. Again, anger surged in Peter. He had heard his whole life not to expect things to be fair, but he still hung onto the hope that if you tried hard enough and were fair to others, everything would work out. Peter put the car in gear and slowly edged out of the parking lot, pausing for a moment so Daniel could lean out and vomit into the snow.

As the play went on, Ivan felt like he was alone on the ice. He was performing better than he ever had. How could he not with what was at stake? But Ivan was certain his luck was going to run out. Later, he thought about the saying that a man brings on what he thinks. Seconds before the period ended, he dove for the puck when he should have stayed standing and let Ernest intercept. The game ended with a 3-2 win for the Flyers. The series was tied 3-3.

Isabel ran out of the house, James at her heels, as soon as Peter pulled into the farmyard. The men got Daniel into the house and hefted him into bed. They then cleared out to let the women see to him.

"Good luck, Mr. MacArthur." Peter waved good-bye and rushed to the car. He felt somewhat bad leaving the older man alone, but Peter was beat, and didn't feel he could withstand a tongue lashing, especially for something not of his doing. He drove the car to the Ramsay farm, parked it and began the long walk home. Alone on the deserted road, he wondered what had unfolded at the rink after he and Daniel left. Were the Rangers enjoying the rewards of winning? He sure hoped so, and wished he and Daniel could be there, too.

However, it was not a victory party the brothers were missing. It was anything but.

CHAPTER 38

Daniel woke with a start. It took a minute to realize he was in his own bed and that the sun was peeking around the blind pulled down to keep the room dark. That meant it had to be late in the morning. Daniel knew by the quietness of the room that he was alone. Slowly, painfully, he lifted himself into a sitting position. The effort made him feel sick and dizzy. His head was throbbing. Daniel waited a minute before swinging his legs over the side of the bed to rest on the floor. He couldn't see that his face was black and blue, but was well aware that his eyes were swollen to slits in his face.

"Shit, what a mess," he muttered, trying to still the panic rising in him.

Daniel tried to stand just as the door opened. Isabel crossed over to him and set a basin of water on the bedside table before speaking.

"What do you think you're doing?" Her voice was controlled, but concerned.

She put her hand on his shoulder and gently pushed him back into a sitting position on the bed.

"I'm going to work." Sweat broke out on his brow.

"I don't think so. Work is the last place you're going today. Doctor McNeil said you have to stay quiet for a couple of days." Isabel gave him her no-nonsense look as she dipped a cloth into the basin.

"We need the money, Isabel," Daniel said. "The mortgage is coming due." He knew, though, that she was right, the pain in his head and body was just too great. He had never experienced anything like it.

Isabel stated the obvious. "Do you really think you can load potato bags in this state? Get back into bed—now." She wrung excess water from the cloth and waited as her husband lowered himself back against the pillows. He winced. Even their softness hurt his head. Isabel sat down beside him and gently washed and dried his swollen face, before rubbing ointment into the cuts and bruises. She rubbed his muscles with liniment and gave him a couple of tablets and a glass of milk.

"Did we win?" Daniel asked as he handed Isabel the empty glass.

She kept it simple, "No."

His spirit crashed. "I'm sorry, Isabel." Daniel reached for her hand as she straightened the blankets.

"You have nothing to be sorry for, Daniel. You were just playing a game you love." Isabel looked down at the man who had her whole heart.

"This wouldn't have happened if I had taken the deal." He avoided eye contact as he stroked her palm with his thumb.

"Just get some rest. You need sleep. We'll talk later." She held his hand and watched him drift off. She lifted his hand to her lips and placed a kiss on it.

Isabel bowed her head. "God, I know I don't talk with you enough," she whispered. "I remember you when something is going wrong and then I am angry and accusing. Reverend Johnson talks about the need to have gratitude and to find the sliver of light in the darkness. I need Daniel to be okay because he is my sliver of light." Her voice caught on a sob. "Please give me that, God. Please give me that."

Daniel woke the next day feeling stronger, but he was still unfit for work. Even though the swelling had gone down in his eyes, his face was still black and blue, and every part of his body was tender to the touch. But he was able to eat and could rest a little easier.

"When is the game?" He wanted to know.

"You won't be playing in the seventh game tomorrow night, Daniel. They will have to win it on their own."

He was too weak to argue with her. Isabel didn't remind him that the mortgage was also due tomorrow. Instead, she gave him one of Aunt Edith's sleeping pills. How ironic that the final game would be the same day as the mortgage was due. Isabel prayed the Rangers would come through on both counts.

The following morning Daniel's first thought was that it was the mortgage due date. Strange how he remembered when obviously he had missed days recovering. Daniel's head was still foggy and then everything flooded back. The Rangers had lost. The seventh game was tonight. Everyone was to have their money to Peter and Wendell by last evening. Peter was bringing it over this morning, and together they would go see Elliott. Though his muscles ached, the throb in his head was bearable, so Daniel got out of bed, dressed himself, and joined the rest of the family downstairs. The girls were excited to see him and wanted up on his knee, but Isabel told them they needed to be gentle with their father for a little longer.

"I'll bet he'd appreciate a kiss, though," she told Mary and Jeannie, and after covering his bruised cheeks with little pecks, the girls settled back on the old couch to resume their colouring.

After Isabel got Daniel his breakfast and he had settled on the rocker by the stove, she set about making bread at the kitchen table. It was usually a job she did in the pantry, but she wanted to be close to the girls and Daniel. Jessie and James were both away for the morning, and Isabel was missing the extra set of eyes to watch for mischief. But Daniel couldn't stay put. Every few minutes, he would gingerly get up from the rocker and limp to the window to pull back the light cotton curtain and look across the farmyard. Where was his brother?

"That's not going to get Peter here any faster, Daniel," Isabel said, sharply, just as anxious as he was. "Just sit down and rest."

But Daniel could not be still. He let the curtain drop and began to pace back and forth in front of the stove. "What's taking him so long? With the mortgage due today, I figured he would want to be at Elliott's at daybreak."

"Look, Daniel, we all know the mortgage is due today. He'll be here. You know Peter. He probably wants to string Elliott along as long as possible." Isabel tried to quiet the unease in her stomach.

"What did he say when he called earlier this morning?" Daniel wasn't convinced.

Isabel kept kneading the bread.

"He just said he and Wendell were double checking the total and then he would be here. You must be patient."

"I just want it to be over, and the quicker, the better." Daniel closed his eyes and sighed deeply.

"Seeing the look on Elliott's face should be worth the wait." Isabel gave him her best smile.

"You're probably right." Daniel returned her smile only to wince from the pain it caused. He went back to sit by the fire.

Isabel finished setting the bread, covered it with a clean dish towel and blanket, and placed it behind the stove to rise. She then removed the ironing board from the kitchen closet. She set the board up near the stove and began to iron the basket of clothing. It was a chore that soothed her.

Daniel had joined the girls on the couch and was colouring with them when Peter finally let himself into the porch and came directly into the kitchen. He stood just inside the door, leaving it wide open.

"Quick, shut the door. Are you trying to heat the outside?" Isabel frowned.

Her cutting tone unnerved him. "Sorry. I didn't think."

Peter turned round to close the door. Just once, he would like not to feel intimidated by Isabel. He didn't know what it was, but when he was around her, he lost his confidence. No other woman did that to him, and Peter resented the fact.

"Uncle Peter, Uncle Peter, do you have a treat for us?" Mary and Jeannie attacked their uncle.

"Sure do. Now where did I put that special something?" Peter pretended to give the matter serious thought as the girls wriggled about. "You could try reaching in my coat pocket . . . but be careful it doesn't bite you!"

The girls squealed with excitement as Peter bent down so they could reach into his coat pockets. They each pulled out a small brown paper package.

"Your Grannie MacDougall made your favourite sugar cookies," he said as the girls ripped into the packages. "Although I think she would want you to share with me." He put on a hopeful face.

"We know you had your cookies on the way here!" They giggled.

Peter grinned. “You girls are so smart. I can’t trick you anymore.”

Jeannie and Mary took their cookies and went back over to their colouring books.

“Are you coming in for a minute, or will we go straight to Elliott’s?” Daniel rose from the couch slowly, trying, as best he could, to hide that he was still in considerable pain.

“We need to talk first.” Peter looked down at the floor, and then back up at his brother and then at Isabel. He took a deep breath.

“You don’t have the money, do you?” Isabel left her place at the ironing board to stand beside Daniel. She put her hands on her hips and looked Peter straight in the eye.

“Relax, Isabel. Of course he has the money.” Daniel half turned. “Right, Peter?”

But Peter took his time. He reached inside his winter coat and took an envelope from the breast pocket of his shirt before he replied.

“She’s partially right. We have $1,145.00 of the $1,200.00. I don’t know what to say, Daniel. If we only had one more week, we could probably scratch up the remaining $55.”

Daniel went as white as the envelope in his brother’s hand.

“It’s really no surprise. What else could you expect of a bunch of hockey players?” Isabel fairly spat out.

“Isabel.” Daniel spoke but one word.

Peter, however, couldn’t hold back. He was as devastated and frustrated by the shortfall as anyone else, and now every past grievance with his sister-in-law boiled to the surface. “It wasn’t just us hockey players, Isabel,” he all but shouted. “You were part of the effort, as were your parents, my parents, and the whole goddamn community. Even Elliott contributed. We raised $1,145 in four weeks ON TOP of working and playing hockey and dealing with everything else in life. That's a lot of money to raise in the dead of winter on PEI, and you know it, so get off your high horse for once."

Isabel went to fire back, but could not think of anything to say.

Peter turned to Daniel. "I'm really sorry, Daniel. You have no idea how much so. There has to be some way we can get the money by day's end."

"And pigs fly at midnight!" Isabel hooted.

"Let's just stay calm." Daniel raised a hand to silence them. "We've over $1,100 in cash. Elliott should be happy to get that. It's likely more than he needs to solve his problems. Fifty-five dollars shouldn't be a big deal. He'll be decent enough to give me a little time on the remaining amount."

"Why do you continue to presume there's any goodness in Elliott?" Peter shook his head in frustration.

"Because there's some good in everyone, however small it might be." Daniel moved across the kitchen as quickly as he could and reached for his coat and boots.

"I sure hope you're right, but I have to side with Peter on this one." Isabel's tone expressed her doubt.

Peter handed Daniel the envelope of money "I sure hope you're right."

CHAPTER 39

From the kitchen window, Isabel watched the two men walk across the yard and climb into Peter's car.

"Mommy?" She turned to her daughters standing next to her.

"Where did Daddy and Uncle Peter go? Not Montreal, I hope," Jeannie's voice was filled with trepidation.

Isabel smiled at the little girl. "No, Daddy has not gone to Montreal." She turned to look out the window to watch the car stop at the end of the lane and then turn onto the road. Under her breath she whispered, "Not yet, anyway."

She looked back at the worried face of her daughters. "He would never go to Montreal without saying good-bye to his beautiful girls."

Jeannie looked up at her mother. "Mary and I will share our piggy banks with you and Daddy."

"Yes!" Mary agreed.

Isabel got down on her knees and pulled the two girls to her in a big hug. "Thank you, girls," she whispered, her heart nearly breaking.

Out on the road, Daniel and Peter drove in silence. Neither could think of anything to say that mattered or could alleviate the tension. Too soon, they were at the store. Peter parked the car and shut off the engine. They sat for several minutes. Daniel was the first to open his door and slowly walk to the store, Peter following right behind. The bell over the door rang when they entered. Daniel quickly scanned the store and saw that Elliott was behind the counter doing accounting work. He was alone in the store, for which Daniel was grateful. Elliott quickly glanced up to see who had entered. When he saw that it was Daniel and Peter, he returned to his books.

Peter stayed by the door and leaned against the frame with his hands in the pockets of his winter coat, while Daniel approached Elliott. The storekeeper continued to ignore him. Daniel reached into his jacket pocket and removed the envelope of money, and laid it on the counter. Elliott glanced at it and then back at his books, still without a word.

"Here is $1,145 of the $1,200 owed on the mortgage." Daniel fought to keep his voice calm, even, and hopeful. "I'd like to ask for a few days more to raise the rest."

Elliott picked up the envelope, removed the money, and flipped through the bills.

He appeared to be thinking as he put the money back in the envelope and placed it on the counter. "Sorry. I called for payment in full," he said.

Anger and disappointment flashed across Daniel's face, before he got his expression back under control. He persisted.

"It's nearly all there. Would a few days' grace hurt you, Elliott?"

"Maybe not, but I'm not willing to give it. You dropped your end of the deal." Elliott looked at Daniel with not an ounce of shame or remorse, then reached for the envelope on the counter. As his hand closed over it, Daniel placed his hand on top of the storekeeper's. As the two men locked eyes, Daniel pressed down with such force, that Elliott could not move either the envelope or his hand from the counter. A flicker of pain passed across Elliott's face, but it was quickly replaced with anger.

"The money's mine," he snarled. "You owe it to me."

Although Daniel was sickened at the actual physical contact with Elliott, he increased pressure on the storekeeper's hand. Peter straightened from his leaning stance against the doorframe.

"I think you've got all you're getting, Elliott," Daniel said.

For a moment, it looked like the older man was going to try and hold his ground. Realizing he was alone with the two younger men, fear flickered in his eyes. "Fine. Take it and get out."

Daniel lifted his hand just enough for Elliott to slide his out. He picked up the envelope and turned to walk towards the door. He handed the envelope to Peter and let himself out of the store. Peter did not follow immediately. He stood looking at Elliott who hadn't moved behind the counter. After what seemed an eternity, Peter took a step towards Elliott who automatically took a step back. Peter paused and unclenched his hands. With effort, he reined in his rage, but not the look of contempt that spread across his face. "You're a small man, Charles Elliott, no doubt about that." Finally, Peter turned and walked from the store, allowing the door to slam behind him. The ringing bell was all that disturbed the silence within.

Daniel didn't say a word when Peter slipped behind the wheel. Peter figured it was best to let the silence be. He started the car, backed it from the parking space, and turned onto the road towards the MacArthur farm. As they approached what was to have been his home, Daniel put his hand on Peter's arm.

"Stop. Please."

Although he wanted to argue with Daniel as to why he was inflicting more pain on himself, Peter obliged. After he parked, they just sat and looked at the unfinished house and the snow-covered land. Tears ran down Peter's cheeks, but he didn't brush them away in case Daniel saw. After a few minutes, Daniel opened the passenger door and got out.

"I'll walk home," he said.

Peter hated the thought of leaving his injured brother, but respecting Daniel's need to be alone, he drove away. More tears came as Peter glanced at his brother in the rearview mirror.

When Peter was out of sight, Daniel walked toward what should have been his family's house. At the door, he stopped to collect himself and then went inside to the kitchen. The room was cold, but the shiver that went through him came from inside of him. Slowly, Daniel walked around the room touching the walls that still had the fine wood finish put there years ago by the builder. He felt the smoothness of the brick in the chimney that he and Peter had started building. He entered the small room off the kitchen that would have served as the living room and thought about how Isabel would have arranged her Aunt Edith's couch and chair. Back in the kitchen, Daniel picked up a chunk of lumber and held one end tightly in his hands, contemplating. It would be so easy to swing it about until he had smashed everything in the place. Elliott deserved nothing less.

But Daniel didn't have it in him to destroy the work that had been done or the beauty of the house. He dropped the piece of wood and climbed the stairs to inspect the second floor. It still waited to be framed up for bedrooms and a small bath. He'd been looking forward to doing it. To creating a beautiful bedroom for he and Isabel to share. For the girls. Daniel stopped in front of a window, and looked out across the field that held his dreams of a future. There were bare patches amongst the snow coverage, a sign that winter hibernation was coming to a close and the earth would again awaken. His gaze stopped at the tree line at the back of the property. The sun filtered through the trees with a whisper of promise.

It was here that Isabel found him. Peter had gone to tell her what had taken place and where Daniel was. He had given her his car to come back while he stayed with the girls. She had rushed into the house out of breath, her coat unbuttoned, fearful of what she might find. Daniel didn't turn when she came up the stairs, but continued to stare out the window.

"Daniel?" She walked over to stand behind him and wrapped her arms around his waist. Together, without words, they looked out.

CHAPTER 40

As dusk fell, Percy's truck waited at the school with the engine running. Everyone was on board except Daniel. The players waited in silence, leaving the chatter to the fans who were travelling with them. They had no wish for the fans to learn what had gone on the past few weeks or that the fundraising mission had failed.

Seeing that they were already ten minutes past the time they should have left, Percy turned to his passengers. "We can't wait any longer for Daniel," he said putting the truck in gear and pulling onto the road.

"He's not coming," Ernest whispered to Keith.

"Why would he? We failed him." Keith closed his eyes and let his head drop against the side of the box.

"Daniel just can't play hurt. Doctor McNeil said so." Peter made a stab at lightening the atmosphere.

The hum of the truck tires was the only response he got. No Ranger had any spirit to play the coming game.

Daniel was alone in the kitchen of the MacArthur farmhouse. Isabel was upstairs getting the girls ready for bed, while Jessie sewed at the dining room table, and James sat by the stove and read the paper aloud to her as she worked. They felt Daniel and Isabel needed the space.

Daniel paced back and forth across the green and white tiles of the floor. He kept glancing at the clock on the wall. He knew exactly what time the truck was leaving, but felt no relief when the departure time came and went. When he and Isabel had finally left their unfinished house, Daniel told her she need not worry. He had no intentions of playing the final game as he had nothing left to give. Daniel said that he would return all the money to the individuals who raised it, and the fundraising money really would be money for the team. Isabel figured she could at least give thanks that he wasn't insisting on playing. Her husband was in no condition and could end up further hurt.

Daniel kept up the pacing though he wanted to settle down, because his head was starting to ache again. He stopped and stood still to centre himself. Suddenly, Daniel knew what he had to do. He walked out to the porch and grabbed the hockey bag and came back into the kitchen to pack it with the gear still hanging behind the kitchen range following the last game.

"What are you doing?" Isabel walked in as he was putting the last of the gear in the bag.

"That should be obvious. I'm going to the rink." Daniel pulled the zipper across the bag.

"You can't play in the shape you're in." She planted herself between him and the door. "To even try is reckless and stupid."

"I'm fine. And I'm not missing the final game." Daniel grabbed his boots warming at the front of the stove, and almost tumbled forward. As he regained his balance, he sat on the rocker to put them on.

"Your family needs you, Daniel." Isabel tried to be the voice of reason.

But Daniel was resolute.

"You're willing to risk long-term injuries for a hockey team that let you down?" Isabel was incredulous.

Daniel tied his laces and stood before replying. "Tonight's game is not about the team, and it's not about my family." He grabbed his coat and pulled it on. “It’s about me. This game is for me.”

Before Isabel could speak again, Daniel picked up the hockey bag and strode out of the house. Isabel was stunned. In all their time together, Daniel had never left for a hockey game without a proper goodbye, a hug, and the promise of “I’ll see you soon.” She ran to the window and caught a glimpse of the taillights of the car as he drove away. She burst into angry tears.

Jessie and James had overheard the whole exchange, but gave their daughter a minute to herself.

“I’ll go,” Jessie said, and James nodded. Though it had been years since she had held her daughter, Jessie pulled Isabel into her arms and let her sob.

“Why is he doing this, Mom?” Isabel said, when her tears subsided.

“Right now, Daniel feels a total failure.” Jessie continued to hold her daughter to her and stroked her hair. “This game is about proving to himself he’s still a man.”

“That makes no sense.” Isabel lifted her head to look at her mother.

“Men don’t make a lot of sense a lot of the time,” Jessie agreed. “But regardless of how you feel, tonight Daniel needs you to be his biggest fan. So, wipe those tears and get your coat on, and your father will take you to the game.” She handed Isabel a tissue.

“The girls?” Isabel struggled to keep from crying again.

“I’ll take care of the girls. Whatever happens tonight or tomorrow, Isabel, remember you have a good man in Daniel.”

Isabel looked at the woman who never failed to surprise her. Just when she thought she had Jessie figured out, she would throw her another curveball. She hugged her mother. “Thank you, Mom—for everything.”

CHAPTER 41

The dressing room of the Rangers was filled with silence though the players were busy dressing and Coach Ramsay was pacing the floor. He eventually came to a stop and turned to the players.

"Who's taking Craig out?" he wanted to know. No one was surprised by the question.

"I want the pleasure." Peter, in the midst of pulling his sweater over his head, said. He already had a plan.

"I'm better able to handle the job," Keith quickly jumped in.

"Craig's mine. Nobody else touches him."

Everyone was startled at the familiar voice. With all eyes focused on Coach Ramsay, none of the players had noticed that Daniel had joined them in the dressing room.

"Daniel!" The team greeted the welcome sight of their captain. "You're here!"

"Yeah, it's me in the flesh—bruised, but not totally beaten." Daniel grinned. "You guys ready to win this championship?"

A resounding YES! filled the dressing room and the boys rushed towards Daniel to hug him, but he raised his hands. "Don't anybody even think of touching me," he said. Everyone backed away and Daniel proceeded to the bench and began to strip down. The other players saw that it was not just his face that was bruised, but his shoulders and chest as well.

"You sure about this, Captain?" Coach Ramsay wanted to know.

"Damn right."

"Keep it clean?" Coach Ramsay looked at the floor and then back at the young man who had lost so much in one day.

"Wouldn't have it any other way." Daniel slipped on his helmet and fastened the strap under his chin.

As with the first six games, the rink was filled to beyond capacity, and the manager was once again both elated and terrified. The only thing that calmed him was knowing the stands were constructed with heavy Island lumber by skillful carpenters. Nothing was going to collapse. Hopefully. People were sitting and standing wherever they could find space. No one was annoyed about being jammed close together or being jostled. It seemed to add to the excitement of what was to come.

Carol, Ruby, and their children were back even though it was a school night. So was their teacher. Catherine thought maybe watching hockey, or at least one particular hockey player, wasn't that bad a pastime after all. The big surprise of the evening was that Duncan and Allison MacDougall were also seated with the Rangers' fans. Rarely did they come to their sons' games, citing the stress of the play. However, knowing Daniel would not be on the ice, they wanted to show Peter their support.

James and Isabel managed to secure seats on the end of a row high up in the stands giving them an excellent view of the entire ice surface, which made Isabel uneasy. She couldn't bear to see Daniel on the ice in his condition, and yet she knew she would not be able to turn her eyes away. She saw Charles Elliott and his wife and children in the centre of the row down from them. Her muscles tightened with anger. She had to force herself to breathe deeply and look away from him.

"Look who else is here."

James touched her arm and pointed out Malcolm MacDonald and his wife, sitting midway up the stands on the opposite side of the rink. Isabel looked at the couple, stylish in their dress and relaxed in their manner. But she didn't want to look at Malcolm MacDonald, either, to be reminded of his offer. Still, she couldn't look away. With sudden clarity, she saw the arrogance in his face, and instinctively knew Daniel was right in refusing the terms. She returned her gaze to Elliott. The two men were cut from the same cloth. Both were opportunistic, justified in taking what they wanted. Her respect for Daniel increased tenfold. Her husband had understood the loss of himself couldn't be balanced with the achievement of a dream, no matter how much he wanted it. Calmness settled over Isabel. She and Daniel would rise again. Stronger. Better.

James then brought her attention to a number of younger fans down front waving small homemade signs supporting the Rangers. Suddenly, Isabel felt at home in the crush of the crowd. She spotted Catherine, a woman bravely building a new life, and Carol, a mover and a shaker, and Ruby, not afraid to make noise with her pots. She saw Percy over by the entrance and wondered what he was up to. Not far from him stood Reverend Johnson, head bowed. Could he really be praying in the midst of a packed rink? Isabel hoped so and added her own silent prayer: "Protect Daniel."

The exact moment the hands of the clock touched eight, the two teams came out of their respective dressing rooms and spilled onto the ice. They had three minutes of skating time to warm up before they were to go to their boxes, leaving only the first shifts on the ice.

The atmosphere of the rink was charged. The crowd pounded the boards, and waved signs that read "Proud of the Mount Pleasant Flyers," "Flyers Show the Rangers Your Might," "Go Rangers, Go," "Flyers take Flight," "Rangers Melt the Ice." The Rangers' fans chanted, "Rangers, Rangers Make it Right. Take the Trophy Home Tonight!" only to have the Flyers' fans respond, "Flyers, Flyers, Show Your Might. Make the Lot 16 Rangers Cry Tonight!" Back and forth the fans faced off in words, each time rising in volume in an attempt to drown out the other side.

Duncan and Allison, upon spotting Daniel, reached for each other's hands, and squeezed them tightly together. Then, they rose from their seats and raised their arms triumphantly, and joined the chanting crowd.

It was obvious to all that Daniel was stiff with soreness and pain, but his bruised face was set with determination. Sticking to the centre of the ice, he slowly skated the length of the rink and back again, giving his muscles a chance to stretch. Daniel didn't look at the fans. He just wanted to shut them out. But, as Daniel made his second rotation of the rink, he sensed something, and began to scan the stands until he found Isabel. They made eye contact and held the look. She flashed him a brilliant smile and a nod of approval. Daniel smiled back before turning his attention to centre ice. A whistle blew, and those players not on the first lines skated to their respective boxes. The opposing players skated into their positions, the puck was dropped, and the game was underway.

The Flyers had their heart in it, and so did the Rangers, now that they had their captain. Daniel was surprised at how quickly he got his feet under him. His skates became an extension of his body, connecting him to the ice. As he pushed the blades hard against the surface, he felt it yield to his strength, and enable the smoothness and confidence of his stride. The joyful connection unlocked Daniel's muscles and set them free.

The bruises lost their power. Daniel felt the lightness and energy that came with passion for the game.

Though the fans were screaming for more, Daniel didn't push himself in the first period, because he wanted to be sure he could last the game. But he still played his position dependably, and covered Ivan skilfully, leaving the hard digging to Ernest and the forward line. Daniel noticed that Craig kept his distance, which made a payback opportunity difficult. But Daniel wasn't worried. He could be patient. There was plenty of time.

The first period ended scoreless. Fans on both sides of the rink screamed "Give Us More, Give Us More. Give Us what we Paid for at the Door!" before visiting the canteen and the washrooms. Many milled about talking and betting among themselves. Thankfully, no fights broke out. Both coaches were in the dressing rooms going over every second of the first period to point out what should have and shouldn't have been done. Daniel downed a couple of aspirin and sat quietly waiting for the siren to announce it was time to get back on the ice.

Peter, unassisted, scored in the first minute of the second period. Ernest assisted Wendell in delivering the second goal. Wendell seemed surprised by his own success. The Rangers held the Flyers from getting on the board. Daniel made certain of that. The Rangers' fans upped the noise level, "You can knock our captain down, but you can't keep our Captain down. Just so you know," which made his head throb a little worse. He hoped the aspirin would soon kick in. But, the noise was feeding him and giving him the energy and strength to channel his rage into something constructive. Daniel knew he couldn't let the anger go rogue.

Well into the period, a Mount Pleasant player got a breakaway and skilfully slipped the puck by Ivan's skate and into the net. Then in the last seconds of the dying period, Chester Craig somehow scored to tie the game. The goal went to his head as he forgot all his earlier caution in the game. Craig displayed his cockiness by saluting the Rangers' bench as the siren sounded and fans stomped their feet and shouted.

"Flyers, Flyers, show your might, make the Rangers cry tonight!"

"Rangers, Rangers, make it right, take the trophy home tonight."

Reverend Johnson had loosened his clerical collar earlier, but now removed it to wipe the perspiration from the back of his neck. Fans seated near Ruby found their heads ringing long after the period was over from her banging on her pots so much. Isabel felt sick and was holding her father's hand so hard he was sure it was turning blue inside his mitten. The tie was where things had gone wrong in game six.

The ritual of the period break was carried out yet again, and the third period got underway. After five minutes on the clock, Daniel seized his opportunity. There was a loose puck at centre ice . . . and from opposite ends, both Daniel and Craig were skating at it. But Daniel was not playing the puck. He was playing Chester Craig. Finally.

Still high from his previous goal, Craig was solely focused on the puck, and went in with his head down. He failed to see the proximity of the Rangers' Captain, leaving him totally unprepared for Daniel's shoulder in the centre of his chest.

"Ouuufff." Craig gasped aloud before dropping to the ice winded. With Craig down for the count, Daniel flipped the puck to Peter who broke over the opposing blue line and, shooting low to the stick side, scored.

"He's our Captain don't you know? Mount Pleasant saw his might when he made poor Craig cry tonight!" Ecstatic Rangers' fans were on their feet in an instant.

Coach Ramsay gave a sigh of relief. Daniel had kept it clean.

"Way to go, Danny Boy!" said Jessie, listening to the commentary on the radio. In the wild frenzy no one, other than his mother, paid much attention to Craig, who by this time was back on his feet and skating off the ice. The last thing he wanted to do was puke in front of the crowd from Daniel's blow.

When he saw that Craig had made it to the Flyers' box, Daniel skated past to give him a small salute. Craig dropped his head. Sick as he might feel to his stomach from the blow Daniel had delivered, he was wise enough to know he had gotten off lightly. He also knew he was done for the night. Chester Craig had no plans to rush back onto the ice, and Coach Dyment had no intention of asking him to do so.

Having settled his score with Craig, Daniel began to play hockey as though driven by a power greater than himself. He put all his thoughts and energy into the game. The Mount Pleasant players couldn't contain him. They were in truth leery, for clearly the Rangers' captain meant business. They knew their teammate had fully earned being brought to his knees, but they were not sure Daniel was in the mood to leave it there. They tried to keep the puck from getting to him, rather than having to take it from him. Daniel's own teammates had caught his intense spirit and were doing their jobs in the right place at the right time. There was only three words the Rangers uttered on the ice, "Cover Ivan" and "Pass."

Behind the bench, Coach Ramsay could hardly grasp the speed of the play. His pacing and gum chewing had also grown faster. His players rapidly passed the puck from Ranger to Ranger making it difficult for the Flyers to take it off any one player. They played hard around the Flyers' net, testing the goaltender to the extreme. But the goalie stayed on top of the many attempted shots, cursing aloud at his teammates to get the puck out of their end.

Finally, Daniel claimed the puck, skated around the Mount Pleasant defenceman coming straight for him, and with a quick backhand shot, aimed for the top right-hand corner of the net. In the stands, Isabel leapt to her feet, her hand to her mouth, Ruby forgot to bang her pots, Reverend Johnson twisted the clerical collar in his hands, Duncan and Allison covered their eyes, and Charles Elliott moved to the edge of his seat. The puck appeared to travel in slow motion, suspended in midair, before it dented the twines of the net. The radio commentator yelled over the airwaves that the Rangers' captain, Daniel MacDougall, had scored.

BUZZZ! The clock ran out. The crowd went wild, and the Rangers piled on top of each other in the middle of the ice as Coach Ramsay came running out onto the ice to join them. Seven games, but the championship was theirs.

Daniel skated around the circle of men.

CHAPTER 42

The Mount Pleasant Flyers skated slowly to their box after the buzzer. Some sat down while others remained on the ice close to the box, fighting back tears for having lost by one goal in the seventh game. Coach Dyment didn't try to speak. He felt it best to stay silent out of fear at what he might say to his players. As he watched Coach Ramsay running around his players, he wondered if he, himself, had another season in him.

"The Lot 16 Rangers are taking home the trophy tonight!" The Rangers' fans kept up a thundering noise of foot stomping, slapping the boards, and chanting, while the Flyers' fans looked miserable.

Eventually, the Rangers also made their way to their box to wait for the rink to be set up for the final award ceremony.

Fans kept the excitement alive while rink rats carried a table and microphone out to the centre line and then unrolled a narrow red runner from the gate at the boards to the table. Finally, they carefully transported a large trophy and set it in the centre of the table.

Two middle-aged men in business suits, dress coats, and hats made their way out and the League President, Jack Simpson, signalled the two teams to skate to their respective blue lines and line up. When everyone was in place, Simpson raised his hands for silence.

"The level of play this season in the C division has been one of excellence," he said, when a hush fell over the rink. "The playoffs were no exception. One couldn't have asked for more in a game than we were given tonight. As league president, I extend congratulations to both our finalists for a great series. Of course, there can only be one winner. Congratulations to the Lot 16 Rangers, winners of the C.C. Baker Trophy and the Island's new Intermediate C champions."

Cheers from the crowd forced him to pause. "I ask Rangers' Coach, Ronald Ramsay, and Team Captain, Daniel MacDougall, to come to centre ice to accept the trophy from Mr. Baker."

Coach Ramsay, a broad smile on his face, moved with Daniel to centre ice. Daniel accepted the trophy from Mr. Baker and both men exchanged handshakes with the league president and sponsor. Though the trophy felt good in his hands, it didn't push aside a deeper hurt, but he determined that no one would know that but himself. Daniel left Coach Ramsay at centre ice and skated back to the Rangers' line to hand the trophy to Ernest, who kissed it and passed it on. It made its way down the line with the crowd cheering.

"This is the moment every coach dreams about." Coach Ramsay was now at the microphone and scanned the arena before looking over at his Rangers. "I thank my team for giving it to me. We have had an amazing season and what a great win tonight." His voice trembled, and he paused to collect himself. "I want to thank the Mount Pleasant Flyers and Coach Dyment for an exciting playoff series. They were worthy opponents," he finished. Fans of both teams clapped.

"Three cheers for Coach Ramsay!" the crowd shouted, and led everyone in a few rounds of cheering. When they finished, the Coach held up his hands, asking for another moment of silence.

"Every one of my players gave 100 percent to the team," Coach Ramsay continued. "They had the passion and the will to win. We especially had great leadership in our captain, Daniel MacDougall. These past weeks have been very difficult for him. His mortgage on the land on which he hoped to build a farm and a home for his family was suddenly and unexpectedly called in, though no payment had ever been missed." You could hear a pin drop when the Coach paused to let his words sink in. High up in the stands, Charles Elliott nervously squirmed in his seat.

"For a while, Daniel thought he would have to quit the Rangers to work another job to make the money he needed," Coach Ramsay continued. Malcolm MacDonald now squirmed in his seat.

Standing on the blue line, shock waves rippled through Daniel's body. What the hell was Coach Ramsay doing talking about his very private business? Had he lost his mind? How could he betray him this way when he had delivered the championship? Isabel would be furious. He found her face in the crowd. She wore a horrified expression. Daniel made a move to skate over to the Coach, but Peter placed a hand on his shoulder and motioned him to stay put.

"Let me go, dammit!" Daniel tried to shake off his brother, but Peter held on tight. Daniel winced as Peter's fingers dug into his injured shoulder.

Coach Ramsay glanced at his captain briefly before looking back out at the crowd. He knew exactly what was going through Daniel's mind.

"The team and I selfishly pressured Daniel to stay and lead us through the playoffs—that's how badly we wanted this championship," the Coach continued. "In return, we said we would raise the remaining mortgage money." Coach Ramsay paused for a moment and looked down at the ice before looking directly back at Daniel. "Being a man who believes in honouring his commitments, Daniel took a big risk and stayed. I have little doubt it is for this reason that we claimed the C.C. Baker Trophy tonight."

"Unfortunately, though the team worked hard to raise the money, we didn't make it. As of this morning, the due date of the mortgage, we were fifty-five dollars short," the Coach said. "It has been a difficult day for everyone involved."

A murmur ran through the crowd. "Unfair!" someone shouted from the stands.

"But where there is a will, there is a way. Our goalie, Ivan, thought of our fans who have faithfully supported us over the years, and are a special part of our family. And so we turned to you. Tonight as you arrived, Percy MacLean, our driver, asked if you wanted to contribute to the cause, and the response was more than we could have ever hoped for. Even the good people of Mount Pleasant contributed, because Islanders help Islanders." The crowd clapped their approval.

"Because of your generous donations, I am holding in my hand the full amount that Daniel owes on his mortgage, which he has until midnight today to pay." The Coach motioned for Daniel to come forward. "Please give our captain a special round of applause while he accepts this gift from all of you: his team, his fans, his friends, his neighbours, and his family."

In the stands, Isabel turned to her father and began to sob. James gathered her to him and let her bury her head in his shoulder just like she had so often done as a child.

Daniel was frozen in place while the entire arena erupted in cheering. His aching head had to be playing tricks on him. No, this could not be happening. But his teammates were motioning for him to skate over to the coach, so surely it had to be true. As he did so, the crowd roared. Coach Ramsay placed the envelope in Daniel's hand and clapped him on the back, then again motioned for silence. "We're really helping two men in our community tonight. Charles Elliott, our storekeeper, holds Daniel's mortgage, and only called it after facing difficulties of his own. Charles has always been a community man, and there for many of us so, I know how difficult it must have been for him to call in Daniel's mortgage. Therefore, it feels really good that not only are we helping Daniel, but we are helping Charles, one of the Rangers' biggest fans. I just want to say thanks to Charles for supporting us tonight and through the years of building this team. Please come down from the stands to receive your money, Charles." Coach Ramsay motioned for Charles Elliott to join them on the ice.

"We're having financial trouble? You never said anything to me." A surprised Mrs. Elliott turned to look at her husband.

"Later," Elliott growled under his breath while giving her a sharp look.

Reluctantly he stood and with all eyes on him made his way down from the stands to the ice surface. As Elliott stepped onto the carpet, he stumbled, but Keith rushed to his assistance and guided him right to centre ice, where the man then stood awkwardly between Daniel and Coach Ramsay. Elliott's tension increased when Daniel moved to the microphone. He was now certain Daniel knew the truth of the matter. Was the bugger going to expose everything and ruin him in front of everyone? A chill went up his spine. Malcolm MacDonald stirred in his seat. Discomfort was not a feeling he was overly familiar with, but he was feeling it deeply at the moment.

Daniel was not used to talking in front of crowds and certainly not about private matters. He felt awkward in responding to an outpouring of generosity. He knew he needed to effectively communicate his deep gratitude.

"I'm not sure I can fully express what I feel right now," he said, his voice trembling. "But it sure feels good. I owe tremendous thanks to everyone who has helped me. I have to admit it is difficult for me to feel worthy of that help, but I am learning that my wife is right." He sought Isabel out in the stands. "There is no weakness in asking for a hand when you need it: rather, it is a sign of strength. There can be no shame in that. So once again—on behalf of me and my family, I thank each and every one of you."

Daniel turned to Elliott and looked directly into his face as he handed him the envelope and extended his other hand to shake the man's hand. The storekeeper held back for a moment and then, knowing he had no choice, tentatively put his hand in Daniel's. The fans cheered and clapped and stamped their feet. Even the Flyers joined in celebrating a good turn. Isabel kept hugging her father, tears streaming down her face.

"Daniel and I will drop by the store in the morning to pick up the signed-off mortgage. Thanks again for your support, Charles." Coach Ramsay informed Elliott who just nodded and then looked for the quickest exit from the building. During the walk from the ice Elliott felt the many questioning eyes on him. He figured that discomfort would likely be nothing compared to what his wife was going to put him through when they got home. He briefly looked up to the cold stare of Malcolm MacDonald directly on him. Elliott dropped his head and kept on moving, just wanting to be back on solid ground.

MacDonald was annoyed but he knew when he'd been outmanoeuvred. He even allowed himself a flicker of a smile. For once he hadn't got what he wanted, but neither had Elliott. At least that counted for something.

On the ice, Daniel shook the hand of every Ranger and Coach Ramsay. Then he skated over to the Flyers' line and went down it, shaking each hand, including Craig's, and thanking them for a great series. Following his lead, the other Rangers did the same, and then both teams dispersed from the ice without incident, much to the relief of the rink manager and the police, who had prepared for trouble.

"It just goes to show that there's unpredictability in the predictable," the police chief was overheard saying.

CHAPTER 43

In the Rangers' dressing room everyone was talking at once about the goals, Daniel's play on Chester Craig, the look on Elliott's face, and the fans helping with that last fifty-five dollars. They pounded Ivan on the back for such brilliant thinking while crediting Wendell with having come up with the team scheme in the first place.

Reverend Johnson slipped into the dressing room and stood against the wall listening to the talk with a grin on his face. He was thankful that Ivan had grasped the idea he had planted in his ear earlier that day about dedicated fans and how far they would go to support a winning team. How fortunate this morning that he had picked up the phone to make a call on the party line and heard Elliott telling someone that the lame duck was fifty-five dollars short and they could finalize the business. The minister had no interest in anyone's business unless they chose to tell him, but today's conversation had caught his attention. And Elliot had no clue he'd been overheard.

Reverend Johnson had learned of the team's deal with Daniel from a fearful Wendell. Every night and morning since he had prayed for a successful outcome. How fortunate Ivan's mother had invited him to tea today, and without betraying anyone's privacy, he talked with Ivan. Now, standing in the dressing room sharing in the victories, Reverend Johnson felt the stress of the day slip from his shoulders. It didn't matter that he could never tell anyone about his involvement.

Leaving the rink, the Rangers' fans couldn't contain their excitement. They hugged and congratulated each other as though it was them that scored the winning goal. But they had a right to be proud and excited. Their energy and support had propelled the Rangers to the winning of the C.C. Baker Trophy. The fans had spent hours travelling in the truck over bumpy roads, and sitting in cold rinks, and wondering if they could end up with a black eye in the stands. They rightly deserved to share in the high of the victory. And they had saved Daniel's dream.

Ruby continued to bang on her pots, while Carol accepted accolades on behalf of her husband. In the stands, Catherine kept children occupied with a spelling bee while their parents socialized. Since it was all hockey words and the names of players, the children thought it great fun.

James hugged his daughter, who wanted to wait for Daniel, and left for home. He couldn't wait to tell Jessie the news that the mortgage was paid. The radio station had not broadcast that part of the evening at the request of Coach Ramsay. Daniel had his land, Isabel, a house of her own, and Mary and Jeannie would be only a short distance away from their fond grandparents. James knew that he and Jessie would miss Isabel and her family and the life they brought to the old farmhouse, but they would also be happy for them. The MacDougalls needed and deserved their own home. James sighed. How wonderful that home would now not be in Montreal.

As James pulled away from the rink, he thought of the new chapter he and Jessie were about to live. They were good friends and maybe now after all these years caring for others, they could concentrate on each other.

As soon as her father left, Isabel slipped away from the fans and all their questions and went to stand outside the Rangers' dressing room. She could hear the noise of the celebration going on inside and wished she could push open the door and go in. But not only was she afraid of what she might see, she was also well aware the dressing room was sacred territory in which men could be boys. This was their party, their victory. She would lean against the wall and wait.

Finally, the door opened. Wendell came out first. He stopped in his tracks upon seeing Isabel, and the other players and Coach Ramsay smashed into him. The laughter and chatter died on their lips when they saw the captain's wife. Isabel felt the urge to laugh when she saw the trepidation on their faces, but knew it wasn't a compliment that they feared the sharpness of her tongue.

"I want to thank each of you for what you did for Daniel, and for me and the girls. He's a rich man to have friends like you," she said quietly. "And a brother like you, Peter."

Peter solemnly held her gaze then smiled.

"I wasn't happy about Daniel making the deal with the team. I didn't believe you would deliver, and for that I'm sorry. Thank you for believing when I couldn't," Isabel continued.

Uncomfortable with the depth of emotion in the conversation, the men stuttered that it was their privilege, and scurried to move past her. Only Daniel remained in the corridor.

"You're a strong woman, Isabel. A real scrapper. Sure you don't want to play hockey?" he said, as he drew her to him.

"I'll leave that to you, Daniel." Isabel let her arms slide up over his shoulders. "Can you believe our land and house is safe?"

"It's going to take time to sink in." he said.

"It's looking like we have a future here. A good one." Isabel murmured before kissing him lightly on the lips.

Together, they walked from the rink, with no need for more words. They could see a steady line of vehicles still trickling out of the parking lot and turning west for the long drive home. Percy had the truck running and some players were on board, while others were meandering their way across the parking lot soaking up the congratulations from departing fans.

Daniel spotted Peter just ahead of them making his way to the truck.

"Get a move on, Peter. We're all starved, and the 4-H Club says they are treating the players at Andy's Diner." Wendell leaned his head out the box door.

Sounds of clapping and cheering broke out from inside the box. Before Isabel realized his intentions, Daniel called out, "Hey, Peter, you want to come with us?"

Peter stopped, looked back at Daniel and Isabel, and then again towards the laughing, joking players, and fans onboard the truck. Isabel had no doubt where Peter wanted to be, making her wonder if her husband's head was okay. She gave his arm a quick shake. Daniel received the unspoken message. He removed his arm from Isabel's and signalled for her to stay put.

Daniel walked over to Peter and faced him square on. "On second thought, go on the truck and have a good time. We'll meet you at Andy's." His voice trembled. "Thanks, Peter. Thanks for everything." Daniel gave his brother a quick hug and backed away before either of them could become embarrassed.

"You're welcome. You would have done the same for me." Peter looked at his big brother, who could only nod back at him.

“After Andy’s, on the way home, please tell the guys for me that tonight was my last game, okay?” Daniel brushed away a tear.

“You can’t quit now. We need you.” Peter wasn’t really surprised by the news, but felt he should at least register a protest.

“Things have changed. I have a new game to play,” Daniel said firmly. “They’re waiting for you—go have some fun. You earned it.”

Daniel didn’t move. He stood watching Peter run towards the truck and jump aboard. Percy put the vehicle in gear and rumbled out of the parking lot, horn blaring and shouts coming from the box. Daniel remained still, looking after the truck until it was out of sight. Isabel remained where she was, just watching him, and respecting that a chapter in his life was over. He had named his game. Daniel turned and looked at the rink for a long moment, then walked over to Isabel and took her arm. Together, they walked to their car, the last one left in the parking lot.